Drama Free 2003

By Josie Leigh

Drama Free 2003

Published by Josie Leigh at Smashwords

Copyright 2013 Josie Leigh

Cover design by Josie Leigh

Cover Art by Cover art from © Kati1313 | Dreamstime.com

This story is for entertainment purposes only. Names, characters, places, events, most businesses and organizations are either a product of the author's imagination or are used fictitiously. Any resemblance to real persons, living or dead, is purely coincidental.

Table of Contents

LUCAS

"I'm ready for this year to be over, Lucy," Brady grumbled in my ear as our friends drank around us.

"Me, too," I approved, looking over at him. "2002 sucked balls."

Luckily, I was drunk enough not to flinch at Brady calling me Lucy. He always does, even though I, now, prefer to go by my real name. I'd had the name Lucas my entire life, but went by Lucy until I was in high school. Once the teen angst took over, having a boy's name was suddenly cool and didn't get me made fun of anymore. Everyone who'd met me since high school called me Lucas, but my family and friends I'd had my whole life still insisted on calling me Lucy. Brady fell into the latter category, not because he'd known me since high school, but because his roommates had.

"10!" My guests started the make shift countdown to midnight, staring at the second-hand of my living room clock. I was positive that it was fast and we were prematurely counting down the New Year, but it was okay. At least this shitty year would be over, finally. I wasn't exaggerating when I told Brady 2002 had sucked. I was banking on the hope that 2003 would be better. If it wasn't, I swore to GOD, I was leaving this God-forsaken state and moving far, far away. The thirty minute move to Tempe had helped, but not enough.

"5!" My eyes slid back to Brady, my 'date' for the evening, a good friend who agreed to pretend to be my temporary conquest so that an auditionee for my boy corral, Trevor, would get the point that it wasn't going to happen between us again.

Brady was nice enough, if not a bit quiet. Good looking, too-long, shaggy, brown hair, beautiful steel blue eyes, which were similar to my own, oval features, a gash mark scar on the left side of his chin. He was taller than me, but only by two to three inches, and I'd learned tonight that I fit perfectly under his arm as we snuggled on the floor beside my living room window.

"1! Happy New Year!" my guests yelled and turned to kiss their dates or hug the friend they came with. Trevor shot me a hopeful smile, prompting me to turn to Brady, giving him a nervous, but questioning, look. With a shrug, he pulled me close and planted a sweet, lingering kiss on my forehead before settling my head against his chest. I could feel the steady rhythm of his heart against my ear. There was something completely calming about being wrapped up in his arms, but I didn't want to dwell on it.

"Here's to a drama free year," he whispered in my ear. My face heated as chills raced through my body when his breath hit my neck. I couldn't wipe the silly grin off my face at the kiss he gave me on my forehead. I'd be appalled at my reaction if I hadn't consumed enough alcohol to take shame off the menu. I knew he'd never be truly interested in me. He'd seen me retreat to my bedroom during my monthly parties with a constantly rotating roster of guys to ever really want to be with me. I'd be lying to myself if I said that before that moment, I'd ever considered being with him either. Yet, through the course of the evening, something inside me had changed and he was all I could see.

Trying to push the thought away, I did my best to enjoy the remainder of the party before saying good night to those not sleeping on my nearly vacant living room floor and collapsing on my, now, lonely queen sized bed. Was there a way I could get Brady interested in me, without

2

compromising who I was? I doubted it. I was destined to be the girl that flitted from hook up to hook up, never able to find the guy she was really supposed to share her life with. I was okay with that, though, because it meant I never had to compromise what I wanted out of life because of someone else's whims.

As I drifted off to sleep, Brady's smiling face was the last thing I saw. I wondered what 2003 would have in store for me when I awoke the next morning to my empty bed and party trashed living room. Would Brady be the first person I thought of in the light of day, too?

CHAPTER 1

BRADY

My first thought of 2003 was 'Why in the fuck is my back so sore?' Then I looked around and realized that I'd crashed on Lucy's living room floor like a few other people who'd had too much to drink last night. I was perplexed to see that I was the only one remaining, even though the sun was barely peeking through her venetian blinds.

I was grateful for the sheet acting as a makeshift rug, because you could tell the carpet in her apartment had not been changed between tenants in years. What she really needed was some furniture, but I could admire her desire to live by herself and doing what she could to make it work for her.

As I folded myself up from the concrete slab she called a floor, my mind drifted back to the last party she'd thrown at her old house in Florence. The party where I'd gotten too drunk to take her good friend, Abby, back to her dorm room and ended up crashing on her sofa. Picking up plastic cups full of half-drunk booze, my mind flipped over trying to find the difference in my reactions to her then and the previous night...

"When's the big moving day?" I asked, trying to get Lucy's mind off her ex-boyfriend's car pulling out of her driveway with Abby in the backseat. She and I had been friends for a while, but this was the first time we'd ever really been alone. In fact, I think this was going to be the first real conversation we'd ever had, not counting questions like who do you think is going to win the Big Ten championship this year or do you want the raspberry or the vanilla vodka from the store?

"Two weeks," she told me, leaning back in the patio chair. I couldn't help but notice the fact that she wasn't wearing a bra under her tank top and that she appeared to be cold. "I like living here, but I need to be on my own for a while. I'm 21 now, and I want to see if I can make it alone. Plus, I started at Arizona State last week and community college isn't even remotely the same thing as a major university. My major is unforgivingly hard, so I need to be close to those tutoring resources at all times! Not to mention the fact that the commute from here to Tempe is a bitch," pulling my focus from her full tits back to her sky blue eyes, her brown hair framing them in a nicely disheveled manner.

"Don't you work in Tempe already?" I asked, leaning forward in the chair and running a hand through my own brown hair, cigarette jumping in my mouth as I talked. I didn't know if my smoking bothered her, but she never seemed to mind at her parties and often hung out with the smokers, even though I'd never seen her take a puff.

"I do," she confirmed. "Yet another reason to make the move."

"I get the need to live on your own," I nodded, feeling the need to bond with her over this decision. "I went from my dad's house after high school to an apartment with my ex-wife and her son when I was 19, back to my dad's after the divorce when I was 21. Two years later, I'm just happy to have my own room in my apartment so that my daughter has a quiet place to sleep when she comes over."

"Yeah, I'll bet Taylor'll want her own room as she gets older," she smiled in a teasing way. "That's got to be rough for her, going back and forth like that."

"That's why I only get her on the weekends for now," I explained. "You know, she turned two a couple of months ago? The whole thing is still feels pretty surreal," I said,

5

looking at her, unfocused. I loved that little girl more than anything.

"I can't imagine having a kid right now," she said, standing from her chair when I moved to crush my cigarette in the ash tray. "My cat is pain in the ass enough," she joked, as we walked back into the house and she started readying the house for the night, turning off the porch light and the kitchen light as we walked toward the living room. "She—" her phone ringing interrupted her train of thought as she went to get confirmation that Abby had made it safely to her dorm room sans company. A look of relief flashed over her features that I didn't recognize before she turned back to me.

"You don't have to take care of that," Lucy's voice pulled me from my day dream as I was dumping the contents of the cups down the sink in her kitchen.

"I know," I looked at her with a smile. "But I thought I'd help since I'm the last guest standing." For some reason, being here after the way she felt in my arms last night was natural. The only thing that felt wrong was the fact I didn't wake up beside her. That thought alone scared the shit out of me, because Lucas Dunn was a one woman island.

She was an incredibly caring and trustworthy friend, and between her, now, blue-black hair, gorgeous and insightful sky blue eyes, perfect rack, and mile long legs, she was also incredibly beautiful. She was also the busiest person I knew and had boys she kept in reserve to attend to her sexual needs, because a relationship wasn't exactly on the top of her to-do list. She could run me over and not even realize it, but she'd be very apologetic while she was doing it.

"I really appreciate it, Brady," she gave me a shy smile I'd never seen on her face before. A smile that made me

6

think she was more vulnerable that what she portrayed to the world and that intrigued me even more. "Do you need a ride?" she asked, pulling on the hem of the tight red t-shirt she wore, trying to cover the sliver of her stomach showing before her red and white cotton shorts started.

"No, my friends and I drove separately last night, that's probably why they didn't wake me," I told her. I was still surprised that she'd called me last night when she was getting off work instead of one of my roommates. She was much closer to them than to me, but they'd been at a different party last night so her choice to call them wouldn't have mattered anyway.

"Cool," her head bobbed, signaling to me that she felt just as awkward about our closeness last night as I did. "So, um, I have plans to go watch this thing this morning…" she tried to segue smoothly that she needed me to leave.

"Oh! Okay," I blinked. "I'll head home then."

"You don't have to rush out, I've got like twenty minutes before I have to go," she back tracked.

"Well, go ahead and get ready and I'll finish in here," I offered, going back to collecting the trash in her living room and dining area.

"Are you sure?" she asked, cocking her head to the side and biting her bottom lip.

"I'm sure," I confirmed, ushering her back to her bedroom to change.

"Okay, then, thank you!" she called out as her bedroom door closed behind her.

**

LUCAS

If I hadn't been unsuccessful in my objective in waking up before the crack of noon these last couple of days, I wouldn't have needed to basically shove Brady out the door with me. Today was the last morning I was going to have this option, and I'd be damned if I missed out because of my evil alarm clock and night owl tendencies. It wasn't every day, or week, or year, that I'd have the opportunity to see my favorite college marching band perform in my own backyard.

As I pulled into a parking space beside Tempe High School, the thought that I could've invited Brady to come with me flitted through my head. Quickly, I squashed it, because that was getting into dangerous territory. He was not the type of guy I normally hooked up with. He was the type of guy who I could introduce to my mom, and possibly my dad if he was ever in town again. I didn't mess around with the real deal because it wasn't worth it. I knew it could never really last, happily ever after in love wasn't something I was capable of. It was in my blood. Plus, he wasn't a marching band nerd like I was, anyway.

I knew that last reason was bullshit, but I liked to lie to myself, and pretend I wasn't freaking out. It was the only way I could see myself getting through the day without a panic attack, so it was okay. I'd felt something for Brady last night, something I hadn't felt in a very long time, something that my heart wanted to pursue. My heart never weighed in on these kinds of things.

Following the small stream of other people, I made my way to the football field and sat as close to the center of the bleachers as I could. I tried to push down all of my crazy feelings to pay attention to the awesomeness I was about to witness.

8

"Welcome to Gray Day!" the band director said from a bullhorn as he stood on the sidelines. The band was standing in formation in the south end zone in matching sweats, beautiful arranged in parade rest. Excitement filled me as a huge smile took over my face, pushing all thoughts, including those about Brady, to the back of my mind. "Welcome alumni and fans!" he continued. "Please enjoy a sneak peek of our Fiesta Bowl halftime show. Let's start it out with the fight song," he welcomed as the drum major called the band to attention and led them onto the field with a flourish, performing a back flip once he reached the center of the field.

As the band started to form the famous script Ohio, I couldn't help bouncing in my seat a little bit. Watching the intricacies of the movement, of how they were able to play and cross through each other, where the drum major broke off a line and started a new one. I'd never seen anything like it. When Ohio was spelled out, the drum major retrieved the Sousaphone player designated to dot the "I" and lead him into position. I was on my feet with the other audience members, cheering and clapping, excited to see that they hadn't spared the pageantry of the moment simply because it was a practice. This was what made The Ohio State University's marching band, truly, the best damn band in the land.

I loved all things Ohio State, the band especially, so imagine my excitement that the football team was playing for a National Championship in two days at the Fiesta Bowl. That excitement doubled when I found out that the hotel I worked at was hosting the members of the marching band. Because of my connections, I'd been able to get a copy of their open rehearsal schedule and had been trying to get to them all week. Watching the spectacle of their incredible performance, I was glad I didn't miss it. I don't think I ever would have forgiven myself.

By the time the practice was called to a close, my face ached from smiling and my toes were frozen because I'd decided to wear flip flops instead of my tennis shoes. Usually a pair of jeans and a light sweater was protection enough against the Arizona winter, but this morning was colder than usual.

The stellar performance I'd just witnessed and my Popsicle toes were enough to keep me distracted from my thoughts until I was back in my apartment. Looking over my clean living room and dining area reminded me of what Brady had done for me that morning and the memory of how he'd ended up at my house last night played behind my eyes.

I hadn't meant to call Brady, but his cell phone number was only one digit different from his roommate's and I couldn't confirm the number from my cell phone before dialing, because personal phones are strictly prohibited behind the hotel's front desk. When Brady answered instead of who I was expecting, I played it off that he was who I'd meant to call. I thought it would be rude to blow him off. It turned out that he and a couple of his friends were driving around looking for something to do and were close by, so they all ended up at my house for a few rounds of Texas Hold 'Em, losers take a shot.

The four of us were nicely toasted by the time Trevor showed up with the hopes of a booty call that wasn't going to happen. At 11:45pm, there was a knock at my door. This wasn't unusual because I'd gotten a couple of calls from friends looking for a place to ring in the New Year last minute. I'd thought that it would just be Brady and his friends, but I underestimated my ability to pull together a party last minute.

"Trevor," I deadpanned when I opened the door. He was not someone I'd been expecting.

"Lucas," he said, grinning at me, lasciviously. "I was hoping we could bring in the New Year with a bang, what do you say?" he propositioned, walking into my apartment without an invitation.

"Come on in," I shot him a brittle smile before looking around the room and finding Brady's steel blue gaze. "Hey, Brady, can I have a word?" I asked, jerking my head toward my bedroom.

"Um, sure," he agreed, confused, but moving toward the back of my apartment.

"Can you pretend to be my date tonight?" I whispered to him after I closed the door to my bedroom. "Trevor isn't going to work out and I don't want to have to fight him off tonight."

"Okay?" his eyebrows furrowed at my request.

"I'm not asking you to make out with me or anything, just hold my hand, let me sit beside you or something. Just a couple of cuddles to get the point across," I clarified.

"Of course," he said, looking relieved. "I can do that," he continued, grabbing my hand and lacing our fingers together. The shock I felt course through my body as his flesh touched mine was something I'd never experienced before. My heart, immediately, kicked into overdrive at the contact. "Maybe you should take your hair down, mess it up a bit so it looks like you called me back here to make out," he suggested jokingly as he lead us out to my guests.

If that response had been a one-time only thing, I could've just written it off as something brought on by all the alcohol I'd drunk over the last hour. However, anytime his skin touched mine, awareness lit through my body. It made me want to do more than just hold hands with him. This was especially troubling because I had a rotating stock of three guys I utilized on a weekly basis to attend to my sexual needs. I didn't need a complication like Brady. It could cost me everything I was working so hard for.

"Degree first, then I can look for a relationship that works for me," I whispered into my empty living room as I headed toward my bedroom for a mid-morning nap. I needed to get my head on straight before I faced the plethora of check-ins I knew we had at the hotel that night.

CHAPTER 2

BRADY

"Where are you just coming in from?" my roommate and best friend, Flynn, asked me from our sectional sofa when I walked through the door.

"Hung out at Lucy's last night with some friends from work," I shrugged, falling on to the recliner part of the sofa near the door.

"Lucy's? How'd that happen?" Flynn looked at me, puzzled. "Usually she calls me. I mean, I was working, so it wouldn't have mattered anyway," he added, quickly.

"Honestly, I think she did mean to call you," I explained, lounging back as he stood from the couch and paced the distance from our bedroom door to the hallway before Becca's bedroom. I could tell the development bothered him more than he was letting on. Lucy and I didn't hang out without Flynn or my other roommate, Becca- ever. "I didn't recognize the number she called from, so I think she just didn't have her phone and tried to go off memory."

"That makes sense, but then she would've tried to correct her mistake, right?" Flynn's large frame stalked the length of our living room behind the sectional, trying to figure out why Lucy hadn't called him.

Flynn was taller than me, much taller, and lanky. I thought he was self-conscious about his height because he was constantly hunched over. His dirty blonde hair was cut into a faux hawk and his brown eyes were narrowed in thought as he paced. The plethora of tattoos and piercings he sported made him look more intimidating than he was. That's not to say that he didn't have issues, because if he were a magazine, volumes and volumes could be produced based his childhood alone. One of his most infamous was feeling like he was being passed over, which, apparently, he felt Lucy was doing.

"Look, man, it's no big deal. I told her you were working, so she probably didn't want to bother you," I tried to smooth over, but I knew that Lucy would be getting an angry phone call from Flynn later.

"Whatever," he dismissed, letting me know that I was right in my assessment.

"Where's Becca?" I asked, trying to sound nonchalant, not looking around the apartment because I didn't want him to think I was trying to plan a hook up. I wasn't. This was a brand new year, a chance to let go of my past mistakes and have a better future. A future that didn't include sleeping with best friend's ex and roommate, Becca, just because she was there and available. I wasn't that guy.

"Working, some big sale at the store today, I guess," Flynn shrugged. "I've got a date tonight with this chick that came into the shop the other night, so I need you to keep Becca from freaking out. You know how she gets when I'm dating, but this girl is obsessed with piercings and one of my co-workers was talking about the ones on my dick," Flynn said, a cocky smirk on his face. Where most guys had either a PA or an APA, Flynn had both, plus ten more piercings from the base of his dick up, called a ladder. Sharing a room with him meant I'd seen it more than I'd ever care to. The thing looked downright scary. "So, I guess it's more of a new booty call. She wants to try it out."

"Good luck, man," I laughed. "I'll do what I can to keep her distracted, but you know what she's going to want," I shook my head. "I don't want to go there with her again."

"Take one for the team, Brady, besides she'd be good for you," he encouraged. I don't think he wanted Becca and I to have a successful relationship, more that he wanted me to keep her warm and occupied until he wanted to get back together with her, again.

Becca and Flynn were what is commonly referred to as high school sweethearts, and had been off and on ever since. They always described it as intense and unbelievably passionate, but I always thought their relationship was a cluster fuck of epic proportions. It was so destructive that it swallowed everyone it touched whole and regurgitated their bones. They'd been engaged more times than I could count, but always broke up. They were good people separately, but together, damn, they were a category five hurricane. I mean, Flynn ended up heavily medicated in a padded room for a while after one of their break ups. If that's not a glaring reason why they shouldn't be together, I don't know what is.

Becca and I hooked up at one of Lucy's parties last summer and it had become a regular thing. We didn't date, unless you call a single trip to the movies once three months ago. I knew better than to keep sleeping with her, because she had a tendency to get attached quickly. I'd question why I got involved with her many times in the last six months, given her long, complicated and on-going history with my best friend and my own desire to never get married again, but I knew the answer to that, it was 80 proof and started with the letter V.

"We'll see. I mean, I'll hang out with her, I'm sure, cause I don't have any plans tonight, but I don't plan on fucking her so she doesn't spend the night calling you over and over again while you are on your date," I mumbled, standing from the sectional and pulling my cigarettes from my pocket. "I'm going to have a smoke."

I didn't wait for a response as I stepped onto our balcony sliding the glass door shut behind me.

**

Much later, I was playing GTA and in the middle of trying to evade the police on a four star wanted mission when Becca barreled through the door, her cherry red hair spilling over her shoulders, her cell phone glued to her ear.

"Holy crap, really?" she asked into her phone so loudly that it actually startled me. Turning back to her, I watched her toss her purse on the couch as she listened to the person on the other end.

"How much did *that* cost you?" she continued, kicking off her shoes and sending me a flirty grin. I jerked my head up in greeting from my spot on the floor and went back to my game.

"You're *kidding* me?!" she yelled, drawing my attention back to her side of the conversation. As I flicked my gaze back over my shoulder, she covered the receiver with her hand and leaned toward me. "Lucy got a ticket for the National Championship game for one hundred and fifty freaking dollars!"

Furrowing my brow, I shot her a doubtful look, "Are they nosebleeders?" I knew Lucy was excited for the tickets, even if she ended up sitting in the furthest corner of the stadium, behind a pillar and the scoreboard.

"27th row, bottom level," Becca relayed with a shrug.

"Holy shit! Are they real?" I shot back, pausing my video game and turning to face Becca fully.

"Brady doesn't think they're real," she deadpanned to her best friend. After a few seconds, Becca's mouth gaped open as she looked at me. "*SERIOUSLY?!* You should totally sell that ticket, Lucas!...But you can watch the game

16

at the bar like you planned, with the other fans that don't have tickets, but with like two-fucking-grand in your pocket…" she continued. "Ugh, I know," Becca frowned and rolled her eyes at me. "You're right," she finally conceded. "It is a once in a lifetime thing. I remember when I finally got to see Phantom in New York that summer with my dad. It was incredible."

I bugged out my eyes at Becca, surprised I was actually trying to ask for an update. Usually, their girly conversations didn't even rate on my scale of interest. I would usually write it off as just being interested because it was football, but I knew it was more than that.

"A couple of ladies needed to sell the extra ticket in their package cause one of their husbands got sick."

"Holy shit," I breathed, my eyes wide. I might hate her shitty ass team, but even I couldn't deny how lucky she'd been to fall into that ticket.

"Brady thinks you should sell it, too," she announced and almost immediately pulled the phone away from her ear. On the other end, I could hear Lucy yelling. I knew she was ranting about how awesome *THE* Ohio State University was and it brought smile to my lips. That woman was nothing if not fiercely loyal to her team, but damn I loved giving her shit.

"Oh, tell her to calm down," I shook my head with a grin. "I don't like Miami either, so I'm cheering for her crappy team this time. Gotta support the Big Ten."

"Did you hear that, Lucy?" Becca laughed. "I know, he does seem to be growing as a sports fan," she giggled.

"Ugh, I'm going to have a cigarette," I groan at their conversation, but I'm secretly pleased at the banter that seems to be developing between Lucy and me. Our conversations have never been forced or stilted, just mostly non-existent.

Leaning against the balcony railing, I could catch small snippets of the rest of Becca's conversation with Lucy and it strikes me again how close we've been to each other for the past seven years, but have only known each other for, barely, two. She and Becca have been best friends since they were in junior high, not as long as Flynn and I have been friends, though. But they've been friends for long enough that it was weird that Becca, Lucy and Flynn used to spend time together in high school and I never met her. Even weirder was the fact that her high school sweetheart was my younger brother's best friend. It's like we weren't supposed to meet until we did.

Taking a deep drag off my Marlboro, my last thoughts race through my head again. *We weren't supposed to meet until we did?* What the fuck does that mean? And when did I start analyzing this shit like a fucking girl? Lucy's not at home right now thinking about this shit. She's probably half listening to Becca, contemplating whether she's going to call up one of her stand-bys tonight.

A deep sigh draws my attention back to the present and Becca plopping onto the one chair we keep on the balcony.

"She could've had two grand easy for that ticket," she shook her head. "I mean, she's going by herself to the game. Who does that? Isn't it always better to go with other people? I mean, or at least with one other person. I wouldn't have gone to see Phantom by myself regardless of how much I'd always wanted to see it on stage," she frowned. "Not to mention, she went to see their marching band perform this morning and didn't even *call* me! She knows I'm always up for that stuff."

"She probably just figured you had to work," I dismissed as the realization of why I was pushed out of her

18

apartment this morning washed over me. "Which you did," I reminded her.

"Whatever, she still should've called. She wasn't being a very considerate friend," she pouted.

"I'm sure she didn't mean to slight you, Becca," I told her, crushing my cigarette.

"I know," she bounced in the chair like all was suddenly forgotten. "She had to go, I guess her booty call number one was stopping by, I think his name is Eric or something like that" she rolled her eyes. "I don't know how she does that."

"What?" I asked before I could stop myself.

"Just sleep with those guys without any real feelings for them aside from getting off," she told me, leaning back. "She has to be lying, right? I have to feel something other just the physical attraction for a guy to let him into my pants. Isn't that how it's supposed to go?"

"That's always been how it is for me, but with girls," I joked, because I agreed with Becca. Even though my list is short, aside from my rebound after my marriage ended, I, at least, wanted to spend time with the girls I'd slept with. Maybe I didn't see some dazzling future with them, but I wasn't the type of guy to just kick them out of bed as soon as we were done. I knew Lucy didn't even let them spend the night.

"Flynn said you wanted to hang out tonight," she prompted, winking at me and pulling me from Lucy thoughts yet again.

"That's cool," I said, very non-committal, following her to my bedroom. I needed to put a stop this stuff with Becca, because even though she was my friend and I liked her as a person, I did NOT see a future with her. She wanted so much more than I was willing to deliver. I'd promised Flynn that I'd distract her, and I was a man of my word, even though I wasn't in the mood to hook up with Becca tonight. Ugh, what did sleeping with her make me? I just told her I couldn't sleep with someone without some kind of feeling, and that's true, only in her case, it's friendship.

I needed to not be "that guy" anymore for Becca. I don't care what Flynn needs, I'm done. I promise this time.

CHAPTER 3

LUCAS

Aside from Trevor, I was also trying to audition a line cook from my work, Adam, because one of my regular booty calls wasn't available as much as I'd wanted him to be. Adam had asked me out for drinks and freaked out when he realized I wasn't a relationship type girl. The double standards on girls having booty calls always pissed me off, and Adam told me this evening that his sister who had never met me had concluded that I was a slut.

Society's rules would dictate Adam's sister was right and I was a slut, but I didn't feel that way. I had standards of who I would and wouldn't sleep with. I preferred sex to relationships because sex always made me feel good, whereas relationships were full of drama and having to meet his friends and blah, blah, blah.

I didn't have time for a relationship, between working two jobs and going to school full-time. I was a couple of years away from a bachelor's degree in engineering, so my books were my boyfriend. I did, however, *make* time for sex. It was one of the best stress reducers I could find that was legal and didn't require a prescription, aside the birth control I needed to regulate my periods anyway. I had three guys I could always fall back on if I needed to get laid and wasn't seeing anyone regularly. My three were, usually, more than willing to drive to my house when I needed and leave before the sun came up. We had an unspoken agreement that it would never be more between us, and it worked out well for everyone involved.

I was so pissed about Adam and his *sister's* opinions that I felt compelled to participate in some sexual debauchery, even though I'd hooked up with my number one last night, too. Pulling out my phone, I dialed as I backed out of my parking space at the hotel. I may work across the street from my apartment, but there is no way I'm walking in this part of Tempe after eleven at night. Someone might argue that it was only 200 yards, but I didn't have a death wish.

"Hey, hot stuff," Eric's smooth voice answered.

"Hey, dude, what are you up to tonight?" I asked.

"Again? I can't remember the last time you wanted to go back to back!" he joked. "but I wish you'd called me thirty minutes ago," he whined. "I was in Tempe, and I would've been sitting outside your door right now like a stray puppy, I'm all the way in Gilbert already."

"Ugh, and I can't convince you to turn around?" I pouted.

"Would if I could, baby girl, but I pulled the early shift tomorrow, so it's straight to bed, no extracurricular activities for me tonight," he lamented. "What happened to Adam and Trevor? Not that it matters, I mean, if you want to hold off 'til tomorrow?" he suggested. Eric, aside from being the best in my boy corral, was also a good friend who I talked to about my 'dating' habits on a regular basis. He was the only one who never judged me, or told me I needed to settle down. "I know your other dudes are still gone for winter break," he added.

"Let's not talk about Adam and Trevor," I growled as I pulled into my parking space in front of my apartment building.

"And now we have to," Eric mused, clearly entertained by my 'dating' attempts this last month. "You not wanting to talk about something always means good things, well funny things."

22

"I cut Trevor loose," I told him. "We were too incompatible. He was weird, I mean, I'm a nerd and all, but who in the fuck thinks it's a good idea to bring a graphing calculator to a party? And don't even get me started on his penis!"

"Gerkin?" he asked, wryly.

"If only," I answered, wistfully. "The thing was enormous. The entire time I felt like he was trying to rip me in half. Not even remotely satisfying, only incredibly fucking painful."

"Gee, way to give a guy a complex," Eric muttered, as I approached my third floor apartment, sending a nod to Ron, the pimp who lived three doors down, sitting in the hallway with one of his ladies.

"This is why I didn't want to talk about it!" I unlocked my door and shoved into my nearly barren living room. "I don't know why guys think a gargantuan penis is ideal, because I'd much prefer one that doesn't bounce off my cervix."

"Well, I accept your seal of approval for normal sized junk, then," he chuckled. "And Adam?"

"Fuck, I hoped we could move on after I confessed that size really does matter," I grumbled, setting my stuff on the card table that doubled as my kitchen table and walking toward the walk-in closet in my vanity area to feed my cat.

"No such luck, kiddo." I pulled a can of food down from the shelf and took a deep breath. As I pulled back the tab, my cat appeared beside my ankles, weaving in and around.

"Fine," I sighed. "He's decided that either I'm a slut, or I'm just begging for a man to come and rescue me. I'm sorry, I mean, his *sister* decided."

Putting the food in her bowl, I moved to my galley style kitchen to toss the empty can in the trash before heading back through the vanity area to my bedroom. My apartment may not have been in the greatest of neighborhoods, but it seriously rocked. It was massive, and cost me less than a dollar per square foot, including pet rent and utilities. It had dingy periwinkle carpets, a pest control problem, and did I mention I lived three doors down from a pimp?, but it was home.

"Wow, Lucas, I didn't know you were a lesbian?" Eric's question pulled me from my thoughts.

"Um, just cause I kiss the occasional girl, doesn't mean I like to visit the lady cave. That one time with you was an exception," I said, pulling off my work uniform and changing into shorts and a t-shirt.

"I just meant that the guy sounds like he's a giant vagina. I wouldn't worry about making room for him in the rotation, he's not worthy," Eric yawned and I couldn't help but chuckle, the dude knew how to make me laugh, but he couldn't be faithful to a girl to save his life. Sometimes I considered myself the female version of Eric, and wondered if I had the ability to stay faithful. Maybe it was the real reason why I'd resisted a real relationship for the last two solid years.

"So, yeah, I can wait until tomorrow for action, I suppose," I agree, trying to sound put out and bringing our conversation back to the original purpose of my call. Heading toward the stack of books on my living room floor, I let out an involuntary sigh. "I've got a test tomorrow anyway. I don't know what possessed me to sign up for an intersession class during break."

"Then you need to get on top of your books tonight, Lucas, not on top of me," he admonished, jokingly.

24

"Fine, see you tomorrow," I said, ending our conversation and turning to the never ending pile of notes on my bare floor. That was the only thing about my apartment that I didn't love: the only furniture in my living room were two seats, a rocking chair and a bean bag, as well as my desktop computer, which was sitting on my floor beside the aforementioned bean bag chair. It did help with parties though, because everyone just slept in a heap where they passed out. I had a sheet spread out as a rug/crash spot, because I was pretty sure my carpet hadn't been changed since the Reagan administration. I didn't want my friends to catch anything from my floor.

Resisting the urge to log onto the computer, I buried myself in my notes until my eyes burned. Later that night or very early the next morning, I drug myself to my cold and empty queen sized bed for the night, content that I'd not spent another day thinking about the way Brady had made me feel on New Years' Eve. I decided to chalk it up to a fluke. I'd never responded to Brady that way before. Just because I'd felt safe in his arms, and could still conjure up the smell of his cologne didn't mean anything. I wasn't thinking about the way his too long brown hair kept falling in his steel blue eyes when he laughed at something I said or the way his touch gave me goose bumps when he absently stroked my arms. I couldn't have feelings for him. I wouldn't.

CHAPTER 4

BRADY

The manufacturing plant where I worked was still shut down for the holidays until Monday, and I wouldn't get my daughter again until tomorrow. However, I was grateful to wake up alone that Friday morning, because unlike my job, retail stores didn't shut down for the holiday so Becca was at work. We'd hooked up again last night, again at the insistence of Flynn who'd had a second date with the chick he met at work. I was pretty disgusted with myself for caving, again, to my best friend's request to fuck his ex-girlfriend so she didn't go ape shit over his new girl.

My head felt heavy as I pulled myself out of my queen sized bed with iron railings and stumbled toward the living room. I startled back slightly when Flynn groaned from the floor of my walk in closet.

"Hey," he graveled out, rolling onto his back and running a hand over his shaved head. "Didn't mean to scare you," He finished, pushing off his palette on the floor and scratching his stomach over a ratty t-shirt.

"Nah, man, it's cool," I told him, pushing beyond him to reach the master bathroom. "I just didn't expect you home this morning."

"I'm not scheduled today. I saw Bec this morning, though," he growled out. I knew she'd tried to rub our hook up in his face in an attempt to make him jealous, not knowing that Flynn had asked me to "take one for the team." Shutting the door to the bathroom, I did my business and washed my hands. When I emerged from behind the door, I was shocked to find Flynn in the same position I'd left him in.

"I wasn't talking about work," I started, avoiding his comment about Becca and bringing the conversation back to him, "I meant your date with I heart dick piercings Barbie."

"Oh, her, yeah," he chuckled. "That was interesting, because I don't think she was expecting me," he said as we breeched the entry to the living room.

"Ok?" I prompted him, not necessarily wanting to hear his tale of tail, but not wanting to discuss my future with Becca or if he wanted me to continue to keep her mind off his burgeoning romance with his little fetish princess.

"I think she would've fine with a PA *or* an APA or maybe even both, but when you add in the ladder, man! She knew it was there, but things change when you are face to face with it for the first time," he started to howl with laughter before looking at my not amused expression and calming himself down. "When I took off my pants, she looked like she was afraid I was going to debone her with my penis."

"I'm sorry I asked," I said, rolling my eyes at him as he sat on the tattered sectional that took up most of our living room and went to start a small pot of coffee.

"So, um, tonight...?" he started, scratching the back of his head and I felt the anger in my gut at his assumptions bubbling up inside me. I was giving Becca the wrong idea by continuing to fuck her even though I would never claim her as my girlfriend, let alone marry her like she wanted.

"No, man," I said louder, moving back into the dining room so he could see my face. "I can't do it anymore and you have to stop asking me. She keeps dropping hints about being a step-mom to my daughter, and you and I both know I'm never getting married again. I'm done with all that bullshit," I finished, leveling him with my look of absolute resolve.

"Ok," he breathed out, shaking his head. "Fine, I'll just have to navigate her jealousy on my own. Thanks for your help, though."

"Sure, maybe the two of you need to sit down and figure out a healthier way to resolve these kinds of jealousy issues, Flynn. I mean, how are you going to be when she finds someone else, too?" I pointed out; his response was a half grunt half nod before reaching for the remote to flip on the television. His attentions elsewhere, I returned to the kitchen to finish my coffee. Flynn and I had lived together off and on since we graduated high school and again after my ex-wife and I separated, but we'd been best friends since elementary school. If anyone could tell when I'm being one hundred percent honest, it was him. I was glad he saw that I wouldn't allow myself to be ensnared in Becca's fly trap again, no matter how much she was available and how much I wanted to avoid everything memories of New Years' Eve had made me feel for the first time in years.

"You think Lucy'd be up for a trip to the strip club tonight?" Flynn asked out of nowhere.

"I think she'd be all over it, but she has plans tonight," I said, the information spilling from my mouth before I could pull it back.

"You seem to know a lot about what Lucy is up to these days," he sneered at me. Flynn didn't like someone knew more about his "girls" than he did. He had women friends he'd marked as needing protection from the world and Lucy had always been at the top of that list.

"Becca told me that Lucy has a ticket to the game tonight," I told him. "It's not like *she* called me and told me," I shook my head.

28

"I'm not liking that you seem to be a Lucy authority lately, Brady," he frowned, his forehead wrinkled in thought. "You aren't into her or anything, right? Because it would be a waste."

"I'm not, but why do you say it would be a waste?" I chuckled, outwardly, but secretly, I wondered why spending time thinking about Lucy was a waste. I mean, it wasn't like I was going to ever act on it or anything.

"She told me that she'd never be with a guy Becca had been with. She said it would probably destroy their friendship or something. Besides, she says that she and Becca have always been attracted to very different types of guys," he explained. "Once you set up camp between Becca's legs once, it dashes any hope to do the same between Lucy's. I wish I'd known that in high school."

"Makes sense, I mean, they're best friends, so they're just trying to eliminate drama," I said, pulling the now full carafe from the coffee maker and filling my cup 3/4^{ths} full so that I still had room for my creamer. "Aside from Becca, don't we, generally, do the same thing?"

"Yeah, but still," Flynn pouted.

"It's not like you didn't get laid last night," I rolled my eyes.

"That's true," he grinned before going back to flipping channels. "There's nothing on, man. I'm gonna go for a ride," he announced. "I'll be back." After shoving his feet into his boots and grabbing his helmet and keys, Flynn took off, leaving me alone with his revelations.

Why was I so upset to learn I didn't have a real chance with Lucy since I hooked up with Becca? I didn't want to be with her anyway. Right? Even if I did think she was capable of committing, I'm not looking for anything like that, right?

As if on cue, I heard my phone ringing in my bedroom. Looking at the caller ID, I had to laugh at the universe's joke.

"Hey, Lucy," I answered, holding back the laugh in my chest.

"Hey, Brady," her shaky voice answered.

"Are you okay?" I asked, immediately on high alert. She sounded vulnerable and Lucas Dunn didn't do vulnerable.

"Um, yeah, is…is it true?" she asked, completely bewildering me as to what she wanted me to confirm.

"Is *what* true?" Walking back into the kitchen, I grabbed my cooling cup of coffee and my pack of cigarettes and headed to the balcony.

"Your brother's unit? Are they being deployed at the end of the month?" she clarified.

"Yeah," I sighed, knowing why she was feeling upset by this news. "Yeah, Lucy, they are. Parker told me a couple of days ago," I confirmed.

"Fuck," she breathed. "I didn't want to call Preston if it wasn't true, but I just heard from my old roommate. I figured if anyone would know it'd be you," she babbled.

"He's going to be okay, they both are," I comforted. "Preston and Parker are going to be in training until the end of April, then they'll head over to Iraq for a year. I'm glad Parker will be there with his best friend. They'll look out for each other."

"I know, it's just…" she started, taking a deep breath. "Preston and I haven't been in a very good place since before I moved and I don't want to let him go overseas without trying to mend fences, you know? Of course, you don't," she sighed again. "Look, forget I called and babbled like a crazy person just now. Thank you, Brady," she said and just like that, the call was over. Dumbfounded, I took a long drink of my lukewarm coffee and pulled a cigarette from the pack. Lighting it, I took a drag and looked out at the parking lot, wondering what the fuck just happened.

**

LUCAS

Of course. Of- fucking- course! Tears stung my nose as I stared at my bedroom ceiling from my position in the center of my bed, the covers bunched up under my legs. I was still basking in the sexual euphoria that only a night with my number one could bring when Carrie woke me up with a phone call. She wanted to let me know about Preston's deployment. My first instinct wasn't to call him to confirm. I didn't want to talk to him unless it was true, so I called Brady instead.

Brady's brother, Parker, had been Preston's best friend since elementary school. They even enlisted together and were in the same reserve unit. If anyone would know if the unit was being sent overseas, it would be Brady. So I fucking called him. Now I wish I hadn't. Now I wish I could live in denial, but I couldn't.

I didn't want it to be true, but deep down I knew it was. And of course, I would find out today, of all days. The day that's supposed to end in the most awesome way possible, at the National Championship game. With an Ohio State victory, even though they are double-digit underdogs.

Instead, I'm starting the day with a phone call I'm not sure I really want to make. My past with Preston is a complicated as they come, but something always keeps us

31

coming back. I knew I couldn't ignore the fact that he was going to war. I knew if I let him leave without even a conversation and something happened to him...I couldn't even think about what that would do to me.

I mean, I will always love Preston. He was my high school sweetheart, my first love, someone who, if I thought I was the marrying kind, I could see him as my happily ever after. And he was going to war, soon. Fuck.

I didn't even know if he'd take my call, honestly. We hadn't spoken since before I moved to Tempe because I realized one night, after he volunteered to drop my friend, Abby, at her dorm after a party, that I no longer trusted him. I spent the whole hour waiting for Abby's call petrified that he'd taken advantage of her drunkenness. I didn't like having that feeling about someone I'd once loved more than anything else in my life. It made me question my ability to trust my own judgment.

Preston was supposed to be my knight in shining armor, but he wasn't. The blinders were off and I could see all the dings and rust on his armor. He couldn't save me from what he'd already done to me, he couldn't save me from the fact that I barely saw my father growing up, he couldn't save me from anything.

It didn't change the fact that he still meant something to me, even though he shouldn't. So, with a resigned sigh, I lifted my phone from beside me and called him.

"Holy shit!" he answered with an uncomfortable laugh. "I haven't heard from you since September, Lucy. And I've called," his voice sounding wounded.

"I, um, I've been busy, you know, um, working full time and starting at ASU, and stuff like that," I hedged.

"I know," he said, sadly. I knew that he knew I was lying. He could read me better than anyone, even when we weren't face to face. "I just, I miss you, Lucy."

"Yeah, phone works both ways. You called twice, Preston," I pointed out, rolling onto my stomach and looking at my solid wood headboard. It wasn't attached to my bed frame, so I had to pull the bed away from the wall enough that I didn't alert my neighbors, inadvertently, when someone was fucking me really hard. I figured the fact that I was a screamer was enough to let them know that I was enjoying myself. The additional sound effects would've, actually, embarrassed me, and that didn't happen easily. I could've just lost the headboard, but it was pretty and having just a mattress and a box spring on a frame seemed way too white trash for me.

"And the polite thing to do is to return your phone calls, Lucy," he countered. I was happy to find that our banter hadn't been sacrificed through all the awkwardness.

"What am I doing right now?" I joked, rolling out of my bed finally and walking to the living room.

"I'm thinking that you heard the news that I'm leaving and wanted to call so you don't feel guilty if I don't come back," he said, calling me out point blank.

"Preston," I warned.

"What? Is it not true? I thought we were headed somewhere last fall, Lucas," he said, his voice thick like he was holding back tears.

"It's not true, Preston. I love you, you know that, it's just," I started, taking another deep breath. I always seemed to need to collect my thoughts a lot when I was talking to Preston. "It wasn't the right time," I finished, falling back onto one of our regular excuses, instead of telling him the truth.

With a deep sigh, he responded, "I know what you mean." I could almost see him pushing his blonde hair away from his eyes and pulling at the roots just a little to remind him of our usual pattern of behavior, the game that we'd been playing for seven years now. "But when I get home, Lucy, and I *am* coming home. I'm done with this game of ours. When I get home, you are going to be mine. We *are* going to be getting married. It's all I can think about," he confessed, taking the wind out of my sails a little, because it wasn't our typical script, but it was close enough.

"I know," I agreed, solemnly, nodding as if I were in agreement, even though marrying Preston was the furthest thing from my mind. "Write me?" I squeaked out, fighting tears again.

"I will," he promised. "Write me back," he whispered.

"I will."

"God, Lucy, I love you, you know that right?" he choked out.

"I love you, too, Preston. Always," I told him, averting my eyes from where I'd been focused as if I were lying. I wasn't though, I *did* love Preston. I just wasn't *in* love with him anymore. I hadn't been for years, and I was sure he felt the same, but our game was more important than the truth. "I've, um, I've gotta go."

"Me, too. I'll talk to you later?" he asked.

"Definitely," I lied, ending the phone call and laying down in a weepy mess on my living room floor. Fuck. Why do I keep doing this to myself? I needed to spend the time that Preston was away finally and completely moving on from high school. I was over halfway through my bachelor's degree. I needed to sac up or uterus up, or

34

whatever girls did when they wanted to prove they were finally taking control over their life.

Going to the greatest football game ever by myself was going to be my first step into the great unknown abyss of adulthood. I'd been taking care of myself for a long time, working, going to school, taking care of my bills on my own, which are things that made me a responsible adult in the eyes of my parents. Emotionally, though, I was still a fucked up teenager and it was time that changed. I just wish I knew how to break the cycle.

The Buckeyes pulling out the victory in double overtime showed me that even when the world counts you out, you are in control of your own destiny. The electrification I felt from the crowd was more than I could've ever imagined. Witnessing that game, feeling hopelessness when I thought we'd lost and exhilaration when we won, experiencing it with my seatmates and the family in front of me. A small part of me changed that night. I was still scared about my future and didn't think I was capable of an actual commitment, but if an opportunity were to present itself, I was going to go for it. I had to.

CHAPTER 5

LUCAS

On my way to meet my friend, Abby, the following week, my phone started vibrating in my purse. Seeing Carter's name on the caller ID gave me a slight pause. I hadn't had a traditional boyfriend since high school, but Carter was the closest thing to that label I'd had. We dated for a couple of months, pretty exclusively, but now we were just friends. We were, mostly, friends… actually, we were still a clusterfuck and I had no idea where we stood, but I answered the call anyway.

"Want a couch?" Carter asked me without preamble. Reminding me that the Preston cycle wasn't the only one I was in. The only difference between what Preston did and said and what Carter did and said was that Carter was usually drunk when he told me he was in love with me and wanted to be with me, only to push me away again when his mind was clear. This is why I decided relationships weren't for me. I was sick of my heart and feelings being used as a yo-yo, even though I was just as guilty as Preston.

"Um, sure?" I said, questioningly, not sure where he was going with the offer, but if there was the possibility of furnishing my living room, I was all in.

"My dad bought me a new living room set for the condo, and my roommate was going to take the couch, but he said he just wants the love seat now," he explained.

"Oh, yeah, that'd be great then, give more people a chance to sit down in my apartment," I joked.

"Cool, well, I need it out of the house in Tempe by the 18th. Can you call a member of your boy army to help me move it?" he asked, sounding more jealous than usual.

It was true that there were a lot of people in my life to keep track of, and the cast list of my life might seem confusing to an outsider. I was just a friendly person with a lot of acquaintances and fuck buddies. I had an ever changing landscape of people flitting in and out of my life, or maybe it was the other way around. I cared about Carter, but he hadn't risen above the rank of occasional friend because he wasn't willing to see me as anything more either. I couldn't make someone a priority in my life when they weren't willing to do the same.

Carter's question seemed like it was an afterthought to the actual reason for his call, he wanted to borrow my truck. I drove a white Ford Ranger, barely big enough to be classified as a truck, but it had a bed with the capacity to haul stuff, so it qualified when people asked for help moving.

"I'll see what I can do," I sighed after we'd settled our business about the pick-up of the couch and the plan for his borrowing of my truck. "Look, it's Tuesday, so I have to go."

"What does that have to do with anything?"

"I'm on my way to get Abby for our weekly date at Antonio's!" Abby, on the other hand, was a friend who always made time for me, so I was happy to repay the favor. Plus, Antonio's was awesome.

"Oh, right, duh, how could I have ever forgotten?" he asked, sarcasm practically dripping down my arm from the receiver.

"Dude, what's up your ass today?" I asked. "You usually aren't so openly hostile."

"Nothing, just another fight with my roommate. I'm going to be so glad to get out of here next month, Lucas. You have no idea," he sighed.

"You can always stay with me, you know that," I offered, turning on to the street that offered overflow parking for the best pizza joint in Tempe.

"That just opens up a can, Lucas, and you know you want to be with someone your own age. Plus, I deserve someone who likes to wear panties, not just wears them because I ask," he informed me, rehashing a tired argument. Carter was a whole eight years older than me and he thought the fact that he was pushing 30 meant that I couldn't possibly have any real interest in him.

"Whatever," I grumbled. "I'll talk to you later," I said, ending the call as I approached the outdoor hostess stand of Antonio's. "Any seats at the bar?" I asked, knowing I'd probably beaten Abby there and would have to stake out our seats; otherwise the wait for a table was an hour and a half. Even though the joint boasted both indoor and outdoor seating, their amazing food drew people in regardless of the weather, but the bar seating was first come, first served.

"I'm not sure, you're more than welcome to go and check, though," the hostess motioned to the cramped interior section of the restaurant. Nodding a quick thanks, I disappeared through the door and made a beeline for the bar, almost colliding with Eric in the process.

"Whoa there," he laughed, reaching out to steady me, his dark brown eyes alight with humor. "There are two near the window," he sent me a smirk, shaking his head of dark hair, before going about his business getting someone's take out order ready.

"Thanks!" I called over my shoulder and walked to the seats he'd indicated. Hooking my leg around the neighboring stool to save it for Abby, I shed myself of my oversized Ohio State sweatshirt. Outside, it was a brisk 54 degrees, a temperature I called 'Arizona freezing', but the heat from the pizza ovens made additional layers unnecessary.

"Jumping on the bandwagon I see, Lucas," Eric tutted in disapproval, indicating my discarded sweatshirt. "I thought you were better than that."

"Do you, seriously, not know how in love with THE Ohio State University I am?" my jaw dropped to my chest in shock. "Do you not see how faded the scarlet is on this?" I practically thrust the sweater into his face. "It's nearly red from multiple washings! Not to mention the tear in the cuff!"

"Chill, Luke! I was joking!" he roared with laughter at my indignation. "I've been in your apartment more than once. You don't think the average person wouldn't have picked up on your love of the Buckeyes? It's more obvious than your cleavage in a turtleneck!"

"Thanks," I grumble as Abby came barreling toward me in all of her ADD glory. She was a good two inches taller than me, rail thin, and my current female partner in crime. It used to be Becca, but lately she'd started to get uptight about hanging out with Abby, so I'd been forced to put my best friend on the backburner. Abby lived closer and we never fought about boys and stupid shit.

"Hey girl," Eric winked as she took the seat I was saving for her. "Anytime you ladies want a do over, let me know," his grin curled wickedly, making my nether regions clinch deliciously in memory.

"Ugh," she groaned, planting her head on the solid oak bar in front of us.

"Come on! It wasn't that bad," Eric chuckled.

"No, it was amazing, but I have a boyfriend now, so no do-overs, Eric! You know that!" she pointed a finger in his direction in warning, but her head remained on the bar, her shoulder length auburn hair spilling on either side of her face.

"I didn't realize I tempted you so much," Eric whispered before returning to his post at the register.

"I don't know why you say things like that to him, Abby. It just feeds his already massive ego," I said, pulling her hair from one side and whispering into her ear. Looking over her head, I saw Eric looking at us like I was going to throw her up on the bar and eat her out for lunch. The way he was biting his lip told me I'd be getting a phone call later.

"I'm not going to deny that it takes skills to rock the world of two girls at the same time, Lucas," she turned her head to the side to peer up at me, the most serious expression on her face I've ever seen. "I know that he rocks yours semi-regularly, so I'm not going to pretend that he didn't rock mine once, too. Thanks for sharing, and I wish I could, but I can't go back for seconds this time."

"You are bad!" I hiss as the waitress comes to take our drink and food order and hustling her way down the bar to make sure everyone is still taken care of. Antonio's has a set lunch menu, so service tends to be quick. You can choose from a never ending bowl of angel hair marinara or a giant slice of thin crust pizza. We usually picked the pizza.

"So, this Saturday, party? Right? I'm dying to introduce Ted to everyone," she said, grinning at me. She was already in deep with this guy, I could tell.

"No, I've gotta move it to Friday, cause I could only find someone to work for me on Saturday, not Sunday," I frown at her.

"That'll work for me! I'll let Ted know!" and just like that, Abby was bouncing in excitement again.

"Why do you always plan parties for when I've got plans?" Eric asked with a fake pout on his full lips.

"I didn't know you were aching for an invitation," I couldn't stop my jaw from dropping at his confession. Eric had met two of my friends, Abby included, and never seemed interested in crossing that line with me. Eric was a fuck buddy, not a friend, not even an acquaintance. For the first few months we were hooking up, I didn't even know the guy's last name, so inviting him to a meet and greet never registered with me.

"Do you already know when the next one is?" he asked, "That way I know?"

"Um, yeah, cause I have to request time off work," I tell him as our waitress slides my order in front of me. "On the 31st. We usually only have one party a month, but I have a friend coming up from Tucson that wants to hang with everyone."

"Buy me a six pack of New Castles and I'll be there," he smiled at me before returning to his post.

"Um, what just happened?" I hissed at Abby as I picked up a piece of my giant slice of pizza.

"I think Eric wants to be moved up in the rotation," Abby whispered back.

"He's already number one," I dismissed.

"Maybe he wants to be the only one in the rotation?"

"God, I hope not," I groaned, shoveling in another bite of ham and pineapple.

"What would be wrong with that?" Abby looked at me, perplexed.

"I wouldn't want to cut him loose, and he's incapable of being faithful. Besides, it's not like that with us," I told her. "I doubt he even knows my middle name or favorite color."

"Aside from the faithfulness, isn't the rest of that stuff you learn at the beginning of a relationship?"

"The faithfulness is mostly the point, Abby. He's cheated on five of his last six girlfriends. Which I might let go if it was just with me, but it wasn't. Plus, the other stuff? We've been sleeping together for three years! I don't know that stuff about him either!"

"Hey, Eric," she called to him at the register. Turning with the phone in his hand, he signaled for her to hold on.

"What are you doing?" I asked, frantic for her to let this go, because, as good as Eric is in bed, I really wasn't looking for a relationship.

"What's up?" Eric propped his head on his elbows in front of Abby. "You change your mind about having another go?"

"Do you know Lucas' middle name?" Abby fired, her expression schooled.

"Um, no? Why would I?" he looked at her like she'd grown an extra head. "But I do know that her middle initial is S, because it's on her debit card when she picks up her to go orders."

"Close enough," Abby shrugged. "It's Spencer, by the way."

"Why, Abby?" I whimpered at the same time Eric turned to me saying, "Lucas Spencer? Your mom a General Hospital fan?"

"Are *you*? How did you guess that so fast?"

"Oh come on, you don't have to be a fan to know about Luke and Laura! But yes, my mom is a fan, too," he confessed.

"Spencer isn't bad. It could've been worse," I said, sitting up taller on the stool.

"And how's that?"

"It could be Lorenzo," I mumbled and he immediately started to howl with laughter.

"I suppose you're right," he said, after calming down. "Mine's Michael, by the way," he threw over his shoulder on his way back to the now ringing phone.

"How boring for you," I yelled after him, turning my scowl to Abby. "Stop, it's not going to happen," I whispered, signaling our waitress for a box. I needed to finish my lunch to-go, because I couldn't go back and forth with Abby over this for the next hour.

"You never know."

"Just because you are all happy and flighty and in love now, doesn't mean you need to set your sights on my love life," I explained, sounding angrier than I intended, but wanting her to know I was serious. "Shadow and I are perfectly happy with things the way they are. I love you, though, and I'll see you Friday" I finished, throwing some money on my bill and waving at Eric as I passed him on my way out the door.

"If you have to bring your cat into your justification, maybe you should rethink your statement," Abby yelled after me, but it only caused me to laugh as I made my way to my truck.

CHAPTER 6

LUCAS

The afternoon of the party, I raced around my apartment trying to make it look presentable. Even with the complete lack of furniture, it was easier said than done. My worst habit was creating clutter, because I didn't like to throw anything away. This held true for books from old classes, same for the notes I took in said classes, bills that needed to be filed away, and random other papers that I really had no reason to keep. I had a large bookshelf bursting at the seams with paperwork and school books.

I guess the same could be said about the people in my life, I tended to collect them, too. I had exes that still hung around after we broke up for years. Guys that I'd turned down that thought there might be a chance, because I hadn't sat them down and told them it wasn't going to happen. I always tried to let a guy down nicely, but sometimes that translated as 'unclearly' shutting the door, but they still thought it was propped open.

Gathering a giant pile of assorted paperwork in my arms, I traipsed to the walk in closet in my vanity and shoved the pile onto a tote in the back corner, careful to balance it correctly so it didn't end up on the floor or in the cat's litter box. I knew that I wasn't actually cleaning anything, just making it less visible, but it made me feel better. Before exiting the closet, I took a visual inventory of my extensive liquor cabinet, making note of anything I might need to pick up before people arrived.

My parties were always BYO because I didn't have the money to bankroll them. Everyone understood the protocol and planned accordingly. I provided the mix-ins and my favorite booze, plus a twelve pack of cheap, shitty beer. If you wanted anything else, you were in charge of bringing it. I, generally, stuck to strawberry daiquiris and pina coladas in wine cooler form, because, though I enjoyed the mind numbing effect, I loathed the taste of alcohol.

Usually, Brady, Becca and, sometimes, Flynn would show up early to help out before everyone else arrived. The tradition had started from my first party, when I wasn't quite 21 yet. Flynn and Brady would grab some cash and a list from me then come back with a backseat full of the requested alcohol. Now, though, we would all go together. Flynn had been hit or miss when it came to wanting to hang out with me lately though, since I'd failed to call him, instead of Brady on New Years' Eve, he'd been incredibly distant and more hostile with me. I didn't understand what I'd done to make him so upset and he wouldn't talk to me. The whole thing puzzled me and made me wonder if he'd show up that night.

As if reading my thoughts, my cell phone started to ring from my card table. Seeing it was Becca, I laughed as I accepted the call.

"Hey!" I answered, brightly. "Are you guys heading over early tonight?"

"That's why I was calling," she started. "Flynn has to work tonight, but Brady and I are coming. We're bringing that guy from his work that he said came with him on New Year's?"

"Oh, yeah, that guy," I laugh, remembering how upset he got when someone had a better poker hand than he did. "That's cool, he's interesting people."

"That's putting it mildly," Becca joined in with my laughter. "But he's going to be a little late, so we won't be there early tonight."

"That's cool, then," I repeated. "I'll just see you when you get here. Carrie is bringing her famous chicken tacos."

"Awesome! I fucking love those things," she squealed. "Alright, I've gotta go find something smokin' to wear!"

"See you soon," I answered, clicking the end button on my phone and harrumphing into a folding chair at the table.

Becca had been my best chick friend since our freshman year of high school. She seemed to think we were in constant competition for things I just didn't care about, though. We'd fallen out of favor with each other a few times over the last seven years, but it was usually because our periods were in sync. Cycle syncing is the number one reason I think girls aren't supposed to be friends with each other, because eventually, you *will* want to rip each other's heads off or throw each other against-or through- a wall. She and I had been getting along great for a while, like for the last six months or so, which meant one false step could change that in seconds. I hated having to straddle that line and filter everything I said or did around her. Eventually, I'd piss her off and then she'd say something so much worse than my initial infraction that I wouldn't be able to overlook it. It was exhausting waiting to fight with your best friend. And it called attention to another cycle I constantly found myself in. Preston, Carter, Becca…was there anyone in my life that I didn't end up going around in circles with from time to time?

Those thoughts carried me through the remainder of the afternoon and my trip, alone, to the grocery store. Before long, the first guests were knocking on my door to party, and it was no surprise that Becca, Brady, and the dude from his work were on the other side.

"Hey guys! Come on in!" I greeted, ushering them into my apartment.

46

"I brought some Rolling Rock," Brady's friend said. He wasn't unattractive, short, slightly round, with dark features, but he definitely wasn't my type. Besides, his poor sportsmanship and whininess was a deal breaker for me. "Where do you want it?"

"Um, probably the fridge, unless you want to drink warm beer later," I suggested, motioning toward the kitchen. "You've been here before, don't be shy."

"That's Mike," Brady nodded toward his friend before hoisting the bottle in his hand. "And this is vanilla vodka. They were out of the raspberry."

"Sounds good," I said, taking the bottle from his hands. "I still have a few shots of the raspberry in the walk in, if you want to claim it," I offered as I set the bottle on the kitchen counter.

"Did you buy any Coke or ice?" Becca teased, knowing that I usually forget ice when we go to the store. No matter how often I tell myself to remember it, I almost always forget, even if the cashier asks if I need any.

As I opened my mouth to shoot her a snarky answer, Carrie kicks my door open in all her Amazonian glory, her hands full of deliciousness, and three more guest trailing behind her. "I found these guys downstairs."

"Tell them to leave," I joked. "That way I don't have to share the tacos," I shoot my friends a smirk over Carrie's shoulder and grab the fixins from her hand while she balanced the container with the meat in her other hand.

"I need your microwave," she said, pushing past Mike and starting to warm up everything. Mike looked up at the blonde haired, blue eyed beauty that just took over my kitchen, his mouth agape.

"I'm going to start drinking," Mike said, shaking out of his stupor and pulling a beer from the pack he just stored in my refrigerator. "I've got a really high tolerance for alcohol, so I need to pre-game before everyone really starts to show up."

**

Two hours later, the party was in full swing. The smokers were outside, the non-smokers were sitting at my card table playing some dirty game someone bought me for Christmas, and those in between were just chilling on the floor of my living room. All in all, everyone was having a great time, except Mike, who was already praying to the porcelain God and forcing guests to find another place to pee.

"So much for his high tolerance claim," Carrie said, hiding a snicker behind her hand.

"I thought he said he had 'Irish blood,'" Becca added, her shoulders shaking with restrained laughter.

"I need to change," I said, pulling at my clothes. I'd started out the evening in my tailored tan pants with the lace and fringe belt, with my blue, white and tan watercolor one sleeve shirt. My hair hung around my shoulders, because I didn't feel like pulling it back.

"Costume change number one!" Becca yelled out to the party guests. Becca and Carrie were already dressed comfortably in jeans and t-shirts, but part of the lore of my parties was how often I changed my clothes. The amount of costume changes was a good gauge at how drunk I was at a given time in the evening. My choices became more and more for comfort and less for style as the party raged on. My guests knew I was nearly done for the evening when I came out in my pajamas.

48

"I think I'm only going to have one tonight, Becca. I'm going straight for comfort over style. Carter's already here, so no one else to see how cute I look before I change into something A LOT more comfortable," I said, dismissively.

"Damn, I've got three changes in the pool tonight," Carrie snapped her fingers in feigned disappointment.

"Are you already *that* drunk?" Becca tutted, disapprovingly before whispering to Carrie, "I had two."

"Well, I'm not drunk enough to have my head in a toilet already, like somebody," I answered, my voice getting louder with each word, hoping Mike heard.

"You mean like the party bitch?" Carrie laughed.

"We should totally write that on him somewhere when he passes out," Becca whispered, trying to school her fit of the giggles.

Sweeping my eyes over my guests, I spot Brady and Carter coming back into the apartment then my eyes swing back to Becca and Carrie with a brilliant idea. "New plan!" I announced. "First, I'm going to change into my comfies, and then I'm going to kiss everyone."

"Everyone?" Becca asked, her eyes slicing to Mike, still puking with the bathroom door open.

"Maybe not everyone, but everyone not currently puking," I smiled. "Is it okay with you if I kiss Brady?" I asked, feeling obligated, since I knew Becca had her heart set on being the second Mrs. Manning.

"Of course!" she agreed, but something told me she wasn't happy about it, maybe it was the fact that the words came out behind gritted teeth and a too tight smile. I was too drunk to care though. I had permission, dammit! I was going to kiss Brady, even if she didn't really mean it. "OH!

Look! Mike's out of the bathroom and shirtless on the vanity floor! Let's grab the whipped cream for the blow jobs and decorate the drunk!"

"Let's do it!" Carrie agreed, grabbing a black marker from my dresser and leaving me in my bedroom to change. Once I was comfortably attired in a tank top and pajama shorts, I set off through my apartment, kissing everyone who crossed my path. The kiss was generally a small peck on the lips, until I finally reached Brady.

"Do you mind if I kiss you?" I asked, with a slight smirk. He'd just seen me kiss nearly everyone else at the party, so I hoped I'd been sly enough that he didn't realize I'd kissed everyone else just because I wanted an excuse to kiss him. I'd been wondering what it would be like since he'd kissed my forehead instead of my lips on New Years'. I was excited at the prospect of finding out if my crush would die right here or if I'd have to try to sleep with him to get him out of my system.

"Why not?" Brady answered with his usual mask of indifference in place. The second my lips touched his, I knew this had been a mistake. My stomach plunged to my toes and I was all too aware of my heart trying to escape through my throat. I didn't know if getting him out of my system would ever be an option.

**

BRADY

Holy fuck! Electricity pinged through my body quicker than I would've thought possible, considering the amount of alcohol I'd consumed over the last couple of hours. Lucy's lips connecting with mine sent an instant signal to my dick that it was game on. I tried to convey to my cock that it shouldn't get its hopes up of sinking balls deep into

50

Lucy, but it wasn't listening as it jerked happily under my jeans. Frankly, it wasn't just my dick that was on board with getting Lucy out of her tiny shorts and tank top and fucking her until she screamed. My heart was beating faster, but my head was telling the rest of me to calm the fuck down. At least, part of it was. The sensible part, but it was only half-assing the argument, so I knew my brain wanted it, too. It had to be the copious amount of vodka running through my system that had me off my game. I was far too eager for this.

The taste of strawberry daiquiris on her lips reminded me that she was just as drunk as I was, but then her tongue connected with mine, all remaining thoughts in my brain ceased and the rest of my body said 'game on!' She'd circled the room and placed chaste kisses on most of the people at the party, some were less innocent. I was glad to get one of the less innocent kisses, but I'd expected something much more chaste, since we weren't the kissing type of friends. Aside from New Year's, I didn't think we were even the touching kind of friends.

She was careful not to press her body against me and I had to fight to keep my hands at my sides and let her kiss me, so I didn't scare her away. Her lips were soft and I could just feel the tips of her breasts against my chest as she explored every corner of my mouth.

As she pulled away, I had to choke back a growl over the loss. I didn't have to wait long to test the theory of whether my response was akin to her or the alcohol, because Becca, apparently jealous of her best friend, yanked my face to her lips as soon as her friend continued on, finding Carter's lips next. Lucy kissed him with the same amount of passion she'd given to me, it seemed.

As Becca's lips connected with mine, I felt the same thing I always did. Nothing. Holy shit, it was Lucy. I hadn't been expecting that. I'd been wondering what kissing Lucy would feel like, and now I had the feeling that it was a door that we should've left closed. Had she been wondering the same thing? Is that why she kissed me?

On these thoughts, a slight frown pulled at my lips as Bec broke the kiss. Her mouth dropped in shock at my expression. With an affronted huff, she stomped back to the Lucy's vanity to resume licking whipped cream from a nearly passed out Mike. Thank fuck he'd finally stopped vomiting! Maybe now someone could actually use the toilet to piss, instead of having to walk down to the convenience store on the corner. Or finding a patch of grass down by the trash can for us guys.

"You okay, Brady?" Lucy asked from her kitchen table, looking perplexed. I wanted to test the connection again, but I couldn't without being overly obvious about being attracted to her. My curiosity was short-lived, as I watched Carter yank Lucy from her chair and pull her into what looked to be a very serious, very possessive kiss. I knew our kiss had bothered him, because he kept one eye on me the entire time his tongue invaded her mouth, as if he were trying to challenge me. If it were me, I'd be focusing on how to get her into her bedroom and out of her clothes, not looking at some dude across the room. Oh well, I shrugged, scratching my head. It wasn't like I needed that kind of headache anyway. After breaking my weird eye contact with Carter, I stumbled out the front door to have a cigarette. I didn't think I could handle watching him pull her into her bedroom. With his hands all over her ass, I had no doubt that's where they were headed next.

Calmly, I enjoyed the quiet of the cool night and listened to the traffic that was still pretty abundant for after two in the morning as it passed Lucy's apartment complex. Just as I crushed my cigarette in the ashtray, Lucy's front door opened and Carter stepped out, trying to look formidable.

"Stay away from her, man. She's mine," he warned.

"Then why aren't you guys together?" I asked, the words spilling from my mouth before I could stop them. I'm not supposed to care about who Lucy's with, I tried to remind myself.

"It's complicated. I'm working out my own shit, but I have her on retainer for when I get it figured out. She can keep fucking her little army of boys, but you wouldn't be up for being one of her fuck toys, so you need to back off," he said again. "You'd want something real with her, but you can't have her."

On those words, I watched, shocked at his observations, as he walked down the stairwell, leaving the party. What the fuck? He just warned me off, and left? How did he expect to keep me from her when he wasn't willing to stick around?

CHAPTER 7

BRADY

The Monday following Lucy's party, I found myself at the impromptu wedding of my brother, Parker, and his fiancé, Celia. It was, for lack of a better term, a shotgun wedding. Not to say that they weren't in love and devoted to each other. They were. In fact, they'd planned to have their wedding much further down the road, but a baby and the US Army Reserves had decided to move their timetable up a few years. I took a vacation day so my daughter and I could be there for him. I may be cynical about ever finding love for myself, but that would never stop me from wishing my brother and his new bride all the happiness in the world. Or, at least, that's what I told them.

After spending the afternoon securing a marriage license and trying to talk Taylor into wearing the dress his fiancé picked out. My two year old folded her arms over her chest and turned her nose up, declaring the dress looked "itchy." After promising her a trip for ice cream, I was finally able to wrestle her into the purple monstrosity that Taylor confirmed was, in fact, itchy. Add to that the actual ceremony at a small wedding house, plus a messy trip to the ice cream shop and the resulting bath, my daughter and I were officially exhausted. About the time I got her tucked into bed and began to breathe again, my cell phone started ringing in my pocket. Loudly. Fuck.

My eyes cut to my sleeping daughter and grabbed the phone, answering it quickly and not checking the caller ID.

"Hello?" I whispered before hurrying out of my bedroom to leave my daughter in peace.

"Hey, Brady. Are you busy? I'm sorry! I thought you were working tonight, I was just going to leave you a message to call me back," Lucy's voice came through the line.

"Hey, Lucy," I answered, trying to keep myself in check. The last time she'd called was to confirm Preston's deployment, so I was pretty sure this call had nothing to do with me either. "I'm good, I was getting ready to yell at you for calling after I'd put my daughter to bed, but I realize you didn't know I wasn't working tonight."

"You have Taylor on a Monday?"

"Parker got married today," I explained.

"Oh, okay," she said, sounding just as confused as she did when the conversation started. "I didn't know he was engaged."

"What do you need?" I prompted, trying to find out if this was another mistaken dial or if she'd meant to call me.

"Um, are you working tomorrow night?"

"I plan to…"

"Well, Carter is giving me his couch, but I need someone to help me move it," she started. The tone of her voice gave away her reluctance to ask me this favor, but I was, secretly, glad that she called me. Absently, I wondered if I was her first phone call or her last resort. The thought of being her last call bugged me more than I wanted to contemplate at the moment. "He has to work in the afternoon on Wednesday and needs me to get it before 10am. You could come over after work and get some rest?" she offered. "He lives in Tempe, too, so you might get a little more rest that way?"

"Yeah, that should be fine. I carpool to work, but I know a guy on my shift that lives that way. I'm sure I could catch a ride with him," I assured her, wondering why agreeing to help her was second nature to me when we'd only ever been casual friends that didn't ask these kinds of favors of each other.

"Oh, thank God!" she breathed into the phone, sounding more grateful for my help than made sense. "I'll see you tomorrow then?"

"I get off work at 2am, so it's more like Wednesday morning," I joked. "But yeah, I'll see you then." Ending the call, a small knot of nerves started to form at the base of my stomach.

I didn't know what to expect in going to her apartment in the middle of the night during the week. I knew she had a rotating stock of guys because she didn't want a relationship. Would there be a guy there when I showed up? Would she make me sleep on the floor in the living room or let me sleep in her bed? Stopping the direction of my thoughts, I sat down in front of the television and turned on the Playstation. Maybe some violence was in order to clear these thoughts from my head. My helping her move a couch was not the sign of anything, and I was stupid to even think that I might want something with her. Neither of us were relationship material.

**

By the time I walked to Lucy's door after work the next night, the small knot had grown to a giant tangle of yarn sitting in my stomach. I had no idea what to say to her nor did I know how we'd interact. I was a quiet, introverted guy and she was like a ray of fucking sunshine. I'd never met a bigger extrovert. She never met a stranger. Maybe she'd just want to go back to sleep right away and leave me to unwind on my own.

Taking a deep breath, I knocked lightly on the green door to her apartment. As I waited for her, I bounced from foot to foot, trying to regain my equilibrium.

56

"Cold?" she asked as she opened the door.

"Very," I lied; hustling into the darkness of her apartment, only a small light from the walk-in closet in her vanity area illuminated the apartment. "Did you fall asleep again?"

"No, I'm not that tired anymore," she answered as I watched her rub her bare arms trying to warm them from the few seconds she stood in the doorway. I watched her eyes as they took in my trademark jeans and t-shirt while I noticed her dye stained gray tank top and blue monkey shorts. I could tell that she was affected by the cold air, as she wasn't wearing a bra and I had to tear my eyes away from her, obviously, erect nipples.

"The cold wake you up?"

"Something like that," she answered, the quiver in her voice betraying something other than just catching a chill. In fact, it sounded similar to nerves. Was she as nervous about us being alone as I was? "Can I get you anything?"

"Can I get a shot of that vanilla vodka? Is there any left?" I responded with the first thought that came to my mind. I would be much more relaxed after a drink or two or three or seven. Then I wouldn't have any problems talking to her.

"Um, sure," she smiled before grabbing the bottle of vodka from her liquor cabinet in the walk in closet and a shot glass from a cabinet above her sink. "Here," she thrust the contents of her hand at me.

"Thanks, um, do you want a shot, too?" I offered, not wanting to look like I was a lush.

"Sure," she grinned, relieved, before pulling down another shot glass. "So, when you're ready to sleep," she broached, biting her lip and taking the shot I poured for her.

I downed mine as she continued to talk. Her words had me pouring us both a second drink. "I don't think it would be cool of me make you sleep on the floor out here, and I've got a queen sized bed, so you're welcome to sleep beside me. I mean, if it's not too weird," she rushed the remainder of her words.

"Sure, thanks," I told her, holding my shot glass in a toast and downing it again. As she followed suit, I caught a whiff of her apple body spray on the heated air of the apartment and my body started to react. Maybe sharing a bed was a bad idea, but it was too late now. Saying no now would only call attention to my possible reasons, of which there were only two: 1. I wanted her and didn't think I could control myself or 2. I thought she was repulsive and thought I might catch something if I shared her bed. So sharing the bed as if the first option weren't playing in my head in a loop was my only real choice.

"So, um, how was your day?" I asked, trying to make conversation while I poured a third shot. I didn't drink like this, but I couldn't seem to stop the flood of nerves in my system. The fact that she'd made no move to turn on any of the lights in her apartment, aside from the light shining from her walk-in closet, added to the quiet intimacy of the moment.

"It was fine," she smiled, seemingly nervously, as she accepted another shot glass of vodka from me. "Work was busy, but otherwise dull."

"I know what you mean," I agreed, giving another small salute with my glass and tipping it back. Over the top of the glass, I watched her do the same.

"So, um, how are things with Becca? She doesn't mind you staying here tonight, right?"

58

"Becca and I aren't together, Lucy," I frowned, twirling the empty shot glass on the table.

"Oh?" her brows shot up at my words, like she was surprised.

"We just hook up occasionally," I grumbled, not proud of my decisions to continue sleeping with Becca after I realized nothing would ever happen between us. Honestly, it was something I knew before I fucked her, but more often than not, a willing female was better than my hand.

"Oh, um, she made it seem like it was more than that," Lucy said, chewing slightly on her bottom lip again. It seemed like it might be a nervous habit, because I'd never seen her do it before.

"Doesn't she always, though?" I sighed, not really wanting to talk about Becca. "I need a cigarette," I announced, getting up from the table.

"I'll grab my blanket and join you," she said, giving me a small smile. I'd never been so happy to have someone watch me smoke. Shit, taking her up on her offer to share her bed had *really* been a bad idea.

**

LUCAS

What was I thinking telling Brady we could share my bed? I didn't let guys sleep over in my bed, like ever. With the random exception of Carter or Preston, a long time ago. Why did it feel so different when I offered the option to Brady? I hadn't even meant to say the words when I opened my mouth, but they barreled out without any real warning.

I went over and over everything in my mind as I watched him smoke. While my blanket warmed my arms, my feet were starting to feel like icicles, but I couldn't bring myself to leave him outside alone. We idly chattered about how his day was and Parker's wedding. Absently, I wondered if Preston had been there. We'd talked earlier for quite a while about his impending departure and how scared he was to go to war. Even though we'd drifted apart after an encounter six months ago, he was still one of my oldest friends and my first love.

"Ready for bed?" I asked Brady when he snubbed out his cigarette and turned to me. He just nodded, looking slightly pale and nervous about the possible implications of my question.

In spite of my inner turmoil, I found myself slipping into my side of the bed and pulling myself as close to the edge as possible. When I noticed Brady do the same thing, after only taking off his jacket before climbing into my bed, and turning his back to me, I breathed a small sigh of relief and let myself relax enough to fall asleep for a few hours.

I awoke later to my alarm and actually felt refreshed. It seemed in those few hours of being unconscious, Brady and I had drifted closer to each other. While we weren't wrapped in each other's arms or anything, I could definitely feel his warmth beside me. A small frown formed on my lips as I realized how good waking up beside him felt. Waking up beside Carter always felt weird, but I didn't feel any of that with Brady which, in and of itself, was weird.

"Good morning," he groaned, his voice gravely from sleep.

"Morning," I muttered back before rolling out of bed and heading to the bathroom. "We have to head over to Carter's in like five minutes, but I really didn't want to wake up. Sorry," I threw over my shoulder on the way.

60

"No problem. I'll be ready after my morning smoke," he laughed, making his way out my front door to the open corridor to have a cigarette. After completing a shortened version of my morning routine, I joined him outside and we set off in my truck for Carter's place. Leaving him in my truck, I hopped out to knock on the door.

"So I see you brought Brady to help," Carter said, dryly, as I walked him back to where Brady was standing. I was glad he seemed to be just out of earshot, because my eyes flew to him and he only smiled at me as we approached. "I knew you were into him."

"What are you talking about, Carter?" I asked as followed him into his townhome.

"Nothing," he grumbled, shaking his head at me before turning to Brady. "It's in here, man. Follow me. Lucas, why don't you put your tailgate down so we can load it up easier."

"Sure," I agreed, wary about leaving the two of them alone, since Carter seemed to be—jealous? That had never happened before. There was nothing to be jealous of; I wasn't going to ever date Brady. I didn't even have a chance. Just as I pulled the tailgate down on my truck, the guys made their way through Carter's front door with a long black couch covered in white cat fur.

"I'm letting you borrow my shampooer to get the cat hair off," Carter called to me as they approached the bed of the truck. "It should come off easily."

"No problem," I shrugged, getting out of their way. "It's not like my cat won't shed all over it, too, but it'll be nice to get the scent of *other* cats off it so she doesn't try to mark her territory all over it."

"Probably a good idea," he grunted, stepping into the bed while pulling the couch as Brady pushed.

"It's a tad too long," Brady announced as they were now both pushing the sofa into place and running out of room.

"Did you bring any ties?" Carter asked, slightly annoyed.

"I've got like two little bungees behind my seat we can try," I answered, reaching into the cab of my truck and pulling back my seat to grab the ties.

"We'll just have to drive back to your place slower than usual, Lucy. It'll be fine," Brady smiled.

"I'll meet you guys over there," Carter said, walking to his car.

"Sounds good," Brady and I said, ducking into my truck.

"I'll watch it and let you know if there are any issues, cool?"

"Perfect," I told him, cranking the truck and starting to back out of the driveway slowly.

An hour later, my apartment officially had a couch in the living room, and Brady was lying on my bed again to get a few minutes rest before I had to drive him back to his place. This allowed me the ability to walk Carter to his car without an audience and get to the bottom of his supposed issues.

"Why'd you call Brady?" Carter asked as we walked down the stairs.

"Why not?" I shrugged. "He's a friend who mentioned he would be up for it when we were all talking about it at the party."

"Yeah, but you'd just kissed the shit out of him, Lucas. He probably would've agreed to be a surrogate mother for you, too," he paused on the steps and focused his chocolate brown eyes on mine so that I could see he was serious.

"He's not into me like that, Carter. It was just a kiss," I dismissed. "Besides, I kissed everyone at that party and you don't see a line of people helping today, do you?"

"I see the way he looks at you, Lucas. I'm not stupid," he said. "He's closer to your age, too. I think he'd be really good for you, better than me, anyway," he finished, before leaning in to give me a kiss good bye.

"God, you're confusing," I said, rolling my eyes and suppressing an exasperated groan as he settled in behind the wheel of his car.

"I know," he grinned. "Call me when you are done with that shampooer and I'll come and pick it up."

Instead of answering, I shot him a quick salute as he stomped on his accelerator and screeched out of the parking lot.

CHAPTER 8

BRADY

Waking up beside Lucy had fucked with my head all day. I didn't think it would really be that big of a deal to sleep in her bed, but I hadn't expected it to feel so natural to climb in beside her, to feel her warmth permeating the mattress, to feel her ice cold feet against mine the next morning. The whole thing should've had me spinning in directions I didn't even want to fucking think about.

After she said good bye to Carter, she came back into her apartment and crawled in bed with me. We slept another two hours before she needed to give me a ride back to my apartment to catch my car pool. I woke up before she did, and damned if I could keep myself from watching her sleep. I felt like a jackass.

Her black hair was peeking out from under the covers, but her entire body, including her head, was cocooned under the blanket. I'd never seen anything like it. She always seemed so strong, but she slept like she was hiding from the world. After being friends for two years, this development confused me. It, also, intrigued me.

That small amount of vulnerability I saw when she slept beside me haunted me the rest of the day. Is that the reason she never let anyone sleep over with her? Because she didn't want them to think of her as weak?

"Hey, man," Xander said, slapping me on the back and sitting beside me on the picnic table. "Light me?" he asked, holding up a cigarette.

"I should make you suck the pole, but I'll show you some mercy," I said, grabbing the cigarette and lighting it with my own. Xander was my work best friend. He'd looked out for me when he was my supervisor, because I'd been going through my divorce and dealing with Lori's demands and inconsistent parenting schedules with regards to Taylor. If he hadn't been so understanding about the whole thing, I doubted I'd still have a job. We worked at a manufacturing facility with explosives used for commercial mining and blasting and other fun stuff, so carrying a lighter to work was an offense punishable by death. And the death of your fellow co-workers because you were stupid enough to think it was okay to bring a lighter into a building with enough gun powder to take out a small country. The first person to make it to the smoking patio had to light their cigarette from a pole the company provides for those of us with the disgusting habit.

"Well, thank you for taking pity on me," he said, miserably, taking a long drag from his newly lit cigarette. "It's been a rough day, man," he sighed, shaking his head. "Just found out my girl's cheating on me."

"No shit!" I said, but I wasn't actually surprised. "Mike?" I asked, knowing that the ass that couldn't hold his liquor had been crashing on their couch for the last couple of months.

"Yup," he confirmed, taking another drag from his cigarette and casting an evil eye at one of our co-workers that looked like she was going to join us at our table. She, quickly, reversed course and left us alone. "Great way to pay me back for taking his sorry ass in, right? Now I need a place to crash, cause I'm sure as hell not staying there."

"No doubt," I agreed, flicking some ash to the ground. "This is why I don't date."

"I'm joining the club. It's been far too long since I got myself some strange."

"Not to sound like a dick or pussy or anything," I started, wanting to be a good friend and ask the obvious questions. "But are you okay? I know you have kids together, man."

"Yeah, it sucks, but I'm going to be there for the kids," he nodded, resolutely.

"If it makes you feel any better, I think Lucy got a picture of him naked, with just a pillow covering his junk at the last party," I offered. I don't make it a habit to assess guys, but I looked at Xander and wondered who could've ever picked Mike over him. He was a good four inches taller than me, and looked every bit the biker badass he was raised to be. He was his father's son, right down to the tats and goatee. Mike was barely five foot eight and resembled a hairy troll.

"Why the fuck would I want to see that?" he graveled out. "If it weren't for my ex and the kids, the dude would be in a shallow desert grave by now."

"You wouldn't, I know, but I doubt he'd want anyone else to see it either," I answered, staring, unfocused, at the metal building in front of me. "It's more legal than what you want to do."

"Good point," he chuckled. "Who's this Lucy you're always talking about?"

"She's a friend," I shrug, not really knowing how to describe her. "She's cool, not a typical chick. You'd like her."

"Isn't that where you were today? Hanging out with her?"

"Well, I went over after work last night so I could help her move a couch into her apartment, yeah," I said, taking a drag from my Marlboro.

66

"Oh?" he lifted his eyebrow in question. "Is that a euphemism? Like you delivered her a pizza or cooked her some sausage?"

"It's not like that with her," I shut him down.

"You sure? Why'd she call you to help her then?"

"You know, I honestly couldn't tell you," I said, suddenly dumbfounded and questioning why I was the one she called for help.

"She have an extra room or did you sleep on her floor? I mean, I'm assuming she needed the couch cause she didn't have one."

"No, we shared her bed. Her carpet is like concrete and looks like it hasn't been changed by her complex in the last twenty years," I said, as a means of explanation.

"Oh?" he repeated the gesture of lifting his eyebrow at me.

"I told you, it's not like that with her."

"Sure, it's not," he scoffed, taking a drag from his Camel.

"Change the subject, bro," I said through gritted teeth. I didn't know why I was getting so defensive over some fairly innocuous questioning about my sleeping arrangements with Lucy last night.

"Fine. How'd she get this picture of the asshole?"

"Drunken truth or dare. Mike was so blitzed at the last party, I doubt he even noticed. He spent most of the laying on the floor of her vanity and occupying her bathroom," I snickered at the memory. "He proclaimed that his supposed Irish heritage made his alcohol tolerance really high, and then puked like it was his job after half a twelve pack of Rolling Rock. Holy shit, man, when he finally came up for air, he'd burst a couple of blood vessels in his eyes from spewing so hard."

"Classic, I wish I could've seen it."

"She's having another party next weekend, you should come with us," I offered. "Even if you don't get laid, you are sure to see, at least, one set of boobs and girls making out with girls."

"Fuckin' A, man! You've been holding out on me," he grinned, slapping me on the back. "Reminds me of the parties my dad used to have."

"Not holding out on you, at all," I dismissed. "You've just been busy with the kids and all that."

"Sounds just like what I need! I'm in!"

"If you want to crash on my couch in the meantime, I don't think my roommates would mind."

"I don't want to impose, but if they are cool with it, I'm sure I can pitch in with the rent," Xander grinned at his new possibilities. "I can't wait to meet this Lucy chick though, she sounds awesome."

"She is pretty cool," I mumbled more to myself, but Xander's eyebrows shot up and I could see the wheels start to turn in his head. "I already told you. It's not like that with us," I graveled out.

"Sure it isn't," he agreed, sarcastically.

"She's not the type to settle down, man. Believe me. When you meet her, you'll get it," I said, stamping out my cigarette and headed back to my machine to finish out the night, wondering why the reason I gave Xander was that she wasn't the type to settle down. I didn't want to get married again, so why the fuck did Lucy's inability to commit bug me so much?

68

"I'll be the judge of that, my friend," I could hear Xander's laughter following me the entire way and I knew the gears were turning in his head. Shit, I needed to figure all these new thoughts about that girl before the party, or Xander might think it was up to him to play misguided matchmaker.

**

LUCAS

Because of the couch moving extravaganza, my regular lunch date with Abby was pushed back a day, guaranteeing a run in with Eric. When we pulled up, I could tell she was already giddy with the prospect. I still didn't understand what it was about being in a couple that made you suddenly want to pair up all of your friends, even if the thought of being in a relationship made them want to claw their eyes out. Or in my case, gave them hives and caused their throat to close up.

"Stop bouncing, Abby, before I have to tell Ted to stop giving you sugar in the morning," I growled, wanting to head home before lunch even started. A deep sense of dread came over me when she giggled, so I continued with my threat, "I didn't mean in the metaphorical sense. I literally mean I'm going to tell him to stop buying you donuts."

"You wouldn't dare," her green eyes widened and I hid my grin behind a curtain of black hair as I bent to pick up my purse from the floorboard beside her.

"Just behave, okay? I don't have the time or desire to turn my arrangement with Eric into something more permanent," I warned again.

"I think you protest too much, but fine," she pouted, but exited my truck with her head high. "But, that's not going to stop us from partying like crazy this weekend, right?"

"Fuck," I groaned, when the date flashed in my head. "I told Dennis I'd work Saturday at the other hotel to make up for the time I'm taking off for my party next weekend. I'm sorry! I totally forgot you wanted to drink your way through Mill Ave!"

"Fuck is right!" Abby's pout seemed to grow deeper at my words. "But, if it's slow, he'll let you leave early and you can meet Ted and me wherever we are? I don't know how you work two jobs and go to school full time."

"You know why I work as much as I do, Abby," I reminded her that although one job would cover my bills sufficiently, the extra money kept me from feeling like I was living paycheck to paycheck. I liked knowing that I had savings to fall back on if I ever ended up jobless or something.

"I know," she moaned, "but it's messing with my birthday, come on!"

But how am I supposed to help you drink your way down Mill if I have to drive afterward?" I asked, going back to her previous suggestion of meeting up with them.

"Ted and I will pick you up and we'll get trashed!" she grinned at the new plan, volunteering her boyfriend for an unnecessary trip. "I can't promise I won't be already trashed though."

70

"I didn't expect you to wait, Abs, believe me," I chuckled as we made our way to the familiar bar top and two empty chairs against the wall. Part of me wondered if we were really that lucky to always find bar seats right away, or if we had help from a guardian angel answering the phone.

"Hey, Eric," I greeted, flipping him a salute as we sat down.

"Hey, Lucas, am I up tonight?" he asked, winking at me with his dark brown eyes sparkling.

"Do you want to be?" I flirted.

"I already am," he stage-whispered to me across the bar.

"Well, I get off work at 11 tonight, if you want to swing by," I offered.

"Sounds like a plan," he smiled. "I'll be the puppy scratching at the door at 11:15. I tried to call the other night, but you didn't answer."

"Oh, I had someone over," I answered, dismissively.

"Auditioning another newbie, Lucas?" Eric asked, something like disappointment flashing in his eyes.

"Oh, nothing like that," I laughed, but it came out harder than I intended, sending a questioning look from Abby. "My friend, Brady, stayed over to help me move a couch Carter gave me."

"Look at you all fancy with your furniture from ex-boyfriends."

"Carter isn't an ex, well, not really."

"I couldn't see you for like three months when you met Carter, Lucas. Even if there were no labels, he was your boyfriend," Eric said.

"I've seen you guys together, Lucas. Carter was your boyfriend," Abby agreed, making me feel cornered.

"Doesn't matter now, does it?" I sneered at them. "I tried to show him I could commit, but he wasn't interested," I continued, trying to shrug it off, but knowing that my initial reaction had sold me out.

"That guy is straight up in love with you, Lucas," Abby shook her head. "Mark my words, if he starts to feel like someone is a threat to his tentative claim on you, he'll get aggressive."

"Maybe I should meet this guy, size him up, make sure he's worthy of you," Eric offered, his eyes suddenly distant.

"Thanks, but—"

"You're still coming to the party next weekend, right?" Abby asked, starting to bounce in her chair again.

"Um, I was planning on it; you're still getting me a pack of New Castles, right?"

"Yeah," I nodded, but wondered why I was agreeing to buy Eric a six pack of beer that I wouldn't normally buy my other guests, especially expensive premium beer.

"You can meet Carter then! He'd never miss one of Lucas' parties, too much lady on lady action."

"Good to know," he rubbed the shadow of dark hair on his chin as the phone at his station started to ring and he excused himself to get back to work. Our waitress came to grab our usual order and Abby and I fell into a companionable silence until our drinks came.

"So, how did everything go with Carter and Brady?" Abby asked before taking a sip of her Coke.

"Fine," I shrugged, puzzled about her line of questioning as I plunged my straw into the glass of ice cold Dr. Pepper in front of me.

"Fine? Really? Cause Carter had murder in his eyes when you kissed Brady last weekend."

"I know," I sighed, with an eye roll. "He kissed me hard enough to bruise after I kissed Brady, like he was trying to prove something," I continued, flatly.

"So, nothing's going on with you and Brady?" Abby asked, her tone disbelieving as the waitress brought us our lunch slices. Ordering from Antonio's lunch menu ensured prompt service, especially the pizza. It was a huge slice of thin crust pizza, cut into smaller squares of deliciousness.

"Carter asked me that yesterday, too, and the answer is no," I shut her down, picking up a stray piece of pineapple and popping it into my mouth. "Brady is a good friend, he doesn't think of me like that."

"Oh, convenient little phrasing there, Lucas," Abby smirked over the chunk of pizza in her hand.

"What do you mean?" I frowned.

"*He* doesn't think about you like that? What about *you?*"

"What about me? That doesn't matter; neither of us is looking for anything. I think his divorce turned him against relationships. Plus, he's been hooking up with Becca, and that's usually a big no-no spot for me," I rambled, knowing I was getting her one too many reasons why I couldn't be with Brady. Abby didn't miss much when it came to that stuff and her 'Lucas has obviously thought about this' radar had to be pinging like crazy.

"Hmmm, sounds almost perfect to me," she grinned a little too brightly.

"You really don't care who I'm paired up with, do you? Carter, Eric, Brady? You just want me to have a boyfriend."

"Um, HELLOOOOO?" she said, as if what she was about to say was the most obvious thing in the word. "Double dating?"

"It's not my fault you want me to come on your dates with Ted, Abs," I groaned. "I don't want to be in a couple, so what makes you think there is even the *remote* possibility that I'd want to be a part of a couple's night? That's like double the commitment," I choked out, disgusted at her suggestion. "I'm afraid something like that would actually cause my death, because I would be suffocating on my lack of freedom."

"Don't knock it 'til you've tried it, Lucas," she warned before we turned back to our lunches. I was beginning to wonder if I was going to have to distance myself from Abby until she realized that Lucas Dunn and relationships were like oil and water or maybe I should just double down on the debauchery until she got the point. Yes, this was something that could only be fixed by calling in the rotation in succession. I'd only been calling Eric for far too long and people were starting to get ideas.

Though, my heart gave a little kick I didn't want to acknowledge when I thought about the possibility of adding Brady as a pinch hitter. I couldn't fight the visions that flooded my brain of having him as the only player in the dugout, and how it almost brought a smile to my face.

Fuck! I've gotta get rid of this crush, because it was more dangerous than I ever thought possible.

CHAPTER 9

LUCAS

After knocking out my goals for the week, at school, at work and personally, I found myself still daydreaming about Brady. I was starting to piss myself off, so I made sure to get the time off I needed to celebrate Abby's birthday with her and get completely and totally trashed. Three solid nights of sex with my rotation hadn't helped me forget, so alcohol was my only remaining option.

We'd made our way inside the third bar of the evening, and it was a favorite of mine. The waitresses all dressed in school girl uniforms and you could dance on the bar. After settling into a booth, I announced that I was going to grab us some more shots. We'd been alternating between blow job shots and Seven and Sevens since the first bar.

After stepping up to the crowd and trying to get the bartender's attention, I smoothed down the black skirt that Abby had picked out for me that barely covered my ass, and pulled up the baby blue halter she paired it with. That, coupled with my knee high black boots, was turning more heads than I wanted to think about, as everything I had was on display.

"Hey," a guy at the end of the bar called.

"Are you talking to me?" I asked, pointing at myself and looking confused. Looking him over, I knew I didn't know this guy, nor was I sure I wanted to.

"I don't see any other goth hotties in here, do you?" he asked, now openly leering at my chest like it could grant all his wishes.

"Just cause I have black hair, it doesn't mean I'm goth," I growled, tired of this stereotype that goes along with my new hair color. I still wore bright colors and refrained from heavy eyeliner, so, honestly, I didn't get the correlation.

"Can I buy you a drink?" he asked.

"No, thanks, I'm here with my friend, Abby and her boyfriend. It's her birthday, don't want to bail out on her. I'm just grabbing her a blow job," I told him, wondering why I told him the name of the shot I'm buying or any of that entire diatribe. I must be more drunk than I thought. I knew he's going to think it was an in when it totally wasn't.

"Wow, sounds hot! Can you take it with no hands?" he leaned closer to me and I caught a whiff of the beer he'd apparently been rolling around in and decided to mess with him a little.

"Of course, but I don't take the shot from the bar like an amateur," I scoffed, stumbling slightly on my too high heels. "I can take it from my cleavage," I whisper and right on cue his eyes widened like he'd won the fucking lottery with me. Holding up two fingers, he signaled the bartender and ordered two blow job shots for me.

"I'm Shamus," he said, running a hand through his orange hair and winking one of his beady green eyes at me.

"What the hell kind of name is that? Are you a leprechaun?" I asked, discovering that the four shot and two drink mark was when my filter disappeared. Suddenly, the bartender set the shots in front of Shamus, who handed me one expectantly.

"It's the name of the guy who wants to see your parlor trick so you can take this other shot to your friend for free."

Growling slightly, I grabbed the shot from his hand and exposed another half inch of my cleavage by pulling on the bottom of my halter top. Placing the shot on the outer edge of my breasts, I put my hands behind my back, letting

76

my head descend toward my tits. Securing the shot glass in my mouth, I throw back the shot and yank the glass from my teeth, slamming it back on the bar top. Smiling triumphantly, I wiped the excess whipped cream from my lips with my tongue slowly.

"Damn that was hot!" he exclaimed, handing me my trophy shot. "You know, I know a few tricks myself," he lowered his voice suggestively.

"Like what? You know how to blow yourself? I knew that wasn't just a myth."

"No, but I *can* make my cock disappear."

"Like in a cold lake? Shrinkage?" I could tell he was slightly irritated at my apparent prejudice against his wiener, so I let him get to the punch line of his pick up attempt.

"No, baby, it can disappear and reappear from this tight little hole called your ass. Wanna see?"

"You go straight for the anal? Wow, Shamus, I expected better from you. Thanks for the shot though," I held up the glass and turned toward my friends.

"You didn't tell me your name!" I heard him shout behind me.

Turning again, I yelled back "You're right, Shamus, I didn't." Shaking my head at his presumptuousness, I went back to the refuge of my friend and her boyfriend who agreed to drive us around so we could get balls ass drunk. I wondered if he was regretting the decision as I set the shot down in front of Abby. "Free shot bitch! Happy birthday! Suck it down!" I yelled as I plopped down beside her. As disgusted as I was over Shamus' overtly inappropriate pick up, I was glad that my interaction with him had kept all thoughts about Brady out of my head for a whole five minutes. Fuck, there he was again...

"Thanks bitch!" she screeched before she dove head first toward the table to suck back the shot in a more traditional way.

After the next bar, Abby's night took a turn and she didn't feel so great, so we headed back to my apartment. Unfortunately, she couldn't refrain from gastronomical pyrotechnics and turned the passenger side door of Ted's white SUV pink from the atomic cherry I'd told her it was a bad idea to consume after everything else we'd had that night. And even though I assured her that walking me to my door was unnecessary, she insisted and stumbled up three flights of stairs.

"Thanks for coming out tonight, lady!" she shouted.

"Shh," I giggled as I grabbed my keys from the strap of my tiny purse.

"You two are so drunk right now," Ted laughed. "I love being the only sober guy with two hot drunk chicks."

"Oh shit!" Abby shouted and made her way to the railing across from my apartment before hurling over the side, to the courtyard below.

"Hey, man, is it raining?" a very stoned voice echoed from two flights below before we all erupted in laughter and practically fell into my apartment.

"Hmm, this isn't how it usually happens in my dream," Ted groaned as Abby and I stumbled around.

"Oops! Hey, Lucas, you can be honest with me," she slurred, finding her way to my new sofa and pointing at me as she flashed me her red lace thong in her attempt to find the most unlady-like way to sit on a couch.

"About what, Abigail?" I tripped and fell into my rocking chair, pulling off my boots. "Fuck, that's awesome," I groaned, massaging my feet, now semi-conscious of the fact that I was probably flashing my lady clam at them.

"Eric, you want to be Mrs. Eric the pizza guy, don't you?"

"No, Abby, I don't, but I am having feelings for Brady," I confessed, leaning my head against the high back of the chair, and pulling my legs back together.

"HA!" she pointed at me again, like I'd just fallen into her trap, "I knew you weren't a one girl island with no feelings!"

"What the fuck does that even mean?" Ted asked.

"It means she wants love, too, just like everyone else," Abby said, sweeping her pointed finger across the room accusingly, and I could tell we were getting close to the weepy stage of her drunkenness.

"Ted, you should get her home before she starts blubbering, man," I giggled. "It's not pretty."

"I'm not pretty? Why would you say that, Lucas? I'm just trying to find you love!"

"You are beautiful, Abs, but it's time for sleep," Ted soothed, lifting her from the couch and walking back to my door. "She won't remember you told her how you feel about Brady in the morning if you want to deny it when you're sober," he said, understanding that I'd let down a wall I didn't intend with my drunken confession. I nodded, solemnly as I closed the door behind them and left a trail of clothing on my way to my bed and its cold sheets.

**

When I finally woke the next day, I was grateful that I always remembered to alternate between something alcoholic and water. I never really got hung over because I stayed hydrated while I was getting trashed. While I was aware that I shouldn't exactly be proud of that fact, I was glad to have a clear head when Becca's name showed up on the caller id of my cell phone.

"Hey," I answered, brighter than I had the right to be.

"Brady's friend is crashing on our couch and he's so freaking hot, Lucy! I don't know if I can keep my hands to myself!" she gushed. I groaned, inwardly, knowing this was going to be a very girly and self-serving conversation on her end, but I was her best friend, what could I do?

"You guys got another roommate?" I asked, trying to sound interested in Brady's friend, who I, instinctively knew wasn't Mike.

"His lady was cheating on him, with Mike of all people. Seriously, can you picture it? Xander is all towering muscle, light brown hair, gorgeous brown eyes, and a goatee covered chin that was chiseled out of fucking marble, and Mike, well, Mike is a pansy gnome who can't hold his booze," Becca scoffed. "Can you imagine giving all that up for a mousy little dude that drinks until he pukes like a pussy?"

"Wow, that sounded like a direct quote, Bec," I laughed, sitting up in my bed and wrapping my sheet around my chest. While I was comfortable sleeping nude, there was something about talking on the phone while I was exposed that made me pause.

"Yeah, Xander didn't deserve that. They'd been together for *years!* They have *kids* together for God's sake!" she said and I knew she was still parroting what her new roommate was probably lamenting daily.

80

"Just, be careful, Becca, okay?" I warned. "I thought you were still angling to be the second Mrs. Manning?"

"Ugh, no, Brady doesn't want to hook up anymore," she whined. "He cut me off right after the new year. I don't understand it, either. He's said he wanted to stop before, but never actually followed through on it. I think something must've changed because I've tried everything."

"So moving on to more, um, fruitful pastures, I see?" I asked, as my cat jumped on to the bed and started sauntering toward me in an attempt to get me to notice she was hungry.

"I don't know, we'll see," Becca sounded unsure of herself.

"Like I said, be careful. Don't get all twisted up in it, cause he's probably just looking for a rebound lay right now," I advised.

"You don't think I can turn a rebound lay into something more? Do you have no faith in me, Lucy?" she asked, like she was joking, but I knew she was fighting not to take my harmless observations personally.

"What about Flynn? He wasn't happy about you hooking up with Brady, isn't he going to be upset?"

"The fuck I care," she growled, and I knew I'd just touched on a very sore subject.

"What'd he do this time?"

"He's fucking that chick he met. Thank GOD he's not doing it here! I don't want to hear that bitch screaming about how amazing his piercings are," I could practically see the sneer on her face.

"And, as of earlier this month, you were regularly fucking Brady…in the apartment you all share," I pointed

81

out, sliding out of bed and securing the sheet around my body as I went to the walk in to feed Shadow.

"Fuck you, Lucy. It's not the same."

"Whatever you say, Becca."

"I should have known you'd get all high and mighty about this. Who'd you fuck last night?"

"Um, no one, but we aren't talking about me. And I'm not trying to have a relationship with anyone, presently," I said, calmly, knowing that I would just frustrate her further with my nonchalant answer.

"Whatever, I'll talk to you later," she sighed. "And Brady and I are bringing Xander on Friday, so be nice."

"You know he's welcome, Becca. I don't know why you're all angry, but I'm excited to meet this chiseled statue of a man you are all a twitter about," I laughed.

"Back off, Lucy."

"I'm not interested, Becca. I promise," I rolled my eyes and ended the call before heading back to my room to get ready for work.

**

BRADY

"I'm just telling you, be careful with her, man," I warned Xander as he watched Becca bend over in the kitchen to pull a pan from under the stove. He was practically drooling and anyone who knew Becca knew she was in full on 'seduce this guy' mode. It was disgusting to watch, but I was more than a little glad she wasn't using these moves on me anymore. "If you are really just looking to get your dick wet, she's not the girl."

82

"She said you two had a thing, are you sure that's not why you're trying to warn me off?" Xander arched an eyebrow. That fake inquisitive face was starting to annoy me.

"No, but you know what? You'll learn," I laughed, fake clapping dust off my hands to show him that I was distancing myself from whatever was going to happen next. I knew there wasn't anything I could do except let him make the mistake and figure out how crazy and clingy Becca was. "Playstation?" I asked, signaling to the gaming system. "My mom'll be here to drop Taylor off from their lunch date soon."

"Fuck yeah, let's blow some shit up," Xander howled.

"Oh, Xander, you're too funny," Becca giggled from the stove. "Are you guys sure we want to go to Lucy's party on Friday?"

"Um, yeah, we're sure," Xander answered for us, grabbing a controller and sliding down the couch to sit on the floor with his legs crossed.

"But why?" she whined, petulantly. "I just talked to her and told her Xander was going to come and she acted like a total bitch."

"I'm sure you misread things, Becca. Did you wake her up?" I asked.

"Besides, I was told there are boobs everywhere at her parties," Xander threw in, jokingly, but I could feel Becca's pout reach astronomical levels without even turning around.

"When did you start taking *her* side, Brady? I thought you were *my* friend."

"I am, Becca. I was just asking a question," I shrugged and went back to my game. I was almost positive that

83

Becca probably called gushing over Xander and Lucy had told her the same thing I was warning my friend she would do. Becca didn't like it when people told her not to get attached to something or someone.

"Fine," she conceded with a huff. "We'll go to the party. Eric is supposed to be there and I've been dying to get a glimpse at Lucy's number one."

"Seriously? She invited Eric?" the words flew out of my mouth before I could stop them. What the fuck was wrong with me? I didn't care if she invited one of her booty calls to a party. It didn't mean anything anyway. I mean, Carter was at every party and Trevor had come to a couple parties when she was auditioning him, but Eric was always an enigma to everyone.

"Well," Becca started, moving to sit on the sectional behind us. "I don't know that she invited him. She said something about Abby trying to push them to be something they aren't or something."

"Ah, the classic 'I'm in a relationship, so you need to be in one too' thing," I laughed, knowing that Lucy hated when her friends tried that crap on her.

"Yeah, I don't know why Abby can't just leave her be."

"Oh, come on, Bec! You're guilty of doing that to her, too," I pointed out. "You still don't like Abby because she had a slight flirtation with Flynn that one time months ago."

"That's not the only reason I don't like her," she shot back.

"Oh, I forgot. You also think she's competition as Lucy's best friend. Man, girls are mean to each other," I rolled my eyes.

84

"I know," Xander agreed.

"Whatever, you two suck," Becca said before heaving herself off the couch and stalking to her bedroom.

"Man, she's hot when she's angry," Xander said, after the bedroom door slammed.

"Seriously, man. I'm warning you one last time. Don't go there. You. Will. Regret. It," I foreshadowed.

"She said she's just looking for some fun, man. I think I'll be okay," he dismissed, pausing the game before standing up and walking to the patio door. "Smoke break?"

"Yeah," I nodded, jumping off the floor to join him. I'd said my piece, now it was up to him. The way he was eye-fucking her whenever she was in a room, I had a feeling things were about to get really ugly.

CHAPTER 10

BRADY

By the time Friday rolled around, the sexual tension and testosterone in the house was so thick between Flynn, Xander and Becca that you could cut it with a knife and I was more than ready to party my ass off at Lucy's. I wanted to forget that I was positive that my safe little apartment was about to turn incredibly toxic.

Becca, Xander and I arrived at Lucy's just in time to help her carry her party supplies up from her truck. Flynn decided to sit this party out, again, which was probably best for everyone, Lucy's neighbors included.

"This is Xander," I nodded back as I put the bags I'd carried on her card table, introducing my newest roommate to her. "Xander, Lucy."

Lucy smiled, politely. "It's great to meet you," she threw over her shoulder before starting to pull groceries from the bags.

"You, too. Thanks for having me," he smiled.

"The more the merrier or whatever," she said, brightly, as Becca and Xander stood in her living room, watching us unpack her supplies. After grabbing her requisite case of Bud Light from the table and shoving it in her refrigerator, I noticed another six-pack of beer still sitting on the table beside her favorite strawberry daiquiris.

"New Castles, Lucy? Did you take up drinking beer since the last time we did this?" I asked, trying to sound unaffected, but a flash of jealousy I wasn't expecting lit through me, because I knew who they were for. They were for him, her number one. Eric. Fuck, maybe Abby was right? Maybe she did want more with him.

Um, no," she said, evasively, no longer looking me in the eye as she continued to unpack items from bags. Her sudden shiftiness confirmed my suspicions, but also made me curious as to why she wouldn't just say they were for him. Guilt dripped from her as she continued to unpack her groceries and it made my ears prick up a little at what she wasn't saying.

"New Castles? I thought you said she never bought real beer? That's why I brought the Coronas," Xander frowned, watching Lucy pick up the six-pack and scurry into her kitchen.

"She doesn't, usually, what's going on?" I asked, hoping my voice wasn't betraying the jealousy growing in me with every dodging motion she made, from not giving a straight answer off the bat to immersing herself in her tasks and ignoring the question looks at her back.

"Eric's coming tonight," she admitted with a defeated sigh as she stowed the beer in her refrigerator, before turning to face us again, a contrite little frown on her beautiful face, her hair covering just enough of her eyes to not give anything away. Not that they would anyway, her eyes were like a vault of secrets. Idly, I wondered what it would be like to unlock them as I watched her.

"Becca mentioned that he might, but I didn't think he'd actually show up." I said, trying to hide my own frown. I needed to be disinterested, because I couldn't go there again, especially not with her. She would eat me alive if I let her, and I'd probably beg her to do it, too.

"Yeah, I was just a surprised as you," she chuckled, nervously, bringing me back to the conversation. "He's never wanted to come to one of my parties before, but I think it's more about the promise of a super topless lap dance than anything else."

"That's why I came!" Xander yelled from the living room with a chuckle, followed by a loud smack that I knew came from an angry Becca hitting him in the arm because she moved to stand next to me, folding her arms over her chest with a huff.

"Well, then," Lucy smiled, "I'll see what we can pull together for you," she finished with a wink. Briefly, I registered that Becca had gone stiff beside me, boring angry holes into her best friend at her words.

Lucy was just being nice and welcoming. I knew this and Becca knew this. She wasn't flirting with Xander, but that didn't mean that either of us were okay with it. It felt odd to be on the same page with Becca, even though I'd spent nearly six months hooking up with her, and, arguably knew her better than I'd ever known Lucy.

"Lucy," Becca's tone held a firm warning.

"What, Becca? I didn't mean me!" she let out a light laugh, as if her friend's jealous was the most absurd reaction on the planet. The frown from earlier was still in place and something told me this was her way of trying to get beyond the elephant in the room when she'd been questioned about the beer. She was putting on an act so that we didn't see there was something working in her head, something she was fighting against. Did she feel something for me, too?

"I was just trying to make our new friend feel welcome," she continued giving Becca a frown and rolling her eyes, before pulling a bag of plastic cups from a grocery bag, seemingly able to finally shake off whatever she'd been thinking..

"As long as we're clear," Becca whispered, pointedly, throwing her hair over her shoulder and moving to join Xander in the living room again. "This new couch is so comfortable, Lucy!" she exclaimed, rubbing herself against the cushions and settling in beside Xander, thrusting her cleavage in his face. The foreboding feeling that had been nagging at me all week was about to hit astronomical proportions. I knew something was going to happen tonight that I wasn't going to be happy about. The news that Eric was going to be here, in addition to Carter, I, suddenly, wished I'd stayed home with Flynn.

By the time I passed out from all the alcohol I'd downed like water, I was positive I should have stayed home. Lucy had kissed me again, and it had been even hotter than the last time, harder and full of passion, but when Eric arrived an hour later, I was just a memory, forgotten. It hurt more than I'd imagined when she disappeared with him to her bedroom for a good forty-five minutes. If I hadn't been so drunk, I would've left when she came out looking thoroughly satisfied and smiled at Becca. It wasn't long after that that Becca and Xander commandeered Lucy's bedroom for their own purposes. The adorable frown on her face about her sanctuary being defiled almost made the impending drama worth it, and I nearly danced a jig when Eric left an hour or so later. I was happier than I had a right to be that she wouldn't be sharing a bed with that asshole.

One thing had become glaringly obvious over the course of the evening that I didn't want to think about. I had real and undeniable feelings for that girl. How the *fuck* had that happened?

**

LUCAS

I knew I was late before I even opened my eyes. The position of the sun streaming in my bedroom window was too bright. After a power outage kept me at work longer than I'd expected last night, and a visit from my number two, Shawn, I'd been more tired than normal when I crashed at 2am.

"FUCK!" I shouted at no one as I bolted upright and grabbed for my phone on my nightstand. I don't know why I bothered, though, it only confirmed that I'd slept through my first two classes. Even with a teleporter, I wouldn't make it in time to get to my last class of the day.

Two weeks into the actual semester and I was already an absence behind on my Spanish class. We were only allowed five for the whole semester before we automatically failed the class. Plodding to my computer, I sent off an email to my Physics professor about going to his office hours later in the week to clarify anything I didn't understand from the homework the syllabus showed would be assigned that day.

After dressing and grabbing something from my fridge, I set up my books to get started on my homework. I buried myself in notes to make up for my lack of responsible behavior and made a note to myself that it was time to quit my second job. Being down on sleep was something I could handle, but endangering my grades... The extra $300 a month wasn't worth my education. After being so absorbed in my work for the rest of the afternoon, I was shocked to see darkness beyond my blinds when my phone started to ring.

If the time on my living room clock was shocking, then the name flashing on my caller ID when I made my way into my bedroom was nearly stroke inducing, "Brady?" I asked, wondering if he'd butt dialed me. He'd acted weird at the party Friday, but I'd assumed it was because Xander and Becca decided to lock themselves in my bedroom and go at it on the floor. The only thing weirder than their hook up was Eric's unusual attentiveness to me. I figured he'd come to the party to socialize with my friends, but he'd stuck to me like glue and it had me slightly worried.

"Lucy! Thank GOD! Are you working tonight?" his voice came through the phone frenzied.

"No, I'm home tonight, is everything okay?" I asked, sitting on my bed. Whatever he was about to say, I knew that I probably should be sitting to hear it.

"Can you go pick up Becca from the apartment for the night? Can she stay with you?"

"What's going on?" I asked, suddenly on full alert.

"It's Flynn," he leveled. "Xander and Becca haven't been very discreet about how they are hooking up now, and he's flipping out about it."

"But why? He didn't flip out when she was with you, and isn't he seeing someone anyway?"

"I'm his friend, he sees Xander as a threat for some reason, and yes, he's seeing someone, but you know their history as well as I do," he sighed into the phone. "It doesn't help that she's shouting down the roof anytime Xander touches her," he grumbled. It didn't sound like he was jealous, more that he was annoyed at her overly showy sexual display.

"Unfortunately," I frowned, now moving through my apartment, grabbing my keys and shoving my feet into my flip flops. "What happened?" I dared to ask as I looked for my purse and keys.

"I guess he wanted to go out to dinner to talk and when they pulled back into the complex, he lost it and hit her windshield so hard it broke."

"Fuck!" I froze at his words.

"It's not shattered, but she can't drive the car safely, and neither Xander nor I want her to stay with him in the apartment while we are at work," he kept talking and I found myself almost running down the stairs to my truck.

"I'm on my way," I told him as I slid behind the wheel.

"Just," he paused and took a deep breath. "Just, call her when you get there, okay? I don't want you to go up and get her. I hate to even ask you because I don't want to put you in any danger."

"I understand. I'll call her," I agreed, puzzled over his concern over my safety.

"Promise me you won't go up there. He's not thinking clearly right now," he pushed.

"I promise."

"Good," he said, and I could actually hear him sigh in relief before he continued. "She's made arrangements with a co-worker to pick her up at your place tomorrow, so you don't have to worry about missing your classes."

"Wow, thanks," I said, grateful that he'd thought of my scheduling difficulties.

"No, thank you for doing this, seriously," the sincerity in his voice giving me pause, and making me swoon more than I wanted to admit.

"She's my best friend, Brady. Of course I'm going to do this for her," I told him, merging onto the busy road and heading toward the freeway. "I'm just glad I have a couch now, so I don't have to share a bed with her. She's all elbows and knees!" I tried to joke because the situation felt too heavy all of the sudden.

"Is that so?" he asked, and I could almost see his eyebrows quirk up through the phone. "And how would you know that?"

"High school sleepovers! Get your head out of the gutter, Brady!" I laughed. It felt good, even though I was on my way to rescue my friend from a possibly dangerous situation.

"Hey, it's the end of my break, can you text me when you've got her? So I know you're both safe?"

"Absolutely," I smiled at the way he really seemed to care.

"Thank you," he said, ending the call.

Luckily, Becca was sitting on one of the bottom steps of her apartment building with her bag in hand when I pulled in. Yanking open my passenger side door, she hopped in and a dark cloud settled around us. As I backed out of the parking spot, I saw Flynn sitting on the balcony of their apartment staring holes into us with barely suppressed rage. If I hadn't seen him that keyed up before, I might've found myself frozen in fear. That menacing look had become second nature to me over the years of dealing with the Becca and Flynn show.

"Fuck, Becca, what the hell? Are you okay?" I asked when I'd merged back into traffic.

"Oh, Lucy! It was awful! I don't understand why he doesn't see that Xander and I are meant for each other!" she wailed, tears starting to fall from her eyes. "He said he'll never let me go. He said he'd kill us both first," she whispered so softly, I almost missed it. Fuck, this wasn't going to be pretty.

**

BRADY

93

Call me when you can. The simple text from Lucy had me tied up in knots when I snuck a peek at my phone while my machine was running before my last break. A million and one different scenarios played in my head in vivid detail between the time I got the text and when I was able to make the call. Every ring jolted through my body until she finally answered.

"Sorry I couldn't call any earlier, I had to wait for my break," I explained. "I'm surprised you're still awake."

"It's fine," she breathed, her voice hesitant. "I'm not sure Becca and Flynn should..."

"I know, Lucy. They are so toxic, but they feed off the drama, you know that," I said.

"I do know that, but it seems really bad this time," she whispered.

"He's broke things before when she's tried to, um, I don't want to say move on, because Xander is rebounding like crazy right now, so let's just say hook up with someone else," I said in a rush, because Xander was usually on his break not long after I started mine and I didn't want him eavesdropping on this part of the conversation. I just wanted to assure him that the girls were fine. "I stopped trying to figure out their patterns a long time ago, but breaking a windshield with his palm is something I couldn't ignore. Do you have any idea how much force that takes?"

"I'm glad you called me," she said. "Becca's asleep on the couch now, but she seemed really scared when I picked her up. I guess he threatened to kill her."

"He's said that before, Lucy, so I wouldn't read too much into that particular threat. I know it's scary, but it's their pattern. I'm actually surprised she'd never told you that before," I scrubbed my hand against my eye trying to clear my vision. "I wish I hadn't needed to send you after her at all. It would kill me if I sent you into danger and something happened to you," I told her, hoping she didn't read too much into my words, even though I meant them. "Flynn'll sleep it off and get used to it, then it'll just be over and we'll have worried over nothing."

"You're a great friend, Brady, but I'm used to their crap, too. Flynn watched us leave, but didn't make a move to follow us. I think he's just glad she left where he could see who was picking her up. He knows where she is tonight, in case he wants to find her. Maybe it'll help him get past everything if he knows she's not going to be fucking Xander tonight," she explained, seemingly trying to assuage my guilt of sending her into Flynn's firing line. She knew as well as I did that he wouldn't soon forget that she'd come between him and Becca tonight. Forget the fact that she was removing her friend from a volatile situation; he'd only see that she'd taken Becca away from him. Lucy knew her friendship with Flynn was about to take a very sudden and southward turn, because of what I asked her to do.

"I really wish I hadn't needed to call you, Lucy," I said, taking a drag from my almost burned out cigarette. "I really am glad you are okay, though."

"You keep saying that, Brady, but it's fine! I'll always be there for Becca. Please, if it happens again, call me," she pressed. "I'm not afraid of Flynn showing up on my doorstep. My place can be her sanctuary if she needs it."

"Thank you," I said, simply, meaning what I was saying in the purest sense of the words.

"You're welcome, but it's almost 1am, and I have a 7:40 class, so I should try to get some sleep now," she yawned, but I could hear the smile in her voice.

"Of course," I said. "Sweet dreams, Lucas," I finished, and as I hit the end call button, I swear I heard her inhale sharply in response to my using her full name.

"They okay?" Xander's voice asked, startling me from my thoughts.

"Yeah, they're at Lucy's," I said.

"Good. Lucy's a good person."

"Yeah, she is," I agreed.

"You care about her," he stated.

"She's a good friend."

"No, man, you *care* about her," he emphasized.

"What's not to care about? She's a cool person," I wrote off his implication.

"Why do you say that?" he asked, suddenly looking at me more intently. It made me nervous. "Not that I disagree, but I want to hear why you think she's cool."

"Um," I started, scratching the back of my neck. "Well, she knows more about the sport of football than most guys. I mean, if you asked her to explain what a cover two defense or the pros and cons of a spread offense are, she could tell you."

"Okay, that's a good start."

"She's confident about who she is as a person. She's unapologetic about the things that she does, unless she does something that hurts someone else. And she's fiercely independent, but you can also see the hint of vulnerability just below the surface," I continued. "Plus, have you seen her breasts?" I asked, trying to lighten the conversation.

"They are pretty nice," he agreed with a laugh. "You really have feelings for her," he decided.

"I have a ton of respect for her, don't confuse that for wanting to have a relationship," I warned, trying to convince myself now more than him. "Besides, her dance card is a little full, don't you think? She wouldn't want to slum it with me."

"That's complete horse shit and you know it, Brady."

"Not going to happen, Xander."

"We'll see about that," he said, flicking his cigarette to the ground. "Let's get back to work."

CHAPTER 11

BRADY

After his total meltdown about Becca, Flynn calmed down enough that we could all cohabitate somewhat drama free. After a few days of angry talk and threats, it was just over. I think that the fact that he already had someone else to fuck helped. Whatever it was, though, I was just glad that he'd stopped cycling through his mania and decided to let it go. Everything seemed to be roses and chocolates for Becca and Xander, too- at least, according to Becca. Xander said he was having a good time with her, and they were casual, at best, but I knew that Becca saw engagement rings and forever when she looked at him. Her outright depression that he decided to spend Valentine's Day with his kids instead of taking her to dinner told me she wanted more than he was willing to offer. I hoped it would send a message about his intentions to her, too, but I wasn't delusional enough to expect a miracle.

"Lucy wants to know if we want to come over for dinner tonight," Becca told me, flopping down on the couch like a sullen teenager.

"Why?" I asked, curious because Lucy had never invited us over to eat with her before, just to party, drink, and move the occasional couch, apparently.

"I don't know. I think it probably has to do with sending a message to her boy toys that she's not interested in more or something. I was unclear," she grumbled. "Besides, it's not like either of us have anything better to do."

"Thought she didn't cook," I pointed out, becoming increasingly intrigued by the invitation.

"She doesn't, which is even more puzzling," Becca frowned. "I think she's trying to be protective, you know after everything with Flynn last week. Sometimes I forget how thoughtful she can be when she wants to be."

"So, are we going?"

"Yeah, she promised chocolate torte at her hotel after dinner, so even if dinner sucks, we have that to look forward to," Becca surmised.

"Let's go then," I gestured, hiding a small smile at the thought of spending Valentine's Day with Lucy, even with Becca along for the ride. Unfortunately, I was right, Lucy wasn't the best cook. The spaghetti she made us was soggy and too acidic, but I choked it down, because she'd tried. Becca and I shared a slight grimace, though, as Lucy was cleaning up after dinner.

"Thanks for that, Lucy," I smiled, trying to use all the manners my mom taught me.

"Sorry it wasn't better. I quit my second job, otherwise we could've just eaten at the hotel tonight," she frowned.

"It's okay, Lucy," Becca said, a polite grin on her face, "but you should probably buy a colander if you want to make spaghetti again," she suggested.

"I thought I had one, but it must've gotten lost in the move." Lucy's frown deepened even more before she plastered a smile on her face and gestured toward the door. "Shall we head across the street for some sinfully, decadent chocolate torte then?"

"Oh, hell yeah," Becca pumped a fist in the air. I wasn't the kind of guy that was into desserts and sweets much, but even I had to agree, the cake was delicious and worth forcing down dinner. It was kind of cute that she'd even attempted to cook for us, even though it was something she never did.

After being seated in the restaurant, Becca excused herself to find the restroom, leaving Lucy and I to settle into a comfortable conversation. Suddenly, I felt heat on the back of my head, like holes were being drilled into it by someone's eyes.

"Shit," Lucy grumbled, stabbing at the lemon in her water glass with her straw.

"What?" I asked, peeking over my shoulder to find a guy in a chef uniform looking at us with unmasked interest, and a twinge of anger. "Who's that?"

"That would be Adam," she frowned and bugged her eyes out at the chef in question. He must've gone back to the kitchen, because a second later, she visibly relaxed.

"Do we have to worry about getting served a sneeze cake? Or am I going to have a lougie in my tea?"

"We went out for drinks during the same time I was considering Trevor," she started, "He decided that my 'overt sexual behavior,'" she used finger quotes to emphasize with a sarcastic smirk, "was a cry for a deeper commitment, and now he thinks he's just found me on a date on Valentines' Day. Smug ass probably thinks I'm proving him right," she sighed, frustrated before adding, "Fucking Tom," with a snarl. "He's the one that sat us on the lower level of the restaurant in a dark corner, and probably ran to the kitchen with the gossip the second Becca left the table. There should be a new word for the level of douche baggery he's displaying right now," she continued, her voice getting more and more shrill. I was pretty sure only dogs could hear her at that point.

"Why would he do that?" I asked, completely befuddled by her behavior and every word that just fell from her mouth.

She sighed. "Some misplaced allegiance to his boy; I don't know," she said, exasperated, shaking her head at me. "He's the one who decided he couldn't handle me and the only type of relationship I was willing to offer, so, of course, I was aching for a more meaningful relationship. That angry, wounded bird shit is the most ridiculous thing I've ever seen!" she snorted, throwing her straw back into her water glass. "I wish I could order a fucking drink. Stupid corporate policy."

"That sucks, Lucy, I'm sorry," I mumbled, taking a sip of my iced tea, still not quite understanding why she was so upset.

"He might still be upset at my gloating after the National Championship game, too," Lucy's evil grin caught me by surprise, because it was like someone flipped a switch and her mood changed on a dime.

"Why? Cause you got to go?"

"Well, that, and Ohio State won," she tried and failed to come across as flippant. "I had to hear for a week that the call in the end zone wasn't pass interference- lame!"

"How was the game? I forgot to ask you," I said, wanting to change the subject.

"Freaking amazing," she said, a dreamy haze settling into her features. It looked like my distraction technique was working when she continued, "Not only was I on the Buckeye side of the field, but I was also in the presence of a certain Heisman trophy winning former running back! It was so badass, words cannot describe it! Easily the most amazing thing that has ever happened to me," she gushed.

101

"I just can't believe you lucked into a ticket like that for face value and didn't sell it for a huge profit," I teased, remembering her conversation with Becca before the game. I knew she never would've traded the opportunity to see her favorite team play for a couple thousand dollars. Her loyalty and priorities were something I admired about her. She knew there were more important things in this world than money.

"Supercalifragilisticexpi-asshole-douche bag!" she announced, suddenly, startling me from my thoughts as Becca made her way back to the table. She'd apparently found the next level of doucheyness she was looking for. Our bonding time had come to an end, and it made me feel more than a little sad.

"Who's a douche?" Becca asked, taking her seat.

"Fucking Tom," Lucy rolled her eyes as she watched the waiter she'd been cursing approach our table with our dessert. "Seriously, Tom?" she asked, as he set the cake down in front of us with three forks.

"I explained to Adam that you weren't here on a date when he stormed back into the kitchen," Tom told us, rolling his eyes at Adam's overreaction. "I caught him before he shattered one of the dishes."

"He's the one—" she cut herself off with a growl. I shouldn't have thought her exasperation was cute, but it was. Her blue eyes burned and her nose scrunched up.

"I agree, sorry," he apologized with a smile I would've thought was contrite, if his eyes weren't glued to Lucy's cleavage. I, on the other hand, was still completely in the dark about the reasons for her disproportionate anger about Adam's visible jealousy. I didn't think it was a big deal that he thought we were on a date, but she seemed to be

102

appalled at the idea. Aside from the aforementioned 'cuteness,' the whole thing was a little disheartening.

"It's fine," she growled, grabbing a fork and passing it to me, effectively excusing Tom from the table. "Oh, GOD!" she cried out around a bite of the chocolate torte and I felt my body respond to the erotic sound. "Sorry, I always forget how good it is." Her slight blush was contradictory to her normal outward brashness.

"You're right," Becca moaned. "So good."

"So after this, we're going back to the apartment to get drunk, right?" Lucy asked. "I don't have to work until 3 tomorrow afternoon.

"Sounds good to me," Becca jumped on the suggestion. "We can just crash with you tonight, if that's okay? Xander's staying with his kids and I don't want to have to deal with Flynn."

"Sounds perfect," Lucy shot me a shy smile I didn't understand before returning to the cake.

**

LUCAS

I was nicely toasted when I drifted to sleep that night beside Becca. Brady took the sofa like a gentleman. I was starting to realize I was developing really deep feelings for Brady. I'd known I had a certified crush at this point. I didn't know if I wanted to do more about it than kiss him at my parties until I got it out of my system, but Adam's behavior last night probably ruined any chance of anything more if I changed my mind. I'd just resigned myself to that reality when Becca nudged me from my disconcerting dreams of what it might be like to date Brady.

"Wanna do lunch at Antonio's?"

"Damn straight!" I hopped up and started getting dressed.

"Wanna get some decent pasta with us?" Becca asked Brady, taking a dig at my culinary abilities. I knew I couldn't cook well, but for some reason, I really wanted an excuse to spend Valentine's with Brady without being obvious about my interest. Damn, I had it worse than I thought. Had I really invited my best friend over under the guise of distracting her from Xander's rejection when all I really wanted was her roommate to come, too? Fuck, I totally had. I was a goddamn sap.

"I would, but I've got to pick up my daughter, remember? Saturday?" he prompted, looking slightly uncomfortable.

"Go ahead and take my car," Becca offered. "Lucy can take me home, huh?" she looked at me, expectantly.

"Uh, yeah, that's fine," I nodded, upset that I was just volunteered to drive to Mesa and back before work.

"Great!" Becca bounced in excitement.

"Alright." Brady grabbed her keys and headed to the door. "I'll see you back at the apartment."

We were lucky to find seats at the bar because the restaurant was packed, even though we got there right after they opened. The bigger shock than us finding a quick seat was Eric manning the phones at the register.

"What are you doing here on a Saturday?" I asked him when he noticed us.

"I could ask you the same," he smiled. "Kassie called in and I didn't have plans. Did you have a party last night? Why aren't you working?"

104

"Josh wanted to go out with his girlfriend for their anniversary tonight, so I'm covering," I explained. "I think he's planning to propose, he seemed more twitchy than usual when I worked with him on Thursday."

"Better him than me," Eric muttered.

"Tell me about it," I approved. "He's only a year older than me, and I can't even remotely imagine being engaged within the next year, you know?" The words came out slightly garbled, which was weird, like my head didn't agree with them.

"Absolutely. Get anything good yesterday?" he asked, leaning across the bar. I noticed Becca watching our exchange as if it were a tennis match, her head pinging back and forth.

"Carter gave me a DVD player," I confessed and watched their jaws drop. "It wasn't anything though. He bought a new TV for his condo and the player was included, but the one he already had was better. Well, that and he wants to be able to watch DVD lesbian porn when he comes over."

"Oh," Eric said, still shocked. "Well," he started, looking down at the polished wood of the bar with a look of vulnerability I'd never seen before. "Are you going to let him?"

"Yeah, *are you?*" Becca asked, seemingly hanging on our words, her hands cupping her chin.

"What's up with the Spanish Inquisition here? There's no need to break out the rack and shackles, it's just a DVD player," I sighed, shaking my head and reaching for my glass of soda.

"Yeah, but it's from Carter," Becca pressed, speaking very deliberately, as if I didn't understand their reaction to the gift, but I did. I just didn't want to talk about it.

"And?"

"I thought you guys were over," Eric's brow wrinkled.

"We are, or whatever," I waved my hand in dismissal. "He was just being nice. I don't think it was actually a Valentine's gift, I think he just gave it to me as soon as he got it," I said, not looking at either of them, because I knew it was a Valentine's gift and was trying to figure out what it meant myself. I was also trying to decide why I was no longer excited about the prospect that he might be coming around on wanting to be with me.

"That's a pretty insane gift to just randomly give someone you used to sleep with, wouldn't you agree?" Eric asked, standing up and folding his arms across his chest.

"I don't know, but Carter doesn't usually do things with a motive."

"HA!" Becca snorted. "No guy does something without a motive, Lucy. I can't believe you just said that. I don't think I've ever known you to be this naïve, Lucy."

"It's true, Lucas," Eric confirmed, his dark eyes shimmering.

"New subject, please," I requested, pursing my lips.

"Are you coming next week, Eric?" Becca asked.

"To…?"

"The party Lucy's having," she explained slowly, as if trying to trigger his memory.

"I didn't know she was having a party next Friday. What if I'm not invited?" he whispered, loudly, to her, but keeping his eyes focused on me.

106

"That's ridiculous, of course you're welcome, Eric," I told him, frowning that he actually seemed hurt that he didn't know.

"I'll have to clear my calendar then," he winked at me before running to answer a ringing phone.

"What's going on with you two?" she asked with a hiss as soon as he left us, yanking my head to her ear.

"Nothing, I mean, not nothing, but no more than usual," I explained, rolling my eyes at her over-dramatic response.

"That's a crock of shit and you know it! That guy is into you! How can you not see it?" I was thankful that in her excitement, she was still whispering, mindful of Eric's proximity.

"You are just as bad as Abby!" I scrubbed my hands over my face in annoyance. I was so sick of this type of conversation, defending my non-relationship with Eric or Carter or any of the other guys in my rotation.

"Let's not talk about that skank, please."

"Why not? She says the same thing you do about Eric and me," I explained. "And I'll tell you the same thing I told her, it's not going to happen. He's a serial cheater and a good friend, that's all. The sex is great, but it's all I'm looking for from him," I said each word very slowly, hoping they would sink in, but she looked angry at me for belittling her intelligence by the time I was finished with my clarification.

"You don't have to act like I'm a five year old, Lucy," she snapped.

"Well, then stop asking stupid questions and talking shit about Abby."

"Whatever," she huffed and went back to her lunch.

"You busy tonight, Lucas?" Eric looked at me, hopeful as we paid for our lunch.

"I'm working until eleven," I told him.

"After?"

"Nada."

"See you then?"

"Sounds perfect," I smiled and his returning smile was radiant, confusing me even more about our conversation.

"Just sex! HA! I believe that," Becca chided as we walked back to my truck. In one small exchange, Becca was convinced that Eric and I were going to get together now. Nothing could be further from the truth, but I couldn't tell her who I really had ideas about dating.

CHAPTER 12

BRADY

After returning from her lunch with Lucy, Becca started making noise that Lucy was getting serious with Eric, and that made me really not want to go to her party. It had been hard enough when I knew they were just hooking up, but watching them be a couple…that might kill me. Unfortunately, I was outvoted when I suggested doing something else the night of the party.

After being defeated, I decided it was better to get plastered with friends than by myself. I'd just spend the majority of the night outside smoking. With a game plan in place, I felt slightly better about facing Lucy and her possible boyfriend.

During the drive over, I practiced my surprised face for when Lucy opened the door with Eric on her arm. Though, I think my actual surprised face when Lucy opened the door alone was more convincing than anything I'd rehearsed. She looked beautiful, her black hair hanging loose against her shoulders, her pale face contained no makeup, but she was dressed in a short black skirt and red shirt with a peasant neckline that showed off her amazing cleavage. No shoes, though. I knew from experience that she preferred to party barefoot.

"I thought Eric would be here," I said, nonchalantly as she ushered us in the door and took my usual bottle of vodka from my hand. Her crystal blue eyes looked into mine with a decidedly bewildered.

"Why would Eric already be here?" she asked, biting her lip, confusion etched in her features. "Even *if* he were coming tonight?"

"He's not coming?" Becca asked, also slightly puzzled. "But I thought you guys were getting together? I mean, at lunch the other day?"

"Oh!" Lucy started laughing, as if she finally understood where the questions were stemming from. "Um, no, lunch the other day wasn't anything, Becca," she shook her head at her words.

"But he seemed so jealous!"

"Yeah, because Carter bought me a DVD player for Valentines' Day, but not because he wanted something more from our relationship," she said, dryly. "He was fishing for an invitation to come over and watch porn," she continued as she moved to place the bottle of vodka on her kitchen counter.

"Oh," Becca's voice was even more confused though.

"Just because a guy wants to nail you, doesn't mean he wants a relationship with you, Becca," Lucy said, saying the words that Becca had never seemed to grasp. Lucy was definitely someone who was capable of separating the feelings of love from sex. She understood that the two weren't necessarily mutually exclusive.

"Whatever," Becca dismissed before going about setting herself up with something to drink. Looking over at Xander, I just shrugged and went to do the same. Inside, though, I was so happy to hear that Lucy was still single that I could've ripped my shirt open and pounded my chest like a caveman, but I was sure it would've made my feelings obvious.

An hour into the party, my earlier elation was echoed by Xander when he came outside to join me for a smoke.

"So, she's not with Eric," he smirked at me knowingly.

"I guess not," I said, glad we were alone, because I wasn't sure I was ready for Lucy to know I was harboring feelings for her. I had nightmares of pity in her eyes as she turned me down or just outright mocking me with cruel laughter, even though I knew neither were in her character.

"You gonna do something about it?"

"I'm going to let her kiss me if she wants to," I said, taking a drag off my cigarette and staring, unseeingly, into the darkness that lay beyond her building.

"Come on, man!" Xander said, indignantly. "You've gotta try harder than that! I think she's into you."

"She's not, she's like that with everyone," I shrugged off, even though I wanted to believe what he was saying.

"It's not her behavior I'm talking about, Brady. It's the way she looks at you when you aren't looking at her. It's the same way you look at her. I think you'd be good for her," Xander explained.

"I'm not looking for that and neither is she," I rationalized.

"Bullshit," Xander interjected, stomping his cigarette out and putting the butt in the can Lucy provided for her parties. Before I had a chance to refute his statement, he walked back into the apartment.

Hours later, with liquid courage and the fact that Lucy was kissing me more than normal, Xander and I revisited the conversation in the same place, but Becca was there to witness this time.

"But she's making out with Carter as much as she's making out with me," I tried to resist Xander's argument again.

"Actually, I think *he's* making out with *her*," Becca offered, frowning. "He does this to her all the time. He's jealous that she's kissing you."

"What you need to do is just go in there and kiss her," Xander concluded.

"I've kissed her plenty of times tonight, man. I don't know how doing it again is going to show her anything."

"No, man. She's kissed *you* plenty of times tonight," Xander clarified. "You've just stood there and let her."

"He's right," Becca chimed in, looking at Xander with something like hero worship in her eyes.

"What's the difference?" I asked, actually curious. I'd kissed Lucy back, I hadn't just stood there like a dumbass or something, letting her slobber all over me.

"I guarantee if you walked in there right now, grabbed her- hands in her hair- and kissed her with everything you are feeling, your entire world would change and so would hers," Xander laid out, dropping the gauntlet at my feet, daring me to pick it up.

"Bullshit," I growled, not believing it would be that easy.

"Only one way to find out," Xander challenged as I settled against the railing in thought, dragging more precious nicotine into my lungs.

"What have you got to lose?" Becca asked, her green eyes still focused on Xander. Idly, I wondered why Becca seemed to not only be okay with my pursuit of her best friend, she was encouraging it. Maybe she thought I was jealous of her and Xander? Who knew?

"Fuck this," I said, pushing off the rail and walking toward the front door. "I'm going to show you that nothing is going to change by doing this."

"Famous last words, man," Xander called out behind me, but I barely registered the words as I took a deep breath and pushed the door open. Just as I stepped inside, Lucy appeared from her bedroom in a pair of graffiti print sleep shorts and a dark tank top. Beating down the nerves blossoming in my stomach, my legs chewed up the distance between us. Just before my mouth descended to hers, I recognized a mystified but curious look on her face.

**

LUCAS

I was just coming out of my bedroom when my front door burst open and I saw Brady, stalking toward me with purpose. When he finally reached me, he grabbed my face with both hands and yanked my lips to his before kissing me with more passion and desire than I ever thought possible. This kiss was nothing like the ones we'd previously shared. It felt possessive and demanding, plus *he* was kissing *me*. I was lost to it, responding eagerly, synapses firing through my entire body, as if it was coming to life for the first time because of that kiss. Then, before I could truly register what was happening, it was over, and he was stalking back toward my door, without saying a word. The look of shock on my face was rivaled only by the one of pure and utter devastation on Carter's.

"What the fuck was that?" he hissed, as I remained paralyzed in my dining room, a hand braced on my card table in an attempt to keep my balance, because I was pretty sure my legs had been replaced with jelly.

"I have no clue," I answered, honestly, as Becca came through my front door and snaked her arm through mine, hauling me to my bedroom, backward, and shutting the door.

"OH MY GOD! LUCAS!" Becca screeched.

"Lucas? You're calling me Lucas?" I asked, trying to snap out of the trance the kiss had pulled me in to. "You never call me Lucas."

"It seemed appropriate," she dismissed. "Brady is totally in to you! I had no idea! Did you?!" I didn't understand her excitement over the events, because I would have thought she'd be more jealous.

"None," I shook my head in emphasis, but I knew the dumbfounded expression on my face spoke for itself.

"What are you going to do about it?"

"I have no Earthly idea, Becca."

"What do you mean? Don't you like him?"

"I do, but—"

"I don't want to hear your 'I don't want a relationship' bullshit right now, Lucas," she snapped, wagging a finger in my face. "Do. You. Like. Him?" she asked again, slowly and sharply.

"Carter," I sighed, putting my head in my hands and dropping to sit on the edge of my bed.

"I don't give a fuck about Mr. Can't figure out whether he wants to be with you or not, Lucy. I *do* care about Brady, though, and he doesn't deserve to be hurt."

"You don't think I know that, Rebecca?" I hissed, before standing and yanking my bedroom door open. As I stormed to the refrigerator to grab another drink, I felt someone zip behind me at a clipped speed. I was pretty sure

114

Becca was already on her way outside to share her newfound knowledge and my confusion with Brady and Xander. Drink, finally, finally in hand, I felt a presence behind me. Perhaps Becca hadn't gone outside after all. Turning around, I came face to face with a very upset and very drunk Carter.

"I'm in love with you, Lucas," he slurred, grabbing my face and kissing me just as hard as Brady just did. Usually, I lived for the kisses he gave me, but this time, it felt wrong. It no longer fit, and, even though I wasn't ready to admit it to myself, I knew why. Pushing him away, I settled back against my countertop, while he leaned against my sink.

"Why now, Carter?" I whimpered in irritation.

"I've always been in love with, Lucas. You know that. I want to be with you," he said, his voice desperate, his hands clinging to my wrists. Yanking my hands from his, I schooled my anger at his words before looking into his eyes.

"Carter, you've said the same thing to me every time you drink like this. Every. Fucking. Time," I growled. "*I love you, Lucas, I want to be with you, Lucas, Why aren't we together, Lucas.* And then you pull me into your arms and pass out. When we wake up the next morning it suddenly becomes: *I love you like a friend, Lucas, You deserve someone your own age, Lucas, One day you'll thank me, Lucas.* I can't do this with you over and over and over again, Carter," I finished before storming out of the kitchen and practically running out my door. The cool, late night air settled over my skin as I blindly handed my closed drink to someone smoking against the railing to open. I didn't trust my shaking hands to pry open a twist top in their current state.

"Here," Brady's soft voice startled me as he pressed the bottle back into my hand.

"Thanks," I smiled at him, weakly.

"What's going on, Lucy, you seem out of it?" Becca asked, putting a hand on my shoulder.

"Um, Carter," I closed my eyes and took a long pull of my drink. "He's pulling the same shit he always does, except this time he seems frantic to get my attention."

"We're gonna go inside," Xander suddenly said, pulling Brady behind him into my apartment.

"What are you going to do, Lucy?" Becca's question echoed through my brain as I continued to suck down the drink in my hand. I wasn't thinking about the consequences of liquoring myself up even more, I just wanted to quiet the war that was being waged in my head. I just wanted to be numb.

Although the answer came quicker than I would've expected, I still turned to Becca and said, "I don't know."

"The fuck you don't," she sneered before retreating into my apartment, leaving me alone in the walkway, just now registering that I was standing outside in February in a tank top and shorts, barefoot. Polishing off my drink, I sighed deeply and schooled my features to return to the chaos of two guys making a play for me in one night. The sight that greeted me was shocking, Brady and Xander chatting animatedly, Brady with a plastic cup in hand and Xander tilting back his beer. Sitting at my card table, with his head down in what felt like defeat, was Carter.

"Hey, are you okay?" I asked, nudging him.

"Yeah, just a little tired," he smiled up at me, expectantly.

116

"Okay," I said, moving to throw away my bottle and walking to my bathroom. I hadn't wanted to break the seal, but it was time. Upon my exit from the restroom, I noticed that Carter was no longer at my table. In fact, he wasn't in my apartment at all, it seemed. I couldn't help but notice that Brady, Xander and Becca were missing again, too.

"Where'd Carter go?" I asked no one in particular.

"He said he was going to go lay down," someone answered from my living room.

"Fuck," I grumbled and marched into my bedroom, finding a passed the fuck out Carter on his normal side of my bed. Feeling the anger rising, I, once again, stormed through my apartment and out into the crisp, late winter air. "FUCK!" I growled, louder. How dare he try to make this decision for me! He had no doubt that I would pick him, why else would he be so territorial as to fall asleep in my fucking bed? He knew that I'd need to sleep, eventually, and I'd just join him. That he would win. Deep inside, I knew that if I got into that bed with Carter, I'd never have a chance with Brady. Before I knew what was happening, my drunken anger got the best of me and tears started to fall down my face.

"Hey," Brady said from beside me. I startled and swiped at my eyes as I turned to face him. "Look, I didn't mean to pressure you or anything."

"You," I started, taking a deep breath, a sad look crossing my features. "You didn't. It was 100% Carter's doing."

"If you two still have a thing…" he trailed off.

"We don't," I said, resolutely. "In fact, he can have my fucking bed, I'm sleeping on my new couch," I stomped my foot and went back in to my apartment, seeing that the pass out portion of the evening was definitely upon us.

Becca had remained sober and was pushing a very inebriated Xander out my front door, a lascivious look on her face. Jack and Liz were cuddled together on an empty patch of floor, and others were taking up valuable real estate throughout the living and dining areas.

"Get up," Brady barked at a party-goer, who was trying to settle into my couch. "Lucy's sleeping there tonight."

"She has a bed," he murmured before sliding off the couch onto the floor.

"Yeah, but someone decided they needed to share it with her tonight, but didn't ask permission. We're on guard duty," he said, lying perpendicular to where I was now lying on the sofa and indicating to the guy who'd vacated my couch that he needed to flank my other side.

"Thanks, Brady," I smiled before I shut my eyes and fell promptly to sleep.

When I awoke a few hours later, I found the guys still lying, dutifully, on the floor beside the couch. Carefully, I tip toed toward the bathroom to answer nature's call, then I snuck a peek in my bedroom, which, thankfully, was now empty. After that discovery, I made my first step in making my choice known by nudging Brady awake.

"Hey," he said, groggily. "What's up?"

"Hey," I smiled. "My bed is empty; want a more comfortable place to sleep?" I asked, tilting my head toward my bedroom.

"Sure," he whispered, getting to his feet and following me to my bedroom, where we slipped under my comforter and crashed again. We weren't cuddling or really touching in any way, but I hoped he knew this gesture meant something to me.

118

CHAPTER 13

BRADY

I woke up again about 10am, my heart racing from the realization that the night before had not been a dream or a car crash or a hallucination. *I'd* kissed Lucy, and she'd kissed me back. Even though she hadn't dropped to her knees and declared her secret love for me, I could tell that she felt something because of the way she'd agonized when Carter decided to pull his shit on her. If her sleeping on the couch and not with him hadn't shown me that she might want to explore the idea of *us*, then her inviting me to sleep beside her after he'd vacated her bed surely did.

Glancing over at her sleeping form, her head buried under her blankets again, I felt light and settled. Something about the possibility of waking up like this every day did things to me that I wasn't sure were entirely sane. The emotions bubbling inside my head had me questioning my status as a man.

"Hey," she grinned at me when she opened her eyes. Looking out through a tunnel in her sheets, her cheeks reddened when she caught me staring. Languidly, she stretched her limbs and extracted the comforter from her body. Fruitlessly, I tried to keep my eyes from trailing down her body to the tops of her breasts being pushed up in her tank top or the way her shorts were riding high over the tops of her thighs.

"Good morning," I grinned back as I stretched, too. "I need a cigarette," I announced, standing up and heading toward the door. I was surprised and excited to see her get up from the bed and follow me.

"So, what are your plans for today?" she asked, leaning against the railing, trying not to act as if the February air wasn't too cold for her to be outside in her barely-there pajamas.

"Gotta get my daughter from her grandma's, then we'll be at the apartment," I said, taking a drag from my cigarette.

"Oh yeah," she smiled, lightly. "The weekend warrior dad thing- how does that work?"

"It's both awesome and sucks," I professed. "I mean, I love my daughter so much. She's amazing and hilarious, but I feel like I miss out on so much because I only see her on the weekends. I mean, she's two, so I feel like she grows so much between my visits," I rambled, lamenting my lost time with my daughter when the need to clarify my response popped into my head. "I don't regret the divorce, though," I blushed. "Lori and I were just bad for each other. Taylor is the best thing that came out of us being together."

"That's what Becca always says."

"I'm sure she does," I couldn't help how sardonic the words sound as they fly from my mouth.

"Stop that," she admonished with a chuckle. "Becca doesn't seem to harbor delusions about becoming your wife anymore, so let her gush over your daughter if she wants."

"It was never me she wanted, Lucy, it was always Taylor," I grimaced.

"I hear that she's a very special little girl, and adorable," Lucy said, lightly, as if realizing how much would be involved in dating me, how complicated it would be.

"What are you up to today?" I changed the subject. I wasn't sure I wanted to continue talking about Taylor because I didn't know what Lucy's role would be. I hadn't dated since the divorce and my daughter had the tendency to get really jealous of the few girls she'd met that were just friends. They weren't even girls I was interested in and she'd latch on to my neck, glare at them with her bright blue eyes and say 'My daddy.' Though Becca fancied herself an authority on Taylor, I was pretty sure my daughter would like nothing more than to never lay her eyes on Becca again. On the other hand, I knew the sooner Taylor met Lucy, the sooner I'd have my answer about whether our budding relationship, if you could call it that, would ever be an option for me.

"Meeting my mom for lunch at the mall," she groaned.

"You don't want to spend time with your mom?" I asked, watching her give up the pretense of not being cold as she folded her arms over her chest tightly.

"It's not that," she shook her head. "I love my mom, but she hates my hair and she's been trying to convince me to dye it back, but it's black. There's really only one way to fix it, and I'm not ready to do that yet."

"I love your hair like this." Hesitantly, I grabbed a lock of her shoulder length black hair and twirled it between my fingers. I was taken off guard by the silky feel of it and had to take a deep breath to come across as unaffected.

"Thanks," she whispered, that uncharacteristic blush settling on her cheeks again before she cleared her throat and added, "Um, I have to go get ready for lunch." Stepping back and away from me, she made her way to the door again, stiffly, breaking whatever moment I thought we were sharing. Maybe I'd read her wrong, maybe this wasn't what she wanted after all. Contemplating that, I finished my cigarette and went back into the apartment to help her straighten up.

"You don't have to do that," she smiled when she saw me gathering empty bottles and plastic cups from her living

121

room. She was wearing a pair of well-worn blue jeans and blue top that provided full breast coverage, but she looked more beautiful than I'd ever seen her. "Wow!" she said, pointing at something and pulling me from my reverie and toward the wall she indicated between her kitchen and living room. "I didn't realize we'd drunk that much last night!"

Depositing the trash, I absently counted the bottle caps stuck to the wall by static electricity. "I think I both love and hate Xander for showing us that trick," I laughed. "I remember a time when I could lie to myself about how trashed I got, but you can't argue with this, can you?"

"You certainly can't," she said, softly, looking up at me again, her eyes sparkled with something.

I started to raise my hand to caress her cheek, but stopped myself at the last minute. I could see apprehension in her gaze. She was still holding back, just a little bit, like she wasn't sure if I was trying to tell her something with that kiss last night. She actually looked downright vulnerable, and if I weren't a little nervous about her reaction, I would've kissed her again to make sure she understood how serious I'd been. Luckily, I knew Lucy well enough that I could see any further progress would be up to her. Otherwise, she'd bolt and we'd be over before we even began.

With a slight cough, I stepped away from another shared moment. "Looks like everyone already cleared out and I've gotta go, too. I've got about forty minutes to get to my ex-mother-in-law's house," I said in a rush as I looked around at the empty apartment, now just a little bit cleaner.

"I was headed out, too," she nodded, grabbing her keys and the small cell phone holder she called a purse before shadowing me to the door, awkwardly. "Um, I'll call you

122

later?" The nerves in her voice rocketed through me as the words gave me hope.

"I'd like that," I gave her a soft smile as she locked her door behind us and followed me down the stairs.

"Good," she said, unlocking her truck and sliding behind the steering wheel, unable to look me in the eye. "Later, then, I guess."

"Yeah," I agreed, moving to my own car as she backed out of her space and headed out of the lot. Maybe I was something she was interested in pursuing after all.

**

LUCAS

"So, you disappeared this morning," I said into the phone as I exited the freeway.

"Don't I usually?" Carter snorted, flippantly, but there was an edge in his voice that gave me pause.

"Yeah, but, I don't know..." I trailed off, wondering if he'd mention the fact that I never crawled in bed with him last night.

"I had to meet my mom for breakfast," he justified.

"Oh, I'm meeting my mom for lunch right now," I told him, signaling the left turn to get into the mall.

"Sounds like fun," he said, frustrating me with his continued evasiveness.

"About last night, Carter?" I spat out, sick of waiting for him to bring up his behavior.

"That was nothing, you know I love you like a friend, Lucas. Brady's a good guy, and your own age," he rationalized, causing me to bite back a sigh of relief that he was so damn predictable and I hadn't decided to blow it with Brady by getting into bed with Carter last night. "Just—just do yourselves a favor."

"What?" I asked, annoyed that he was about to attempt to give me any kind of advice.

"If you really like this guy, wait to sleep with him, okay?" Carter said, sounding more serious than I'd ever heard him. "You have the tendency to jump into bed too quickly."

"It took me a month to get into bed with you," I countered.

"Yeah, but you were actually looking to have a relationship with me," he sighed. "If you want the same from Brady, you'll wait."

"I don't know what I want," I told him, honestly, parking near the food court. "I don't even know if I'm capable of having a functional and monogamous relationship."

"I'm not sure if you can either, Lucas. It's another reason I've always held back," he agreed, readily. I wasn't looking for reassurances, but his outright support of my fears bugged me in a way I couldn't really understand.

"Thanks for the faith," I mumbled, slamming my truck door behind me. "I've gotta meet my mom now, Carter. Talk to you later," I said, hanging up before he could respond and stalking toward the food court.

"Hey, honey!" my mom squealed as I approached the Panda Express, our usual meeting spot. Cheap and fast Chinese food was the best. "You would look so beautiful if your hair color didn't wash you out so bad!" she announced, frowning as she pulled me in for a hug.

124

"Don't you think the black makes my eyes pop?" I pulled back and folded my arms over my chest like a petulant child.

"Of course, but you are so fair skinned and pale. The black is all wrong for you. It makes you look sick," she shook her head as we got in line to get our lunch.

"I'll keep that in mind," I said, turning to place my order. Even though things had gotten off to a rocky start, catching up with my mom had ended up being exactly what I needed. She always had this amazing way of making me forget any craziness or drama going on in my life. We usually focused on how school was going, and she never asked me if I was seeing anyone, nor did she think it was important for me to try to find a husband. I was grateful for that.

As I walked to my truck, I had an overwhelming desire to call Brady. Now that the Carter question was answered, I wanted to see what last night meant, if anything, but I didn't want to come across as desperate. Therefore, I did the next best thing: I called Becca. Yes, I am a fucking coward.

"Hey, Lucy," she answered, brightly. I could tell right away she wanted to know what happened after she and Xander left, but wasn't going to come out and ask me.

"Hey, Bec, how's it going?" I asked, balancing my phone on my shoulder as I cranked my truck.

"It's dead over here, but we were thinking about playing a game later, wanna stop by?" she invited, as if she were actually daring me to say no and confirm her suspicions about whether or not I'd blown off Brady.

"Um, if it's okay with your roommates?" I squeaked.

"They'll love it," she rejected my weak excuse. "Xander is here, and Brady just got back with Taylor. Flynn'll be home before dinner and he's bringing Travis. I could really use some extra estrogen."

"Okay, then. I'll be right there," I told her, more cheery than I intended, as I backed out of my parking space and headed toward their apartment.

"Brady'll be happy. He's been kind of quiet today," she whispered.

"Isn't he always quiet?" I chuckled.

"Well, more than usual. Just get here, then the two of you can figure out what happened last night, and what you are going to do about it," she chastised before she hung up on me. Ugh, she knew everything was still in limbo. Had Brady told her? Or did she just know because I hadn't volunteered any information?

Becca answered the door with a box of hair dye in her hands and thrust it at me, immediately, "I'm so glad you came! These assholes refused to help me."

"Oh, I see how it is," I laughed. "You manipulated me into coming over so I could re-dye your hair."

"Yeah," she looked down at the floor, at least having the decency to look repentant before her lips curled up into a devious smile.

"Whatever," I rolled my eyes and grabbed the box. "Where are we doing this?"

"Patio, I don't want to stink up the apartment," she bounced toward the sliding glass door. "I'm going to run to get a towel," she announced, suddenly, and cut toward her bathroom.

"Hi," a small voice said from the floor. Looking down, I saw the most beautiful steel blue eyes I'd ever seen, aside from the ones I knew belonged to her father.

"Hi," I smiled. "You must be Taylor," I continued, sweetly. I'd babysat before, I knew how to act like I wasn't nervous to meet her, even though I knew if she didn't like me, it would be nearly impossible for Brady and I to have a relationship.

"Yup," she said, smiling back at me. She had a halo of hazelnut hair, the same color as Brady's, cut into the cutest shoulder length bob. It even curled under, giving her an almost angelic appearance, which was only enhanced by her cherubic cheeks and heart-shaped lips. Looking at this three foot nothing girl who had the ability to make or break my relationship with Brady, I waited for my usual response to the idea of children, which was to run like crazy, but it never came. Instead of being freaked out about what her presence would mean or if she would like me, I just smiled. Two words and this gorgeous little girl already had me wrapped around her finger.

"I'm Lucas," I told her. "I'm happy to finally meet you, cause your daddy talks about you all the time."

"I love my daddy," her smile only got brighter. "My coloring him a picture." Taylor lifted a crayon from the page she'd been working on. I couldn't believe how well-spoken she was for two years old. Although, I remembered Becca mentioning that her birthday was soon, so maybe her being nearly three was the reason she spoke so clearly. I didn't have enough kid experience to know the difference.

"I'm sure he'll love that," I let my eyes wander to Brady, who was playing some snowboarding video game with Xander, but his brows were creased as he watched me interact with his daughter out of the corner of his eye.

"Got the towel," Becca breezed through the living room and opened the patio door, ushering me outside.

"I'll talk to you later, okay, Taylor?"

"Okay! My going to finish this," she nodded and went back to her picture as Becca closed the door behind us.

"Oh my God, Becca! She's so freaking cute!" I gushed, quietly, as I wrapped the towel around her shoulders and released her hair from the elastic band it was in.

"You can have Brady, but you can't have her," Becca bit out, obviously jealous at how nice Taylor had been to me.

"Of course, Becca. She's known you longer," I accepted. "Besides, I think her attitude will change if Brady and I get together." After pulling the bottles and instructions from the box, I retrieved the gloves and began mixing the dye.

"*If?*" Becca prompted with a slight sneer. "You aren't going to lead him on, are you? He doesn't put himself out like this, *ever.*"

"I'm not going to lead him on, Becca. I like him, a lot," I frowned as I realized how much I was starting to care about Brady in the non-friend capacity. "I just don't know what he wants."

"Then you need to ask him that, don't you? Just... if you think it might be heading somewhere... don't sleep with him right away," She said, absently, before she started shivering in the chair. "That dye is cold on my scalp," she laughed.

"Are you sure it wasn't a pee shiver? Cause if it is, you'll have to wait until I'm done now." I squeeze a large dollop of dye onto her roots and started to comb it through.

128

I tried to ignore her words about sleeping with Brady, because it seemed to be what everyone thought I would do. I'm not saying I wouldn't get bored if I slept with him right away, but I could already feel it would be different with him. I didn't want to let anyone know that before I found out how he felt though.

"Damn, now all I can think about is how I have to fucking pee," Becca's leg started to bounce with need and another shiver passed through her body.

"Being out here in the cold probably isn't helping either, so I shouldn't talk about waterfalls and river rafting?" I teased.

"You bitch!" Becca shouted, jokingly. "Back to the subject at hand. Brady... you don't get to change the subject, because now I need you to distract me from my pressing need," she blindly swatted backwards swiping my forearm with her nails.

"Watch it, Cruella, or you're going to end up with a big red splotch on your forehead," I threatened.

"Ugh," she folded her arms across her chest and pouted. "This is supposed to be *less* messy than when we were drunk, Lucas Spencer!"

"Then don't tempt me, Rebecca Lou!" I continued to massage the dye into her hair. Luckily, she continued to pout for the remainder of the session, leaving me off the hook in answering anymore questions about my uncertain future with Brady.

CHAPTER 14

BRADY

Taylor had fallen asleep on the couch after she'd finished coloring. After letting her nap on the couch for nearly thirty minutes, I decided to move her into her bed in my room so she might sleep longer. As I exited my bedroom, I nearly collided with a very distracted Lucy.

"Oh shit!" she froze, pressing her hand to her chest, as if she were trying to calm it. "Becca's in the other bathroom, she told me I could use yours? She made fun of me for having to go so badly since I teased her so hard when I was dying her hair?" she explained, but it sounded more like a question. I caught her country apple scented hair as she moved it from her surprised eyes and struggled to get her breathing under control.

"I'm sorry I scared you, of course you can use mine," I smiled and gestured for her to pass.

"You didn't scare me," she whispered, thickly, looking into my eyes. Slowly, I watched her pupils dilate, hopefully, from desire and her breathing speed up again.

"Good," I whispered back, equally husky. "So...," I looked at her, suddenly unease. "Are we going to, you know, um, talk?" I stammered out.

"Um, yeah," she started, slowly, like she was considering her words carefully, "but I seriously have to pee," she smiled, hopping from foot to foot indicating she wasn't trying to get out of the conversation. "You can even wait right here for me," she offered.

"And have to listen to you pee? No, thank you," I snorted, teasingly, trying to lighten the implied heaviness of the conversation. "I have to listen to that enough when you get really drunk and don't shut the door when you go."

"That's drunk level five," she laughed, pushing passed me to get to the bathroom door, which she, thankfully, shut after she was inside. Shaking my head, I grabbed my pack of cigarettes and headed for the patio. After lighting my Marlboro, I sat down on the kitchen chair Becca hadn't moved back to the table where it belonged and watched the wind blow the flags near the office of the complex.

"Hey," Lucy said, hesitantly, as she opened the sliding glass door to join me. She looked unsure of herself, more than I'd ever seen or thought she was capable of, that air of vulnerability was back. It was hot, and let me know that she was just as nervous about this as I was.

"Hey," I answered, giving her a reassuring smile that she mirrored, almost as if she were grateful for it.

"So, um, last night was, interesting," she cleared her throat after her words and started picking at the end of her hair.

"Yeah," I agreed, scratching the back of my neck, trying to find the words to start this conversation.

"I had no idea, you…," she confessed, after a few beats, a wistful smile settled over her lips and her eyes went soft.

"You're beautiful, Lucy. How couldn't you know?" I asked, thunderstruck that she actually looked mystified by the fact that I was into her.

"But, what you've watched me do…" she sighed, looking over my shoulder. "The guys… you aren't like other people, Brady," she explained and I couldn't help but laugh at her high opinion of me.

131

"Thank you for thinking of me as someone of pedestal level moral fiber, but you'd be surprised at the things I've done," I dismissed. Never in a million years, would I have suspected that she thought she wasn't good enough for me. I was completely bowled over by the realization.

"And you want this? *With me?*" she tried to clarify, biting her lip and giving me a dubious look. "You really want to be with me?"

"Are you sure this is what *you* want? I mean, you told Becca you weren't looking for a relationship," I took a drag of my cigarette, trying to give her an out that I hoped she wouldn't take.

"I don't—I mean, I didn't, but something keeps telling me that I have to go for this with you, whatever *this* is," she swallowed. "I'm not going to lie though, I work full time and go to school full time, so I don't know how it'll all work, but I think I want to try. I'm more than a little freaked out to admit that, if you want the truth," she laid out.

"I know what you mean," I said, crushing my cigarette, catching her by her neck and pulling her lips to mine. She didn't resist, at all, and melted into the kiss. "Exclusive or I can't do this," I told her, after breaking the kiss but not moving away from her. In hindsight though, I probably should've spelled that out for her before I stuck my tongue down her throat again, but I couldn't hold myself back anymore.

"Wow," she breathed against my mouth. "It was amazing when I was drunk, but it's just as intoxicating sober," she continued, dreamily. "Exclusive," she confirmed with a determined look in her eyes that lit up my insides. I never thought she'd agree, especially so readily.

"Good," I agreed, kissing her again, letting her deepen the kiss as she clung to me. My heart thundered in my chest and explosions detonated behind my eyes during that kiss. I'd wondered what it would be like to kiss her if she decided to give us a chance, and now I knew, it was better than breathing.

"Daddy?" Taylor's voice came from the patio door, startling both of us.

"Hey, baby girl," I grinned down at my daughter's sleep rumpled face after I pulled away from Lucy, hoping that Taylor wouldn't get upset or possessive of me, even though I loved when she was. Her acceptance of Lucy was more important to me that I had been willing to admit, which is why I had to stop myself from being too triumphant when Taylor walked over to Lucy and hugged her, lightly.

"This mean I get to see Lucy again?" her blue eyes blinked up at me.

"I think so, baby," I told her as she walked over to me and lifted her arms into the air, signaling for me to pick her up.

"Good," she nodded as I hoisted her onto my hip and her hands clasped behind my neck to hug me. "She a nice lady. My colored *her* a picture, daddy."

"That was really nice of you," I told her. "What about my picture?" I asked.

Taylor made a surprised face at me then looked down in thought, "My forgot! My do it as soon as I finish," she nodded, resolutely.

"I'm wounded! One afternoon and I'm already being thrown over," I said as if I were agonized by her revelation.

"Oh, daddy, don't be silly," my two-year old tsked me as if she were someone much older. "I still love you!" she declared before she started to squirm to be let down.

"Whew!" I exclaimed, wiping my brow, exaggeratedly as she went back into the apartment.

"You're such a good dad," Lucy observed.

"Thank you, I know you don't have much time, but are you sure you are up for *this*?" I reiterated. "I may only get her on the weekends, but I love my daughter. You have to know that she'll always come first."

"I'd be more concerned about dating you if she didn't," she censured.

"If you want to be a part of her life, this can't be a passing fancy," I winced as her face changed at my words. "This isn't an admonishment of your past, Lucy, but I want you to understand that she won't understand if we break up and you aren't in her life anymore. I would say this to any girl I wanted to date. You need to know what you're facing."

"I understand," she frowned, taking in everything I was saying. A montage of emotions seemed to cross her face as she considered my words carefully. Just as I thought she was going to tell me she couldn't do it after all, she started talking again. "I still want to…try. I mean, I can't make any promises about what our future is going to be together, but I can't just let this go. I feel like we have something real here."

"Good," I exhaled in relief, loudly. "I think so, too."

"So, we're a thing now?" she asked.

"We're more than a thing, Lucy," I confirmed. "We're going to be amazing," my confident words slipping out of my mouth easier than I would've expected. What was she doing to me? I was a derisive asshole, not someone who thought dating someone could end up being amazing. One look at her blue eyes and I morphed into someone I didn't know I was capable of becoming: an optimist.

"I'm glad *you* have so much faith," she chuckled, her nerves from earlier making a dramatic reappearance. "With my history, I just…"

"One day at a time?" I offered. "Do the other guys bother me? I'm not going to lie, Lucy, they do. I mean, I have a lot of history to compete with, but I'll try to put aside if you promise me that you can, too," I finished, feeling like I was laying all my cards on the table.

"Okay," she looked at me through lowered lashes. "And we'll take it slow? It's been over a year and a half since I had a boyfriend."

"It's been since I got divorced for me, which I guess is about the same as you, so slow is good." I could tell there was more that she wanted to say, but she kept quiet, so I just held her until I saw Flynn coming up the stairs to our apartment, anger glinting in his eyes at the scene. Fuck, this was going to be awkward.

**

LUCAS

Flynn pushed past Brady and I, a mask of pure rage in place as his disapproval oozed from the tension in his body.

"I didn't know you'd be here, Lucy," he snarked before shoving his way into the apartment, letting me know that he was still angry with me for picking up Becca a couple of weeks ago.

135

"Maybe I should go," I pulled out of Brady's embrace and searched for my purse.

"You don't have to leave because of him," Brady grabbed my arm and pulled me back toward him. "Please, stay. I want you to. We just made a huge decision together and I want to enjoy it for a few more minutes," he smiled at me and I caved, immediately. The steel blue of his eyes weakened me more than I thought possible.

"Okay," I said, cautiously, "but if you really think I should go, it's not a big deal. I mean, I know he's still angry about…you know."

"That's not it, Lucy. Not completely anyway," he tried to tell me. "He's mad at me for letting Xander stay with us, he's mad at Becca for sleeping with Xander and he's mad at Xander for taking what he thinks will always be his, even if he's dating someone else. He's mad at the world right now, so you aren't his *only* target."

"Oh," was the only word I could say. "I- I had no idea."

"The only person he's not mad at is himself," he said, pulling me back into the apartment and steering me to the couch while he went to check on Taylor, who was coloring at her desk again. Why was watching him tend to his daughter such a turn on? I didn't plan on having kids of my own, but the protective, nurturing father thing looked smoking hot on Brady. Subconsciously, I crossed my legs and bit my lip to stifle a moan as I watched him. I wondered why his attentiveness wound me up so much. The only thing I could come up with was something I'd never had growing up. My parents were never married and my dad lived in another state my whole life. I knew I had daddy issues, but, damn, this getting turned on by a good dad thing was disconcerting. Just not disconcerting enough to change my mind about wanting to be with Brady.

136

"You can't have her, Lucy, don't forget," Becca growled from beside me, pulling me from my thoughts.

"I didn't forget, but damn, he's pushing all my buttons right now, Bec…buttons I didn't even know I had," I whispered, honestly.

"I've seen that look before, Lucy. Don't sleep with him right away, seriously. I thought we talked about this," she huffed, quietly. I decided enough was enough. Shooting Becca an angry scowl, I jumped from the couch and walked over to Brady and Taylor. I wanted to stay and spend more time with them, but the overall tension pulsing in the apartment was too much.

"Hey," I started, softly. "I've got some homework I need to finish. Do you mind if I head out?"

"Are you sure?" he looked at me, confused.

"You can't go yet, Lucy! My not done with my picture," Taylor frowned. "But, my almost done."

"That sounds great, Taylor," I told her, taking a seat on the sectional closer to them. "I'll wait for you to finish," I smiled, not wanting to disappoint her.

"HERE!" she shoved a haphazardly colored fairy into my hand with a triumphant smile.

"Why thank you, Taylor! It's beautiful," I returned her smile, feeling Becca's anger radiate from behind me. "I'll see you next time, okay?" I promised.

"Okay!" the two year-old smiled. "My have to go potty, daddy!" she shouted.

"I'll take her!" Becca shouted as she bolted off the couch and grabbed Taylor's arm before Brady could answer.

"I'll walk you out," he looked at me with shadowed eyes.

"Okay," I agreed with a small smile. As I gathered my keys, I heard a shout of good bye from Xander, who'd been in the kitchen. I waved, absently, as we crossed the threshold of the front door and silently walked down the stairs to my truck.

"Everything okay?" Brady asked when we reached the drivers' side door.

"Yeah, there was just too much drama in that apartment and I really do have a ton of physics work to do," I explained, taking a cleansing breath.

"Okay," he sagged with apparent relief. "I was afraid you changed your mind about us."

"No," I hoped the horrified look on my face at his suggestion was clear. I couldn't believe he would even think that! "Never."

"Good," Brady mouthed before pulling me in for a goodbye kiss that sent my mind on vacation again, reminding me of why I wanted to take this risk with him. "So, I think I left my jacket at your house last night," he broached with a twinkle in his eye.

"You did?" I looked at him, perplexed as to why he hadn't told me this earlier. "Do you want me to bring it over after work tomorrow?"

"No," he grinned like he had a secret. "I'd rather pick it up after I get off work on Monday."

"Oh!" My eyes widened in understanding. I wasn't sure if he was angling to get into my bed, it didn't quite feel like it, but after everyone questioned whether I could really keep it in my pants with him for a while, I decided to be extra cautious. "Um, what did you have in mind? I mean, I

138

thought we said we were going to take it slow?" the words came out before I could hold them back with my usual iron-fisted desire to never look vulnerable, but he was blowing away all of my usual defenses.

"I just wanted to spend time with you, Lucy, since you don't have much in the way of free time. I wasn't trying to go where you are thinking. Not yet anyway," he held up his hands in surrender. "I mean, unless you can't picture a physical relationship with me at all, then we might need to have a different conversation"

"Oh," I chuckled, lightly, "I *want* a physical relationship with you. Like, more than you know," I scooted close enough to put my arms around his waist before I tilted my face up to look into his eyes, "but it's been pointed out to me, repeatedly, that I have a tendency to rush the sexual aspects of a relationship and sabotage it by moving too quickly. I don't want to do that with you, which is why I said I wanted to go slow. For some reason, it's really important to me to not screw this up."

"Hey," he said bringing my attention back to his face, his voice low as his blue-gray eyes turned liquid silver. "How about we don't listen to how everyone else thinks we need to behave in our relationship? How about we make the decision to have sex right away or to wait together, instead of taking up a vote amongst our friends? It's not really their call, is it?" he pointed out, a slight edge present, that quite frankly, did nothing to cool my libido where he was concerned.

"You're right, it's our call, but I see the point they are trying to make," I sighed. "I move fast and burn out even faster and for some reason, everything inside is telling me it's important that I keep you," I whispered.

"Then we'll make it work," he rebuked. "I want to be with you for who you are, not someone you think you need

139

to be. Don't ever think that who you are isn't good enough for me. Okay?"

"Okay," I said, my voice thick with the emotion of the moment, glad that he understood my fear of needing to change who I was to keep him.

"Good, now that's settled, Monday?" he quirked an eyebrow at me in question.

"Sound good," I smiled.

"See you then, but call me tomorrow?" he prompted.

"Absolutely," I nodded as he bent down to place another chaste kiss on my lips and released me to get back into my truck. "Talk to you later," I told him as I slid behind the wheel and waved before turning the key and backing out of the parking space. I tried to resist looking at him standing in the parking lot as I made my way toward the street, but I couldn't. As I merged with traffic, I gave into my urge to do a small happy dance as I grinned from ear to ear for the first time in a very long time. I hadn't felt this optimistic about the prospect of an actual relationship since Preston. Maybe 2003 would be a decent year after all. Maybe it would be the year I stopped going around in circles and finally found the right path.

CHAPTER 15

BRADY

"What was *Lucas Dunn* doing here last night?" Flynn sneered at me when I got home from dropping off my daughter on Sunday night, blindsiding me as soon as I walked in the door.

"Um," I started, rubbing the back of my neck, trying of think of how I was going to break this news to him. "Well, um, Lucy and I are together now?" Even though I said it like a question, there is *no* question that's what we are doing. I wanted to grin, but I knew any sign of actual happiness would be met with disgust by Flynn.

"Really?" he scoffed. "Lucy doesn't date, Brady."

"You should've seen them, Flynn. They both wanted this, but were so clueless! It was adorable!" Becca gushed.

"Sleep with her yet? I mean, you've been together longer than five minutes, right? I've been told it's that easy for everyone else, but I'm surprised she'd let you, because she always told me she wouldn't *ever* be with someone her friend had been with first," he spat. Suddenly the real reason for bearing the entire focus of Flynn's anger flashed in front of my brain. He's been trying to get in Lucy's panties for almost seven years and had been continually shot down. She had branded him untouchable because of his previous relationship with Becca. Apparently, he was going the bitter route about the whole thing, since he was already pissed at her and it was easier. His words did make me wonder how I was able to get her to go back on a rule she'd held steadfast for nearly a decade. Not that I was complaining...

"No, Flynn, I haven't," I growled.

"That's shocking. Usually, she tries out the goods *before* she decides to buy. Even though I haven't seen her *willing* to 'buy' for years now. Maybe she's just trying to string you along until one of her studs wants to commit."

"Carter made a power play for her the other night and she straight up shut him down!" Becca announced.

"For now, she shot him down, Becca. For now," Flynn interjected, with the skepticism in his voice so thick it was like a blanket over our conversation.

"Watch it," I warned, my fists clenched at my sides as I sat on the sectional. It took everything I had to remain seated at his words. "I'm pretty sure I have real feelings for this girl and I don't want to hear this right now," I finished, not backing down from the challenge my words threw out.

Out of the corner of my eye, I watched Becca's jaw drop as I declared my feelings for Lucy to my oldest friend. Even though she encouraged me to go after Lucy, I don't think she ever considered that I'd defend her best friend in a way I'd never defended her. She might be with Xander now, but I could tell she could see the difference between what she and I had and what I was building with Lucy. The look on her face told me that she was obviously hurt by my declaration. Seeing her reaction to my words also triggered Flynn to ratchet up his ire another notch.

"Are you seriously trying to go there with me over *her?!* The only thing Lucy is good for is planning parties that would make Caligula blush and getting fucked like the slut she is. I can't believe you would pass up higher quality and much higher class girls for that whore," he stopped and shook his head. I had to keep reminding myself that Flynn was my oldest friend and everything with Lucy was still too new to fully go toe to toe with him, yet, all I saw was red. I'd never wanted to beat the shit out of my friend so badly, but I was a master at controlling my emotions, so I bit my

142

tongue as much as I could and waited for him to finish trashing Lucy. "I feel like I don't even know you right now," he finished, getting up from the couch and stalking toward the door.

"She never fucked you, so obviously, she has *some* standards," I graveled out as the door slammed behind him, losing out on my battle to stay quiet.

"He's just scared," Becca said, more quietly than I'd ever heard from her.

"What?" I asked, angrily, trying to calm the inordinate amount of rage pulsing through my blood by taking a deep breath. I'd never reacted that way before when a buddy teased me about a girl. The back biting comment had escaped mostly involuntarily. After he called Lucy a whore, I couldn't just let it go and the consequences of agitating a very volatile Flynn never occurred to me. I don't even want to think about what would've happened if he'd doubled back at my words. We were lucky he continued on his way and didn't break anything or anyone.

"When you married Lori, you turned into a hermit," Becca explained, calmly, like she was trying to soothe my ire. "He doesn't want to lose you again."

"Insulting Lucy is a pretty good way to lose me, Bec," I fired back, standing from the sectional and pacing the length of the living room in an attempt to calm down. "Besides, Lori hated Flynn and the feeling was mutual, keeping them apart helped me avoid the headache of listening to her complain about one more fucking thing. She already complained enough about everything else, not hanging out with Flynn made my home life a lot fucking easier. You can't even compare the two, Becca. He used to consider Lucy a friend."

"I've never seen you become formidable like that with Flynn, Brady. You are usually so passive," Becca looked at me with awe.

"Thinking of me as passive was a mistake Lori made, too," I said, stopping and narrowing my eyes at the wall. I wasn't upset at Becca, she wasn't the first person to underestimate me. "I may come across as a push over, but if I don't fight you on something, it only means I don't care enough to put in the effort."

"Good to know," she huffed and heaved herself off the couch before leaving the living room in favor of her bedroom. I knew she was overanalyzing everything in our so-called relationship now, like I'd just said I never cared about her. It wasn't true, I'd always cared about her as a friend. She just wanted more from me than I was able to give. Regardless of what she had now, seeing me so willing to try with Lucy had to be weighing on her.

Sanity returned to the apartment a few minutes later when Xander walked in from his day with his kids. "Wanna snowboard?" he asked, gesturing toward the PlayStation.

"Fuck yes," I breathed a sigh of relief as the tension in the room seemed to finally clear. Walking to the machine, I fired it up and sat down in front of the television beside Xander.

"What happened? Where is everyone?" Xander asked, after the game finally loaded, picking up on my body language. Xander's history as an Army Ranger made him an expert at picking up on non-verbal cues. It was how he knew I was into Lucy and how he knew she felt the same.

"Flynn threw a tantrum—"

"Is Becca okay?" he interjected, looking dutifully concerned.

144

"Yeah, actually, the tantrum was aimed at me and my budding…whatever…with Lucy," I tried to explain as he selected the race he wanted us to play. We'd been racking up tons of achievements in two player mode on this course, so I was on board.

"Why?" he said, after a few minutes, letting us get into the groove before continuing the conversation.

"You know, it's so mind numbingly stupid and histrionic, I don't want to even give it brain space," I said as we raced to the end of the first fake snowboarding course.

"Understood. And Becca?" he asked, prompting me to pause our game.

"Cigarette?" I asked. He'd probably had one before he came in the apartment, but I was surprised I hadn't already chain smoked half a pack after Flynn left.

"Great idea," he agreed, folding himself off the floor to follow me to the patio balcony. Becca outed herself as an eavesdropper when she joined us on the patio before we could even light up and perched herself between Xander's legs. She wrapped her appendages around him like a vine, cooing into his ear a little too loudly to be discreet, about what she wanted to do to him. With the two of them distracted, I took the opportunity to look forward to spending time with Lucy after work the next day. We'd agreed to take things slow, but I wasn't sure what her definition of slow was. I could admit, however, that I was looking forward to finding out.

**

LUCAS

For the next week, I did everything I could to balance my crazy busy school and work schedule with the very little sleep I was getting because my boyfriend didn't get off work until 2:30 in the morning, and I wanted to spend time with him. And yes, I was actually using the word boyfriend. I knew it was a big deal, but if everyone could have picked their jaws off the floor and moved along, that would've been awesome.

The nights I didn't have to work, I'd try to go to sleep early so I could get up when he came over, but the nights I did work, he just curled into bed beside me. I know that giving him a key after the third night was probably rushing it, but it was just easier than him calling me when he got to my apartment. I had a hard time finding motivation to go to my 7:40 class every morning because I wanted to cuddle close to him and not leave.

Talking to him was incredible, as was making out with him, but we hadn't progressed much physically beyond that. That was okay with me, because I'd been reminded at every turn to abstain and wait.

"Flynn already thinks you and Brady are fucking, Lucy, and I have honest money on that being true, too. Brady denies it though, so I'm just going to say…if you aren't sleeping with him yet, wait," Becca offered her advice on Sunday evening. "If you want things to work out with him, you know it's for the best."

My mother and I are really close, having been mostly on our own for the last two decades, so I wasn't surprised when her words echoed everyone else's. "Lucas, I know you have issues with your father that need to be worked out, but don't move too fast with this new guy. You seem to actually care about him," she told me on our Monday morning phone call when I was on my way to school. "You bury your abandonment issues by never letting a guy get

146

too close to you emotionally, and you perpetuate that by moving way too fast physically," she counseled, and if she weren't spot on, I would've rolled my eyes. Yet, I still didn't like to hear it over and over again, like a broken record from everyone in my life…and it was literally EVERYONE telling me this.

"As much as I want between your legs again, Lucas, if you want things to work with this Brady dude, who actually sounds like a worthy guy and not a total jack off- keep it in your pants a little bit longer," Eric told me at my weekly lunch date with Abby, who nodded beside me emphatically at his words. "I know you think you can't do it, but I promise you that you can. You are worth more than you think."

"I like Brady and all, but are you sure you don't want to try with Eric?" Abby asked as we left Antonio's that afternoon. "He really seems to care about your happiness."

"Yes, he does, Abby, as a friend," I emphasized once again to my friend. Eric didn't get my heart pumping with just a smile the way Brady did. It wasn't even close.

The problem with all of this well-meaning advice is that it kept the idea of sex in my head constantly. My libido was used to getting action three times a week, at least, and it wasn't happy with this 'waiting' plan, at all.

My lady parts were getting all riled up more and more with every session Brady and I had. I wasn't sure how long it would be before I caved and met Brady at the door wearing only a smile. Although he could be reserved about anything overtly sexual, I had a feeling that once we were behind closed doors that would change. If the way he kissed me was any indication, sex with Brady would be amazing and unlike anything I'd ever experienced before.

However, if I was truly being honest with myself, even though I wanted to be with Brady, I was petrified and not just because everyone thought we should wait. I'd had plenty of sex over the last few years, but none of it had ever held the meaning sex with Brady would. For starters, he was truly and officially, my boyfriend, something I hadn't *really* had since high school. I had guys I dated regularly and exclusively, but that title hadn't been used by me in years.

Second, he was transitioning from being a friend and no one in my corral or otherwise had *ever* been my friend first. Even Carter had gone from a guy I was interested in dating and loved to flirt with to the guy I was sleeping with and wanted to date. Sure, we were friends now, but that came later.

Brady and I, on the other hand, had been friends for years now. This fact brought further into focus the last reason I was quietly freaking out and that was that we had friends in common, best friends to be more precise. I met Carter through work, Eric by chance, Adam at work, Trevor through school. We'd had *things* in common, not people. People, who even with the best of intentions, had the potential to ruin good things under the guise of trying to "help."

I didn't know if I was capable of being a girlfriend- well, a good one anyway. I guess it didn't really take much to be a bad girlfriend, but I had to listen to the voice inside that said I needed to give this thing with Brady everything I had. Yet, I knew I couldn't withstand the pressure I was putting on myself to be perfect at being in a relationship, perfect at school and the perfect employee. Something had to give or I would be crushed under the weight of the expectations I set for myself. These were the kind of doubts and stresses that a good orgasm used to clear out for me. I missed the mindless fucking.

**

Friday was my first official date with Brady. Strange that we'd been sharing a bed together for the last week, but hadn't done the dinner and a movie thing. Brady worked 4-10's and had Fridays off, unless the plant needed him to work overtime. I worked weekend mornings, so I, usually, had Friday nights off as well, because my boss didn't like to schedule us for turnaround shifts.

By the time we were driving to dinner, I was doing my best to hide my nerves, but the butterflies in my stomach were out of control. I couldn't remember the last time I'd been on an actual date; I mean one that involved an actual meal and stuff.

"So, what's this place we are going to for dinner?" Brady asked from the passenger seat of my truck. I knew society dictated that a guy picked up a girl for dates and everything, but Brady had taken the car pool to my house the night before and I wasn't ready to let him drive my baby.

"It's this amazing Mexican restaurant near the hotel I used to work at in Scottsdale," I said with a smile. I hadn't eaten there in forever and I was really looking forward to our dinner, despite my nerves. "The service leaves little to be desired, but their carne asada is melt-in-your-mouth delicious."

"I can't wait," he told me as he laced his fingers with mine on the center console. The physical contact caused a quiet ease to settle over my body. I was surprised and delighted by how something so small could be so calming. After I'd parked in the only empty space left in the parking lot, I stepped out of my truck and smoothed down my dress. The red tank dress I'd chosen for the evening was one of my favorites, but the billowy fabric was prone to wrinkle.

"Have I told you how beautiful you look tonight?" Brady asked, taking my hand again as we walked toward the door. He didn't look too shabby himself in a black button down shirt and jeans.

"Thank you," I smiled at him as we walked through the door the maitre d was holding open for us. We clarified that it was just the two of us and were led to a small table near the bar. "How's Becca doing?" I asked after a bus boy brought us chips and salsa and our orders had been taken. "I haven't heard from her all week."

"She's fine," Brady shrugged. "Better now that Flynn told us that he's planning to move out."

"He is?!" I screeched in disbelief before I could stop myself.

"He said it was hard enough watching Becca and Xander together and didn't want to watch us all self-destruct in our respective relationships."

"Wow, he sounds like he's being a super supportive friend," I muttered, sarcastically.

"Oh, he's being a complete ass," Brady snorted. "He and I had words last weekend about us," he said, nonchalant.

"Us? Like you and me or you and him?" I tried to clarify.

"You and me, Lucy. He thinks it's a bad idea, and had some not so nice things to say about you. It was the first time I'd ever wanted to punch my friend in the face," he admitted, dunking a chip into the mild salsa and sprinkling it with salt before taking a bite.

"Wow," was the only word I could formulate.

"I told him to back off. I think he was just bitter because he'd always wanted to nail you and you kept shooting him down," he shrugged. "He wasn't very happy about that either."

Because I needed to do something with my hands, I picked up a chip of my own and ate it so I'd have time to figure out my response to his defending my honor to his best friend. No one had ever stood up for me like that before and it made me hot, really hot. Really, really, really hot.

"Thank you, Brady, but you didn't have to do that. Flynn is entitled to his opinions of me," I said quietly, looking down at the table, deciding to go with humble.

"No, Lucy," Brady said, drawing my eyes back to his as he leveled me with a look I'd never seen before. "No. one. is allowed to talk about you that way, ever. Do you understand?" he asked, shortly.

"Yes," I whispered, my cheeks heating with a blush. "Um, so, are the movie plans set in stone, or would you rather head back to my place after dinner?" I asked, clearing my throat. At his words, I'd decided that waiting any longer was stupid. Sex wouldn't change what Brady and I were destined to become together. We'd been friends for so long that it wasn't the same as rushing into the physical aspect of a relationship with someone I'd just met. It couldn't be compared.

"Hanging out at your place sounds fine," Brady's voice squeaked slightly at the implication my question had brought to our table.

CHAPTER 16

BRADY

Somewhere between the drive and our entrees, the mood shifted between Lucy and me. I got the feeling that her desire to change our plans meant that her desire to wait was coming to an end in a big way. I would be lying if I said I wasn't really happy with this, not because I was dying to get into her pants, but because I hadn't been happy that she was letting other people dictate the progress of our relationship.

Getting through dinner, knowing we were going back to her place proved difficult, though. I was excited and nervous about what the night would bring. I knew that Lucy's list was much longer than mine, because my ex-wife was my first and I only needed three more fingers to tick off the other names on a very exclusive list. Not that I judged Lucy for hers, after all I knew her, her issues with her exes and the underlying daddy issues at play that made her who she was. It was those very reasons I was drawn to her in the first place.

"Are you sure you're okay with foregoing the movie?" Lucy asked, her blue eyes looking skeptical about the new plan.

"Yeah, why wouldn't I be? Do you just want to rent something on the way back to your apartment?" I asked, trying to clarify her intentions without calling attention to the fact that I knew what we'd be doing when we returned to her place.

"I've got a few movies at home, if that's okay?" she offered, nibbling on her lower lip and looking down at her newly acquired plate as if she were more nervous than I was.

"That sounds good," I tried to give her a reassuring smile as I dug into the chimichanga the waitress had just delivered. "This place is incredible," I said around the bite I'd just taken.

"I know," she moaned as she chewed on a bite of the cheese enchilada on the combo plate she ordered. "I haven't been here since the last time my dad was in town. I'm so glad we came," she told me, her eyes smiling at the memory. I knew she didn't get to see him much and basked in the time they spent together. Lucy's insecurity about relationships came from the fact that her father never asked to spend more time with her than he was allotted and he hardly made the extra effort to come and visit her, even when he was in town on business. I knew it made her feel like she wasn't worth it, but she deserved more than she was getting. She was worth more than she knew.

The rest of the meal was spent in anxious and anticipatory mini conversations that were nice, but had no real point. We both knew we were skirting our true desires vocally, but the way Lucy's tongue caressed the straw on her soda as she looked into my eyes showed me neither of our thoughts were rated PG.

By the time we reached her apartment, we seemed to have hit our boiling point. Between the flirty glances and my hand on her bare thigh during the drive home, the air between us was buzzing with sexual tension that felt like it was going to explode any second. Unlocking the door for us, she hurried inside after nodding at the lanky guy down the hall limping our way with a cane in hand.

As soon as we crossed the threshold, she walked toward her walk in to feed her cat, leaving her keys and purse on her coffee table. She walked with purpose; like she wasn't quite sure how to transition the evening into the reason we both knew we'd skipped the movie theatre.

153

After cracking open a can of food for Shadow, she moved toward her bedroom, nervously. Before she could get too far away, I gripped her waist and pulled her flush with my chest.

"I had a really great time," I whispered into her neck as I buried my head in her hair. The scent of her country apple shampoo overwhelmed my senses.

"Me, too," she whispered back, her lips just grazing my ear, sending an involuntary shudder through my body. "So, what do you want to do for the rest of the night?" she asked, slipping her hands under my button down shirt and sliding her finger along the waist band of my jeans.

"I can think of a few things, but it seems like you have a good plan of your own," I said, lifting my head to smile down at her and moving my hands down her sides slowly as I lowered my mouth to hers in a lingering kiss that held promise for more. I felt like I was being electrocuted every time my lips touched hers, but in the best way possible. It made me feel more alive than I'd felt in years.

"I think you've got a similar plan," she said her lips still against mine as she pulled me tighter against her, letting me know she could feel my erection between us.

"Shit, Lucy," I bit out as she wiggled against me, turning my breathing ragged almost instantly. I knew she was just as nervous as I was, but she was trying not to let it show. "I thought you wanted to wait," the words flew out of my mouth, but I knew that waiting was the last thing I wanted to do, even if her ministrations would make it nearly impossible to put in my best performance. I'd been dying to be able to show her everything I'd started to feel for her this week. The realization that she and I really had something together was more mind blowing than I could've ever imagined.

154

"I'm done," she breathed. "You were right. This is between us and only us. We can't let others decide how fast or slow we progress," she finished, emphasizing her point by slowly unbuttoning my shirt. Once the shirt was open, she started to trail kisses down my neck to my collarbone, heating my blood past boiling.

"Fuck," I panted as I pushed her toward her bed, gently, but urgently, grabbing the hem of her dress and pulling it over her head. "God damn!" I couldn't hold back my reaction as her dress slipped from my fingers and I came face to face with why I was so nervous about being with Lucy. She wasn't like most girls I knew or had been with; she knew how to be the total package, sweet, seductive, surprising, every guy's fantasy. If the virginal white lace bra under the sinful red dress she'd been wearing hadn't proved it to me, the naughty little bare pussy I also found did.

"No panties? Are you trying to kill me? I'm so fucking glad I didn't know that until this moment." I watched Lucy look down at herself with a slight blush and shrug. God! That small amount of red on her cheeks was incredible and drove me crazy.

"Just so you know, I never wear them," she whispered, trailing her hand down to the button of my jeans, again, only this time, she wasn't teasing.

"I don't know when I'll be able to be in your presence without a hard-on again, Lucy. You're always wearing dresses, how can I not constantly think about what you have or don't have on underneath," I gasped as she made work of the button and lowered my zipper, her hand reaching into my boxers to take me in hand. Her fingers glided over the tip, collecting the dew gathered there and using it to coat the head of my dick. She wasn't timid anymore; she knew how to make me squirm. "Shit!" I growled, pulling back slightly as a realization dawned on me. "I don't have a condom. I thought we weren't going to be doing this for a while," I confessed.

"The mailbox," she nodded toward a festive metal mailbox on her dresser beside her television. I'd seen the Christmas themed box before, and wondered its purpose because it was so out of place with everything else in the room. I walked as quickly as I could across her bedroom and opened the magnetized flap. Inside, I found a large pile of assorted condoms, which would've freaked me out even more, if I weren't already a lost cause. Instead, I grabbed one and hurried back to her, forgetting about the neon sign that might've flashed over the box telling me that I might be out of my league with this girl.

"I don't want to ever have the option of being unprotected," she explained. "I don't want a 'just this once, baby,' to turn into a STD or a missed period. It's not worth it," she justified.

"I'm glad to hear that," I mused as she slipped my jeans over my hips as we moved onto her bed. My heart was racing at the thought of slipping into her heat and claiming her for the first time.

"Fuck, I want you so bad. I don't even know why I thought waiting was an option," she sighed again as my hands dispatched her bra and started to tease one of her nipples. Lowering my head, I replaced my hands with my teeth as her hips bucked against my boxer covered dick. The glazed look I saw in her eyes when I looked up at her mirrored my own, as my head was swimming at all the sensations she was bring out with her touch. When her hands started to frantically push down my boxers, I ripped open the condom wrapper and pulled away to sheath myself. As soon as I'd rolled it all the way down, Lucy was pulling me back to her lips. Lining my hips up with her

156

entrance, I started to push my way in. The moment the rounded tip of my cock was finally enveloped in her heat, I knew this would be my last first time. I was done for, she was mine and I was hers.

'*Holy fucking shit*,' I thought as I felt my lungs deflate with the sensation of being inside Lucy. I had no idea how I was going to be able to make this last long enough, because it was too fucking good. '*I will never recover from this.*'

**

LUCAS

The second he started to slide into me, inch by inch, I knew it was all over. I was completely and totally his, meant to be here with him, like this, forever. I closed my eyes as the awareness of being truly claimed for the very first time washed over me. A low groan of satisfaction and awareness permeated the room from the back of my throat.

"I know," he whispered, brushing the hair from my eyes and letting his fingers skate across my cheeks in a gentle caress. "Look at me," he commanded and my eyes popped open, immediately. His slate blue eyes were peering and I saw a softness in them I'd never seen before, from him, from anyone. For once in my life, someone was making love to me and I was making love with him. This wasn't about desire or sexual frustration or a stress reliever; it was beyond all of that. Raising my hips to meet his slow rhythm, I listened to the way our breathing even seemed to be in sync.

"Oh GOD," I breathed, arching my back as our pace deepened and he started to hit all of the right places at once. Everywhere our bodies touched felt like little sparks of electricity coursing through my blood. I felt alive. I felt loved. Sex had always felt good to me, but this…there

157

wasn't even a word to describe how being with Brady in this way was turning my entire being upside down and inside out. We started to pant as we raced toward our orgasm and our movements became choppy.

"Holy FUCK!" Brady roared as I felt my walls convulse around him and I released an incoherent whimper of pleasure. Laying his head between my bare breasts, Brady listened to my heart as we both worked to get ourselves under control again.

"Wow," I said when I could finally talk.

"Uh huh," I felt Brady nod against my chest. "That was…"

"There are no words," I finished, looking up at my popcorn ceiling, trying to calm all the emotions coursing through my body.

"No, there aren't," Brady chuckled and I felt the vibration rack through my body, causing me to shiver. "I'll be right back," he said, getting up to take care of the condom. In his absence, I took a few deep and calming breaths, trying to pretend that my world wasn't spinning around me. It was safe to say that I'd never, ever felt this way after a sexual encounter in my entire life, not even with, Preston, my high school sweetheart and first love. I had no idea what to make of it either. As Brady found his way back into the bedroom, I tried to pull back the freaked out look I knew was on my face.

"That was incredible, Lucy," he started, bringing one of my hands to his lips when he realized I hadn't moved an inch since he left the room. "I had no idea."

"You had no idea what?" I asked, trying not to feel defensive about what he was about to say.

"I had no idea it could be like that," he smiled.

158

"You were married though," my brows knit together.

"Yeah, but I was young, and even though I know I loved Lori, it doesn't even come close to what that just made me feel," he looked at me, his face raw with an emotion completely foreign to me.

"I know what you mean," I whispered and let him pull me to his side as we drifted to sleep together. Several times during the night we reached for each other and made up for the time we spent waiting. I couldn't remember a time before that I'd felt so completely in tune with another person sexually. I'd always said Eric was my best, but Brady was in a completely different class. I knew you didn't have to have feelings for the people you slept with, but damn if feelings didn't make the sex that much better. It had been a long time since I'd been with someone I cared about, and with Brady, I suddenly couldn't figure out why I'd ever resisted relationships.

CHAPTER 17

LUCAS

I love the sound a guy makes when my lips make first contact with his dick. Every guy makes the same part sigh, part groan, part whimper when my tongue snakes out and makes contact with the heated, solid flesh. It happens every time, even if they are asleep when I start. This is not even mentioning the involuntary hip thrust when I wrap my fingers around the base of him and squeeze, when they stop breathing and start panting. I love knowing the power I have over him in that moment, even from my knees. That noise is what makes getting a guy off with my mouth more fun than I can describe accurately.

I was pleased to discover that Brady enjoyed this as well. I awoke the next morning before my alarm, even though I'd gotten very little sleep. I wanted to give Brady a pleasant memory for the day while I was working and he was being a fantastic dad to Taylor. I could still taste the residual flavor of latex on him, but I didn't let that deter me from my goal.

"Lucy?" Brady asked, as his hips bucked in awareness of my actions. "Don't stop," he whispered, running his fingers through my hair and looking down at me with sleepy eyes that were igniting with desire. I'd planned to draw his pleasure out, but as my gaze hit the numbers blazing on my alarm clock, I realized I couldn't take the time I wanted. Redoubling my efforts, I started to work him over frantically until he started to shudder with restrained want. I could tell it was taking all of his control to keep himself from grabbing my head and fucking my mouth until he came, but soon he was shouting my name as his essence filled my mouth. Pulling away, I swallowed before shooting him my most breathtaking grin.

"What was that for?" he asked, seemingly astonished by being woken up that way.

"You'll find that I don't need a reason to do that, but today, I have to get ready for work and I wanted to give you something to remember me by while we're apart," I shrugged as I started to go through my morning routine, grabbing my work uniform and completing my daily hygiene regimen. "Are you leaving with me or are you going to sleep a little longer?" I asked as I pulled my short hair back into a ponytail.

"Um, I'm going to head out. Xander's on his way to get me. We have to go get a few things done before I pick up Taylor at her grandma's," he said, still looking slightly shell shocked in the same position I'd left him in when I started my tasks.

"Then, don't you think you should take a step out of my bed?" I laughed, putting my hand on his bare foot, causing him to jerk it back. "Oh shit! Are you *ticklish*?" I asked, my nose wrinkled in amusement.

"I wouldn't say that," he huffed, pulling himself up to sit with his legs crossed on my bed. "I just don't like it when people touch my feet. I got it from my grandpa, you can't even look at his feet or he'll get twitchy."

"Damn, I really want to explore this with you," I started, a wide grin stretched across my face. "You have no idea! But, if you are leaving with me, you need to get dressed, cause I'm going to be late!"

"You work across the street, Lucy!" Brady said, throwing a pillow at me as he climbed out of my bed.

"Yes, but diagonally on the corner of two very busy streets," I reminded him as I watched him jump into his wrinkled clothing and walk toward the door.

"I should probably bring over some deodorant and stuff, shouldn't I?" he asked, checking his morning breath before shrugging and pulling out his morning cigarette.

"Hey, man, can I bum one of those?" a voice came from down the hall. Ron was walking up to us, sans limp and cane, from his apartment, he was a couple of inches taller than Brady and heroine skinny. His skin was a leathery milk chocolate, but he couldn't have been more than a decade older than me. His hair was slicked back into a ponytail and he wore a pair of ratty blue basketball shorts under an open, thread-bare robe. You could definitely tell he'd lived a rough life.

"Sure, dude," Brady said, handing him the cigarette he'd been holding and grabbing another from his pack.

"Can I use your light?" Ron asked, leaning against the railing beside my apartment.

"Sure." Brady handed him the lighter and waited while Ron lit the cigarette and took a drag.

"Thanks, man. I'll hit you back for this later," my neighbor told him, holding up the cigarette and walking back to his apartment. After exchanging confused looks, Brady and I made our way down the stairs to the parking lot.

"That was random," I observed once we were out of earshot.

"Who was that?" he asked we continued down the stairs to the parking lot. I did not live in a very safe neighborhood, so Brady always seemed more than a little leery about my neighbors.

162

"Oh, that's Ron," I dismissed, pulling my keys from my purse.

"And Ron is?" he prompted, hoping to get more information about the gangly guy he'd probably seen talking to some questionable women outside his apartment at all hours.

"Um, I'm pretty sure he's a pimp," I confessed with an amused smirk as we hit the bottom stair together and stopped to look at him. "I don't know for sure, because I haven't had the guts to ask, but he usually walks with a cane and a fake limp, Brady! He doesn't walk like that unless he's got the cane. And I know you've seen his ladies around!"

"We've got to get you out of this place, Lucy," he shook his head as he started to realize that my apartment wasn't just unsafe, it could be downright dangerous.

"You didn't have a problem with my living arrangements last month," I huffed, crossing my arms below my breasts and popping out my hip.

"I had a problem with it then, too, Lucas, but you weren't my girlfriend then, so I didn't have a right to share my feelings," he challenged, crossing his arms over his chest to mirror my stance. "I care about your safety," he finished, taking the wind from my sails and causing me to drop my arms to my hips.

"I appreciate your concern, but I love it here and I'm under a lease until October," I explained before giving him my back and leading him toward my truck again.

"Okay, I get it," he sighed as we walked by the trash dumpster outside my building. Grabbing my elbow, he pulled me toward him and wrapped his arms around my waist. "I'll try to make sure you aren't here alone much anymore," he whispered into my neck as if he were making a sacrificial compromise.

"I look forward to you delivering on that," I whispered back, a slight smirk on my face that he seemed to care some much about my safety.

"So you're headed to spend time with your dad this weekend with Taylor, right?" I confirmed, changing the subject as I disarmed and unlocked my truck.

"Yeah," he groaned. "I love spending time with my family, but after last night, I'm sad I won't see you again until Monday night," he pouted. "Besides, my mom is in Tucson with her boyfriend, so I'll have to hear those complaints since my siblings aren't big fans of him."

"I've got midterms to study for, Brady," I warned, already feeling completely overwhelmed by the mountain of notes I would be coming home to after work. "The differential equations test alone feels like it's going to be the death of me."

"I know, but I'll call tonight, okay?" he leaned over to give me a good bye kiss before I got into the truck.

"Sounds perfect," I agreed, closing the door as he backed away, taking another drag of his cigarette and watching me back out of the parking space.

"Be careful!" he yelled after me. In the rear view mirror, I watched him watch me pull out to the light before he settled against a wall to wait for Xander.

I pulled into the parking lot at work four minutes later wishing like hell I could be back across the street still in bed, my arms wrapped around Brady. The fact that it wasn't in the cards for the rest of the weekend made my eight hour shift feel like sixteen.

**

164

BRADY

I couldn't stop the grin that took over my face. Lucy put it there with the way she woke me up, even though neither of us got much sleep. My ex's mom even commented on how happy I looked when I picked up Taylor. Thinking about my budding relationship with Lucy, and spending time with my baby, made today one of the best days I'd had in the last few years. I knew I needed to calm down and think about everything, because Lucy hadn't been in a relationship in almost three years and neither had I. I was a skeptic at best and a full on cynic at worst that something like this could ever happen to me, let alone last.

"Wow, someone got laid," my brother said, sing-song, when I pulled up in front of my dad's house.

"Can it, Parker," I tried to growl at him as I helped Taylor from her car seat, but I was in too good a mood for my words to be convincing.

"Holy shit! You did!" he confirmed, his blue eyes bulging out of his head. "I was just joking," he laughed, clapping his hand on my back as I watched Taylor run through the open front door toward her grandpa. "I thought you said Becca was seeing someone."

"She is," I started, trying to decide if I wanted to share the name of my girlfriend with him. Most people I knew had an idea of who they thought Lucy was, based on reputation. Parker was only slightly different, because Lucy had dated his best friend, Preston, off and on in high school. He knew her before all the rumors, but he also half witnessed the push and pull of drama between Lucy and Preston that sent them both through hell and back.

165

I was two years ahead of her, and even though her best friend dated my best friend, we didn't meet until after high school. I'd only heard stories of the legendary 'love' between Preston and Lucy that, apparently, conquered everything, but it was enough. I could see why she tried to stay as far away from relationships as possible. Aside from the call in January about his deployment, she hadn't mentioned his name, but we'd discussed their complex history more than once of the years that we'd been friends.

Their relationship was the definition of mixed messages, according to Lucy. I was glad he wasn't in the state and wouldn't be for the next year or so, because she lamented the fact that every time she seemed to find herself in a position to fall in love again, he reinserted himself in the fray and confused her with promises of forever. Though, she did admit that she wasn't much better and frequently did the same to him. If I were being honest, her past with Preston concerned me and made me incredibly jealous. The only thing that brought me back from the brink was knowing that I was asking her to accept that my ex-wife would *always* be in the picture, thanks to the beautiful child we created together, but Lori and I were over beyond a shadow of a doubt.

Looking up from the sidewalk, I found my little brother looking at me weirdly. "Then?"

"I started seeing Lucy Dunn," I tried to play off, but I knew he'd have something to say. Grabbing my cigarettes from my pocket, I started to walk toward my dad's mailbox. Parker's new wife was very sick and pregnant, and I didn't want her to walk out of the house and be inundated by second hand smoke I knew wasn't good for her.

"No shit?" Parker's mouth was still hanging open in shock.

166

"Yes? We've been friends for a few years now, and lately, we've started to develop feelings for each other. We decided to see where they lead," I explained before pulling a long drag, fortifying drag from my cigarette.

"She break the news to Preston yet? Because you know when she does, he's going to pull out the big guns," Parker threw at me. I knew it would come up, but I'd hoped he would let it go since I was his brother. "Is that what she wants? Another shot with him?"

"I don't know. He's overseas now anyway, right?" I point out. "So it's not like he can make a power play for her like her other ex, Carter did."

"Preston's still in training a few states away until the end of next month, Brady, and they still talk," he informed me. Parker was supposed to be in training with Preston, but because of his new wife's health issues, he'd been moved to rear detachment and would be spending his tour at home. "In fact, I talked to him a couple of days ago and he told me that he'd called her last week to catch up. He said he wants to try again when he gets home. I don't know what went on with her and that Carter guy, but do you think she cares about you enough to stop this crazy carousel she's been spinning around on with Preston for eight years?"

"Thanks for the vote of confidence, bro," I rolled my eyes, flicking my ashes to the ground. "It's literally been a week, so I'm not sure where we are headed, but I care about her a lot," I surprised myself with the admission, because I usually kept my emotions much closer to the vest.

"I can tell," he nodded. "Just keep your eyes and ears open with her."

"Daddy! Aunt Shivy wants know if you's gonna to 'tinue to stand ow-side like a dirty smoker or if you's comin in ta see us," my toddler yelled out the door at me.

"I thought she was two and a half, not a teenager," I laughed. "I'm coming, baby girl!" I yelled to Taylor, to which she nodded at me in acceptance and disappeared behind the screen door to the small one-story house. "I'll trust Lucy until she gives me a reason not to and so far, she's been nothing but completely honest about how out of her element she feels right now. I'm right there with her," I directed at Parker.

"Fair enough."

"Thanks, now let's go devour some barbeque," I suggested, crushing my cigarette under my feet and picking up the butt to throw in the garbage can on the way in. The rest of the afternoon was good family time that helped keep me grounded. Taylor was fawned over as the only grandchild, Parker's wife, Celia, was catered to, because of her health and burgeoning baby bump, my teenaged sister, Siobhan, helped my dad play host, since she was the only one who still lived at home, and I spent the afternoon hoping that I would be able to bring Lucy to a family function soon. I was feeling like the day would finish without another word about my relationship with Lucy and her history with Preston until dessert was served.

"Parker says you started dating Lucas Dunn," Celia sat down beside me, her blonde hair sweeping over her extremely petite shoulders, and digging into a plate holding the largest piece of angel food cake I'd ever seen. "Be careful," she said, raising an eyebrow at me and casting a serious look with her brown eyes. My only response was to sit there, stunned that she'd said more than two words directly to me, because we'd always had a strained relationship. It's not that we didn't like each other, or have

168

respect for each other; it was more that our personalities didn't really mesh. Looking over at me again, she frowned. "Look, I don't think she's a bad girl, she just has a reputation of chewing guys up and spitting them out. I know if you are saying you are dating her, that you are already invested, just make sure she feels the same. I've seen her toss guys aside like they were novelties, and more than a couple of them got their hearts crushed because of the sick game she and Preston play."

"I'm aware; Celia, but I've got it under control. I know you and Parker are friends with Preston, and you've heard his side of things. I've been friends with Lucy for a long time, too, and I've heard her side more than a few times when she got drunk enough and we were waxing poetic about all the ways love sucked and was stupid."

"Was stupid? Are you changing your opinion on that, Brady?" she laughed too hard before it gave way to a coughing fit. "I'm okay," she wheezed when Parker came rushing from the kitchen. "I just never realized Brady could be anything less than cynical."

"I didn't realize being slightly optimistic would bring out everyone's opinions of my actions," I growled, this time convincingly and left the comfort of the couch for the kitchen. My dad's house was not open concept, so I could hide there for a few to get my thoughts together before rejoining a, hopefully, different conversation.

I'd known what I was up against in deciding to kiss Lucy that night, but for some reason, thinking about Preston now… I wished I could strangle him with my bare hands. I didn't want to call attention to the fact that I had no idea that he and Lucy still talked regularly. He was never at her parties, even before he'd deployed, and I'd only ever heard her mention his name in the past tense this last month. I knew it was something I needed to clarify with her

169

sooner, rather than later. Jealously was not an emotion I was used to and I didn't like it.

When I returned from the kitchen, I was grateful that Lucy wasn't brought up again for the rest of the afternoon, and my brother and I resumed our usual super hero debates while Shiv and Celia occupied Taylor. By the time I strapped my sleeping toddler back into her car seat to head back to my apartment, I was daydreaming about ending a day like this with Lucy again. I hoped Parker and Celia were only being over reactionary to my new girlfriend and not rightfully suspicious.

CHAPTER 18

BRADY

I continued to stew over the Preston/Lucy issues my brother had so "helpfully" reminded me off the rest of the weekend. I wanted to run over to her apartment and force her to talk to me about this, but with her midterms coming up and my obligation to my daughter, I knew I had to wait to talk to her about it. Her history with Preston wasn't something we'd discussed since we'd decided to give our relationship a shot, although it should've been clarified, since I was aware of it.

It was something that couldn't be discussed over the phone. We'd known each other for a while and I trusted her to be honest with me, but I needed to watch her mannerisms and physical responses to the questions I wanted to ask her. They would tell me if I really had a shot with her, or if I was a placeholder for Preston.

Parker was right; she and Preston had been way more serious than she and Carter. I may have won out against him, but we hadn't been together long enough to believe that she'd choose me over a past like Preston. I'd already told her my daughter would always come first. That didn't mean that Lori would, that wasn't even an option I'd ever consider again. She and I didn't even like each other when we split up, let alone love each other.

"What the fuck did you think was going to happen, Flynn?!" I heard coming from my apartment as my feet hit the stairs after dropping Taylor off Sunday night.

"I didn't know, Becca, but not that!" Flynn shouted and the sound of glass breaking propelled me into action. Both of them turned sharply toward the door when I opened it and surveyed the scene. Becca was on her toes, as in

Flynn's face as she could be, since he had nearly a foot of height on her, her face red and flushed. If I hadn't just heard them fighting, I would've sworn I'd just interrupted a romantic moment. Looking at the ground, I saw the shattered pieces of a crystal vase and roses strewn through the living room.

"What the fuck?" I asked as they started to back away from each other. I wished Xander were here for back up, because this didn't seem like it was going to be pretty. "I heard you guys from the parking lot. Do you want the neighbors to call the cops again?"

"I'm sorry, Brady," Becca apologized, hastily. "But I got fired tonight, thanks to this asshole," she snarled and indicated Flynn.

"I just wanted to fucking talk to you, Becca," he pleaded. "You were the one that went off half-cocked about your sex life with Xander in the middle of the *children's* clothing store where you worked. Don't put that one me!"

"Again, you come barreling into my work, talking shit about my boyfriend, telling me that you were going to kill him for touching me, for daring to send me roses when that was *our* thing, all while *your* little whore of a girlfriend waited for you, dutifully, on a bench outside my store?! You don't think I'm going to defend myself?" she screamed. "I'm not yours anymore, Flynn. You can't just collect women and say they'll always be yours while you're fucking someone else," Becca raged, picking up her glass full of soda and hurling toward the wall the vase had shattered against. "You wanted me to just fall in line and I didn't. Now I'm unemployed! How am I supposed to pay my share of next month's rent?"

"I have no clue, Becca, and that's not my problem anymore," Flynn scowled at her before turning to me. "This is probably a bad time to tell you that I'm moving out

172

earlier than I thought, effective right now, because I can't stay here while she and Xander are dating. I'll pay my share of next month, but after that you're on your own," Flynn dropped on me. "Don't worry about the glass, I'll get it," he said before going to kitchen to grab a bag to pick up the large pieces and Becca vaulted herself over the back of the sectional and stormed to her bedroom. When Flynn returned, I realized I was still standing just inside the doorway trying to process everything that had just happened. "See what happens when you give your heart to a slut, Brady," Flynn suddenly said, pulling me out of my trance.

"Excuse me?"

"I'm saying Lucas'll break your heart and turn you into a psycho, too. I mean, you've known me since we were in elementary school," he started, still picking up chunks of glass from the carpet. "I never acted crazy like this until she came into my life. Lucy'll do the same to you, I promise."

Nodding more from dismissal than agreement, I walked back outside to the balcony to smoke, because I didn't know if I could hold my tongue on the fact that Flynn had always been just a little volatile growing up. He was right that Becca brought out the worst in him, but they'd been that way from the beginning. They fed on the drama, calling it being too in love, too passionate. I just called it being too unstable and untrusting of each other and being in a dysfunctional relationship, but clinging to it because you love the spectacle.

"The rest of the glass just needs to be vacuumed up," Flynn announced as he joined me on the balcony. "The vacuum is in Becca's closet and I don't want to go in there right now."

"Understandable."

"Are you cool with me moving out now instead of next month?" he asked, hoisting himself to sit on the railing beside a pillar made of pink stucco.

"I get why you need to go, man," I told him. "Xander and I can handle it for a month or so, but Becca really needs to get another job or we'll have to kick her out and find another roommate."

"You guys care about her that little? I thought she and Xander were in love. That's what she says anyway," Flynn's face started to turn red with his words.

"I don't know what's going on with Becca and Xander, but I can tell you that I've got a toddler to take care of, first and foremost, and can't afford to take a twenty-one year old girl I'm not even dating in as a dependent. Sorry," I explained, unapologetically. "Becca's my friend and all, but she still needs to pull her own weight here just like Xander and I."

"If she doesn't get another job right away, I'll help out for a few more months," Flynn offered with a defeated sigh.

"Why would you do that? You guys just scattered glass through our living room because of a jealous fight, Flynn. It's obvious that you two are toxic and shouldn't be allowed within a 20 mile radius of each other," I looked at him, disbelieving.

"Because she's mine, Brady. She always will be, whether she agrees or not, I have to be there for her, take care of her. I still think she's the one I'm going to marry one day. I mean, I'm sure you feel the same about Lori. You don't want to be with her anymore, but don't you still want to make sure she's okay?"

"Um, no, not even close," I said, trying and failing to hold back a shocked laugh. "I want Taylor to be taken care

174

of; I want her to have a happy childhood, so I want Lori's life to be good because her mood trickles down to my kid. That's as far as it goes. I pay child support so that happens, but I don't feel any obligation to help if she does something stupid unless it directly effects my daughter."

"That's it?"

"Well, yeah, man. If we didn't have a kid together, I wouldn't give the smallest of shits about what was going on with her."

"Wow, I don't understand how you just let go like that," Flynn shook his head and headed for the door. "I'm going to grab the vacuum now, Becca's probably done brooding enough that I don't have to worry about flying objects anymore."

"Good luck," I gave him a mock salute as he disappeared through the sliding glass door. As soon as the door clicked back into place, my mind went right back to wondering if Preston and Lucy's relationship was similar to Flynn and Becca's but with much less violence. I needed to discuss this with her and I knew I couldn't chicken out, if our relationship was ever going to move beyond dating. We had only been together a week, but something told me that Lucy and I were destined for something bigger, and I had to make sure we were headed in the same direction, together.

**

LUCAS

By the time Monday came around again, I was aching to see Brady and counting the hours until he got off work. We'd talked more than a few times over the weekend, but between my work and homework and his time with Taylor, we didn't find a time to sync up. I could sense that something was off during our conversations and hoped that he wasn't going to end things with me because we moved too far too fast. As much as I didn't want that I knew it would be much better if he wanted to end things now, before things went any further, even though I was already feeling things for him that I hadn't felt in years.

When I heard the key in the lock, my heart started thumping in my chest so hard it hurt. As he appeared in the doorway, I greeted him with a tight hug and felt more relaxed as soon as he buried his head in my hair and inhaled. He'd miss me, too!

"That's quite a greeting," his words reverberating in my chest.

"What can I say? I missed you," I looked up at him, coyly, from my place in his arms.

Moving an errant hair from my face, he lowered his mouth to mine in a heart stopping kiss that I felt in every part of my body, but spoke to one part louder than the rest. "I missed you, too," he said against my lips, "but, um, I have to ask you something," he pushed away from me and took a seat on the couch, looking serious. "And I want to you to be brutally honest with me, okay? Don't tell me what you think I want to hear," he leveled me with the apprehension in his steel blue eyes.

"O-kay," I said, taking a seat beside him and pulling my knee on to the couch so I could face him fully. "What's going on?" My earlier nerves reappeared with a vengeance at his words.

"I told Parker we were dating on Saturday," he started, and I, instantly, knew what he was about to ask, and I wasn't sure I was ready to answer these questions.

"Oh," I said more dejected than interested.

176

"Yeah, he mentioned Preston said he called you a week or so ago?"

"He did," I confirmed. "It was the Thursday before the party."

"Oh," Brady looked at me, surprised, and I wondered if he thought I'd deny it. "Parker said Preston wants to try again when he gets home."

"He's said that before, Brady," I rolled my eyes, as my heart flew into my throat. I knew Preston wanted to try again, and I hoped I was stronger than I was last year when he pulled this shit. "I told him that I was done with our patterns, but I don't want to lie to you."

"What does that mean?" his eyes narrowed slightly.

"There will always be part of me that loves him. He was my first love and we never really got a chance to give it an honest to goodness shot, so we got stuck in this...revolving door of pain with each other," I tried to verbalize the cycles that my relationship with Preston seemed to go through constantly. "We started dating our freshman year of high school, and he told me he'd been in love with me since junior high two weeks into the relationship. I freaked out, and because I wasn't sure I even saw him as more than a friend, I broke up with him. I, almost immediately, realized it was a mistake, but he was heartbroken so it took us months to reconcile.

"When we finally did, I was in it more than I was before, but I still wasn't sure I felt as strongly as he did. My mom was super strict about my grades back then, so when they started to slip, I had to cut back on all my extra curriculars, boyfriends included. So I broke his heart all over again, because he didn't understand my blind trust in my mom's decision. I just wanted to maintain a civil home life.

177

"A few months later, I woke up and knew that I was completely and totally in love with Preston. I couldn't hold back or deny it any longer, so I told him and we got back together again. This time it seemed like it was built to last, but it wasn't.

"When it ended, that was the last time we were ever officially together, but we continued to torture each other by professing our love for one another whenever it seemed like we were getting serious with someone else. It's kind of the reason why I avoided relationships until you. It's just too hard to deal with it without hurt feelings and jealousy."

I looked up to see Brady studying me carefully as I talked, trying to weigh my story. "So, by getting into this with me, are you saying you are done with all of that with him?" he asked, frankly.

"It means that I care about you enough to try," I said, completely honest.

"Why is that not completely reassuring?" Brady mumbled, looking away from me.

"Look, Brady," I called his attention back to me. "I'm not saying I know what the future holds any more than you do. But I really like what we have here, and it's only been a week, but I missed you these last couple of days more than I've ever missed anyone. I want to give us an honest to goodness shot to be together, regardless of what Preston thinks he wants. Is that enough? Is that okay?" I asked, pointedly.

A slow smile started to form on his lips as he looked at me. "I didn't know what I wanted you to say about all of this, but I'm glad it was that. I haven't felt this way so fast either."

"Good, so can we move past this now and head to my bedroom? I'm tired, but I've been missing the quality time we spent together on Friday," I stood and grabbed his hand to lead him to the bedroom.

"Me, too," he agreed, "but I was so worried about how that conversation that I'm completely drained now," he dragged himself off the couch.

"Oh, thank GOD! Me, too! Waiting up for you was exhausting!" I admitted. "So, how about we go to sleep right now, and I wake you up creatively after I get home from my Spanish class tomorrow?"

"After Spanish? I thought you had three classes tomorrow," he pulled off his jeans and slid into my bed, confused.

"I do, but I'm going to come and spend some quality time with you instead. I'd skip Spanish, too, if I didn't have an attendance requirement," I frowned as I tucked myself into his side.

"I don't necessarily condone you skipping classes, young lady, but I'm sure I could make it worth your while," he said, kissing the top of my head.

"I don't doubt that for a second," I mumbled into his shoulder before I drifted off, glad that my baggage had been opened and strewn all over my apartment so that we could, hopefully, put it behind us.

CHAPTER 19

LUCAS

"I know you are with him right now, and I'm dating Monica, but I'm still in love with you, Lucy," Preston said, his eyes pleading with mine. "Understand that I just can't break up with her, not yet, but I'd like to spend more time with you. Just holding you in my arms, smelling your hair, feeling you breath against me. You are everything to me," he begged.

"I..." I looked at him, startled by his words, but I shouldn't have been. He'd said them to me before, so many times. I found my feet walking into his embrace as he pulled me into him. The feel and smell instantly relaxing me, giving me that dose of familiarity I craved. A contented sigh fell from my lips as his hands caressed my back. "I can't break up with him," I breathed as his fingers found their way into my hair, soothing me.

"I know, baby, I don't want you to, I just want this," he said against my ear. "When the time is right, we'll be together again. Tell me you love me," his voice came out pleading. "Tell me you love me more than you love Brady," he continued, imploring me to tell him what he wanted to hear.

"I...I lo-," I started to say what I always said, but my tongue stuck in my mouth like I'd been eating peanut butter. I tried again to force the words out of my throat, but instead, I looked into his eyes and said, "I can't."

My heart pounded in my ears as I shot out of bed at my dream. What the fuck was that? Was it because of what Brady asked? Or was I really stronger than I'd been in the past? Were my feelings for Brady already strong enough to propel me beyond Preston, finally?

With a groan, I looked at my alarm clock and saw that I was supposed to be up in five minutes, so I pulled myself from the warm bed containing the man that was starting to mean more to me than I'd ever expected and got ready for Spanish.

After the longest hour of my life the next morning, I raced home to find Brady still snuggled into his pillow. Quietly, I undressed and cuddled in behind him to take a small nap, because I was still pretty tired from my late night and waking up from my dream for a 7:40am class.

I awoke a short time later as I felt him start to kiss his way down my body, stopping to lave his tongue over my nipples and trail it to my stomach. I knew where he was going, and I'd never really enjoyed it. I didn't want him to feel obligated, because I woke him up this way on Saturday. Plus, the only moisture I'd accumulated there from oral had come from the tongues of overeager boys thinking it was something I wanted.

"You don't have to do that," I told him, breathlessly, grabbing for his hair. "It doesn't do anything for me."

"I need to do this for you," he said from between my thighs. "I want to feel you come apart on my tongue, in my mouth."

"I won't," I asserted, shaking my head. "Many have tried, all have failed," I frowned down at him.

"Many, huh?" he chuckled, propping his head on his hands, still in position above my bare mound. I couldn't believe we'd paused to have this conversation. "How many?" he asked, casually, but I knew he was dying to hear my dirty little number.

"19," I disclosed, quietly.

"Including me?" he asked, astonished by my admission.

"Well, you haven't exactly gotten to business, have you?" I laughed.

"I guess you are right about that," he paused, a small frown on his face. After a moment, the frown morphed into the most confident smile I'd ever seen on his face. "You've gone for quantity over quality I see," he said, smugly. "You've tried quantity, let's see if we can't show you what quality looks like, huh?"

"Okay," I agreed, immediately. As soon as I felt the first swipe of his tongue against my clit, I knew that this time would be different as my hips bucked forward involuntarily and a low moan erupted from my lips.

"I thought you said you weren't going to enjoy this?" he laughed from his spot between my legs, sliding an arm around my stomach to hold my hips down. "I'm glad it looks like I'm not going to be the only one who will get some satisfaction from this," he finished before his tongue went back to work. Aside from feeling amazing, it was also too much, too intimate, something I wasn't used to feeling. I started to try and push him away, but when his fingers breeched me, it was all I could do to not pass out from the ecstasy coursing through my body. His other hand was still holding my hips down like a vice and forcing me to absorb it all.

"FUCK!" I growled, loudly as he started to pump his fingers deeper into me, adding a third, the stubble on his upper lip scratching me in all the right places and I

182

suddenly felt that familiar quickening deep inside my womb.

No way!

I was still in denial as the tension in my hips gave way to the most exquisite orgasm I'd ever felt in my entire life. It was like I'd never had an orgasm before that one, and I knew I was in trouble. That experience only added to what I'd already learned three days ago. I was lost to him, completely, forever. My hips sank down into the bed as I wrung the last of my pleasure out against his face, little whimpers slid out of my mouth. Feeling his grip loosen over my stomach, I thought he was going to move back up my body, but he didn't. Using both hands, he gripped my hips and yanked me back to his mouth, devouring everything between my legs and it was WAY too sensitive from my orgasm. My hips were frantic to buck him off, and I could think of no other response but to laugh.

"Stop!" I gasped, "It's too much, I can't take it," I squealed, peering down at the wicked smile on his face, his steel gray eyes alight with triumph.

"I just had to make sure I got every last drop," he said. "Apparently, that's never happened before," he leaned up and wiped his mouth with the back of his hand. "I felt it was my duty to savor it." As he rose up over my body again, I felt how rigid his cock was against my leg. If it was granite when he slid down my body, it was harder than diamond now. I absently wondered if it could cut glass in its current state before he grasped my hips again, after covering himself, and impaled me with one swift thrust.

"A little sure of ourselves now, aren't we?" I panted out as he set a punishing rhythm. If the pace he set was any indication of how turned on his was by giving me my first orgasm from oral sex, then I fucking loved it. Brady pushed into me harder and rougher than I'd ever thought possible

183

from his mild demeanor, and it was incredible. His body curved into mine as our hips meet, his arms strained in effort to keep himself from crushing me, and his lips attached to every inch of skin they could reach, then he found my sweet spot and I went flying again.

"Holy FUCK!" I gasped out as he stilled above me in his own release, then gathered me into his arms, giving me some of his weight. Once again, I noticed that we seemed to be breathing completely in sync. In together-2-3, and out. How could we be in this kind of place already? I'd never breathed with someone so intimately before. Was that even a thing?

"Yes, I'm that sure of myself now," Brady said after our equilibrium returned and he shifted to lie down beside me. "Holy fuck," he whispered, echoing my earlier words. "That was, shit. Mind blowing? I can't find the words. I thought that the other night was Earth shattering, but this was so much more, Lucas."

I inhaled sharply at his use of my full name. I'd rarely, if ever, heard him use it and I found that I loved to hear it from his lips more than I'd expected. Calling me Lucy inferred that he'd known me for long enough to have earned it, even though I preferred Lucas. Suddenly, I didn't care about anything but hearing him call me Lucas over and over and over again.

**

Days that Brady carpooled to work and to my apartment, I drove him back to Mesa. I was glad I didn't have to work on Tuesday, because I'd planned to spend the evening going over the lessons I missed that day and going to bed early. After our Preston talk, Brady seemed lighter and bubblier, practically giddy.

184

I couldn't remember a time when I'd seen him smile so much. Happy Brady wasn't something anyone got to see very often, but this Brady usually only made strong appearances when he was just beyond buzzed and on his way to flat out drunk at my parties. Seeing it when he was stone cold sober, and knowing I was the one who put the smile on his face brought me more joy than I wanted to think about. I just knew that I'd do just about anything to keep the joy radiating from him, and the brooding Brady at bay. Not that I wasn't smitten with cynical Brady, too, cause a well-placed angry sneer could make my knees part pretty fast, too. I loved every side of my boyfriend I'd met so far.

"You're here!" Becca proclaimed as we walked through the door to the apartment that afternoon.

"I'm here," I repeated, confused. "Shouldn't you be at work?"

"You didn't tell her?" Becca looked at Brady, dumbfounded.

"It's not my news to tell, Bec," he said, continuing on his path to his bedroom to change for work.

"I got fired on Sunday, because Flynn came barging into my work and demanding that I stop seeing Xander!" she bemoaned, throwing herself on the sectional dramatically. "All while the ho he's been screwing sat in her purple haired glory on the bench out front."

"Wow," I sat down across from her in the corner of the sectional, astonished at her news. "That's so juvenile! Did he throw things or something? Cause a huge scene?"

"We both did, kinda," she looked at me, sheepishly. "I let him get to me and I started shouting at him in the middle of the baby section."

"Oh, Becca! You know better than to let him get to you like that," I admonished. "It's a competition with him, and he won cause he got you to break."

"Ugh, don't remind me," she let her body fall to the side on the couch and pulled her legs up into the fetal position. "But, at least, Xander said he'd cover my part of the rent until I find a new job."

"That's good, at least," I said, relieved that Brady wouldn't have to pick up the slack.

"So," she started, lifting up onto her elbows to check for listening ears before turning back to me and lowering her voice. "Brady looks super happy these last few days, how's everything going with you two?"

"Pretty fucking great," I couldn't hide my smile, but seeing Becca's crestfallen look, I tried harder than I normally would've. "What?"

"Nothing, I mean, I love Xander and all," she paused, "but I still wish Brady'd thought of me that way. He should've looked at me the way he looks at you."

"Don't do that to yourself, Becca. You are happy with Xander. Hell, you even encouraged me to give Brady a chance," I pointed out.

"I know, but old habits and all of that," she frowned again, before pasting a giant smile on her face. "So, isn't he amazing in bed?" she gushed, calling attention to the fact that we'd now been with the same man. Fuck, I promised myself that would never happen.

"Yeah, he's amazing, I mean, we even breathe together. It adds this surreal quality to the whole thing, like he's who I'm supposed to be with," I said, a little too wistfully. Was I actually swooning? What was happening to me?

186

"That doesn't mean anything," Becca snapped. "It's probably just because you guys are almost the same height, so, of course, you'd have similar breathing patterns," she finished, rejecting the connection I'd implied.

"Has it ever happened with you?" I asked, honestly wanting to know the answer.

"No, I'm shorter than you and have only been with guys nearly a half a foot taller than me," she rolled her eyes at my question. "I think it would feel weird, like we were too much alike and wrong for each other," she continued, cattily.

"It doesn't feel wrong, though, Bec," I contradicted. "For the first time in my entire life, it feels completely right," I whispered. "I can't even describe to you the emotions that flow through my body when we are together, because I've never experienced them before."

"I'm happy for you two, really," she said, trying and failing to sound sincere. "It's just hard to believe that you could be so devoted to him when you had a contact list of booty calls that you utilized regularly. I mean, weren't you with Eric like two days before that party?"

"Um, yeah, but that was just sex," I looked at her, baffled that she still didn't get my feelings about sex.

"Whatever, Lucy, nothing is just sex to girls," she laughed.

"It is to me, usually, but, I don't know, with Brady, I feel like I finally understand what you say about how much better sex is when it actually means something," I declared, causing her to sit upright on the couch, her demeanor shaken at my words.

"Holy shit, Lucas, are you falling in love with him?"

My jaw dropped at her question, and I searched for a way to deny her accusation, but I found I couldn't, because I was. I felt my eyes start to sting and dry out from my wide-eyed astonishment. After a few second, Becca realized why I hadn't answered and reflected what I imagined shell shocked expression looked like. Fuck, even though we'd only been officially together for a little over a week, I was absolutely falling in love with Brady. Outwardly, I tried to pull my face into a confident smile, but inwardly, I continued in a full freak out mode. How was I ever going to survive this?

"Everything okay?" a voice beside the couch brought me out of my trance. I looked up into Brady's steel blue and concerned eyes and instantly knew. I wasn't falling in love with Brady, I was already there.

CHAPTER 20

BRADY

I was starting to get the distinct feeling that Lucy was avoiding me. She said it was because she was trying to get through mid-terms, but she took her last one on Thursday and was officially on spring break. We still talked every day, several times a day, but we hadn't been able to spend more than a few hours together since she dropped me off at my apartment a week ago. I should've known that it would happen when I saw the look on her face when I came out of my bedroom and she was spacing out, her blue eyes wide as she stared at Becca then at me.

I don't know what Becca said to her, but I could tell she was scared. Whatever it was, she refused to talk about it with me, and immediately found a reason to leave. I tried to grill Becca, too, but she had the same deer-caught-in-the-headlights look Lucy did. Stammering out some random excuse about telling her about what happened with Flynn, she disappeared into her bedroom until Xander and I left for work.

Every time we talked, the conversation felt like cotton candy, pretty and delicious, but not really that filling or satisfying. I've always known Lucy to be incredibly blunt and forthcoming about her feelings, so this development was more than a little puzzling. I couldn't shake the sensation that I was losing her, but I didn't know what I could do to fix it. I kept trying though, because I could already feel that it was going to be worth it.

Sitting on the smoking patio at work, the conversation we'd just ended started to play in a loop.

"Hey," she answered. "How's working going?"

"It's a Monday, so it's slow," I told her, reaching for the cigarette another smoker was kind enough to light for me so I didn't have to suck the pole.

"That stinks, I'm sorry," she said, sincerely. "It's been kind of slow here, too. There is a random night game for Cactus league tonight, so our baseball fans are there instead of milling around the lobby."

"Sounds good," I leaned back against the picnic table and looked at the stars. It was a crisp night, but the sky was clear. "Are you on your lunch break?"

"Yeah, but you are calling right at the end of it," I could hear the frown in her voice. "I have to get back to it in a few minutes."

"Oh, um, what are the plans for tonight?" I asked, hoping she'd invite me over. "You don't have class in the morning, right?"

"Yeah, but Abby was asking to spend some time together after work tonight, since we've both been so busy lately, you know?"

"Oh, well, um, what about tomorrow?" I asked, now hoping I wasn't sounding desperate, even though I kind of was.

"We'll have to play it by ear," she deflected. "My mom wants me to come spend a day with her, because she's on vacation this week, too, and they are going to be bug bombing my apartment while I'm working on Wednesday, so I have to take Shadow to spend the night with her," she continued to list off all the plans she had for the week that didn't include me. "Maybe Thursday?"

"Yeah, that sounds good," I nodded, feeling gutted by her dismissal.

190

"If it works out for sooner, I'll let you know. I really miss you," she whispered, letting me know that someone must've joined her in the back office where the desk staff took their breaks. "Um, I've gotta go."

"Okay, talk to you on my next break?" I asked. My next break was about a half an hour after she was scheduled to get off work.

"Um, sure," she answered, distractedly. "He can't pay with that credit card, it's been declining all night," she said, obviously talking to a co-worker. "I've really gotta go now, Brady." She hung up before I could respond. I couldn't help but dwell on what we were doing. When she didn't answer when I tried to reach her on my last two breaks, I was on full alert and my heart was hammering in my ears at what she'd say the next time we spoke. Was two weeks together all we were going to get?

The scent on the air stopped me dead in my tracks when Xander and I walked into our apartment at nearly 3am after work. Fucking country apple. Even in my apartment, I couldn't escape the thought of her.

"Hey, man, I'm going to turn in," Xander said, pulling me from my paralyzed state. I gave him a nod as he headed to the opposite side of the apartment, and I walked, almost zombie-like, toward my bedroom. The sight that greeted me on the other side of the door was more baffling than the country apple smell in the living room. Tea light candles lined a path to my iron framed bed, and my usually messy sheets were neatly made, but the rest of the room was empty. Becca and Xander were together, so I knew this wasn't one of her attempts at seduction. I stood there, turning in a circle, scratching the back of my neck in thought when Xander popped his head into the room.

"Hey, I think there something of yours in the hall," he jerked his head back toward the living room to indicate that

191

I should follow him. As soon as I stepped out of my room, I saw strappy black four inch heels on the most beautiful foot I'd ever seen. My eyes travelled up her slender calves to her milky thighs, where they met with the bottom of a black silk robe. I continued my journey upward as I took in her curves and the way her black hair met the top of the robe at her shoulders. Finally, I saw the devious smile on her ruby red lips and the sparkle in her smoky blue gray eyes as she gazed at me from under thick lashes.

"You said you were hanging out with Abby tonight," I choked out, too turned on for words and wondering what she had on under that robe, because I could tell it was something special. Her hands moved to the bow on the sash holding the robe together and raised an eyebrow at me in question. A quick glance around showed that Xander had, once again, retreated to his bedroom.

"Well, I wanted to surprise you, so I couldn't just say I was going to be here when you got home," she teased, releasing the bow and moving to open her robe.

"Hold that thought," I rushed to stop her from dropping the robe and ushered her into the bedroom, sliding the sash from its loops as we went. I had a fantastic idea, and I just hoped she would be on board. As soon as the door closed behind us, black silk cascaded to the floor at her feet and I struggled to take in the baby pink satin halter dress that hugged her curves perfectly before coming to a sudden stop where her ass met the top of her thighs. "Holy fuck," I barely whispered before I tucked the sash into my back pocket and started to explore her body with my hands. Starting from the tops of her thighs, I trailed my palms over her bare ass to her hips, over her flat stomach to the rounded swells of her breasts. Using my fingers, I traced her collar bone before burying my fingers in her hair and pulling her lips to mine in a soul crushing kiss. I felt her

192

body shudder at my touch and a low moan erupted from the back of her throat. Deepening the kiss, I brought her body flush with mine, so she couldn't mistake how much I loved her surprise.

"You were a naughty girl," I said against her lips, as I walked her backward toward the bed, careful to avoid the tea lights still illuminating the dark room.

"Oh yeah?" she asked, breathlessly, pulling at the hem of my blue t-shirt and yanking it over my head. "Why's that?"

"Lying to me like that," I said. "You made me think you didn't want to see me anymore," I admitted, pushing her onto the mattress and moving to straddle her, my jeans still in place. "It was very mean."

"I'm sorry," she pouted. "I didn't mean to upset you."

"Oh, but you did, and I think you need to be punished for hurting my feelings," I told her, grabbing her hands and putting them together above her head. Holding them firmly, I retrieved the sash from my back pocket. "Is this okay?" I asked, showing her what I had in mind. I was delighted when a soft hum came from her body as her eyes lit up.

"Oh God yes," she bucked her hips beneath me. Wrapping her wrists in the black silk, I secured them to the railing on my bed. After I was sure she couldn't free herself, I stood up beside the bed and walked toward my CD player. "Where are you going?" she whined.

"I'm punishing you," I laughed as I looked for the album I wanted.

"But, but," she stammered, trying to look back at me. Finally locating the disc, I shoved it into the slot and hit play. I took off my shoes and socks as the dark sounds of Marilyn Manson filled the room. "You weren't kidding," she whispered, sounding more turned on than scared, her hips writhing. Seeing her bound and hot made me shed my jeans and boxers faster than I'd ever known possible. Pulling a condom from our stash under my bed, I started at her ankles. My tongue tasting my way up her calves, I came to a stop on the inside of her thighs. "I've always wanted to do this to this CD," I told her as I looked into her eyes, her pupils dilated by desire.

"Is that so?"

I answered her by kissing the inside of her thighs upward until my tongue finally made contact with her throbbing clit. Sinking two fingers inside of her, she started to rock her hips more violently. Moving my free hand, I held her hips steady as I worked her over with my mouth and fingers, adding a third when she was sufficiently stretched. The moan that escaped her lips sounded so wanton, so close, as she pulled fruitlessly at her restraints. Suddenly, her hips thrust forward and I felt her start to convulse in ecstasy. She said no one but me could to this to her. It was a powerful feeling, being able to make her shake like that with my tongue. The accompanying scream of pleasure told me that she was coming hard, causing me to smile against her slick folds.

"Delicious," I lifted my head from between her legs and grabbed the condom, quickly sheathing myself. The song had switched to a more driving beat, and I smiled at her, wickedly. Grasping her ankles in each hand, I put her heel clad legs against my shoulders and pulled her hips to meet mine, entering her, roughly. "GOD, you feel good," I told her, swiveling my hips as she met my thrust, greedily, throwing her head back.

"Fuck!" she moaned, as I grabbed onto her heels and powered into her at a frenzied pace, she moved with me. I really loved the fact that she couldn't touch me right

194

now, that I was in total control of her body. "I'm close, honey, faster!" she screamed, and I began to slow my pace with the intro of the next song.

"Is that really up to you?" I asked, moving inch by inch back and forth, so slowly I could tell it was driving her mad. It was driving me mad, too. "This is a punishment, remember?"

"Oh, please, please, please," she begged, tilting her hips higher and higher. "Please," she whispered. At her pleadings, I looked into her eyes and started powering into her again as the song kicked into high gear, watching her breasts jiggle uncontrolled under pink silk. I bent her in half so that her legs were nearly nestled behind her ears as I bit at her aching nipples through the dress.

"OH MY GOD!" she screamed and let out a low, rolling moan, her vaginal walls convulsed around me again.

I couldn't control my rhythm anymore and that was enough to send me over the edge after her; I thrust once more and spilled myself into her. "Holy SHIT!" I growled, collapsing my weight onto her, and shifting her legs back down my body toward the bed. As I found my breath, I notice we seemed to be breathing in unison, as if we were one person. As my eyes met hers, something between us shifted and I couldn't stop the words that spilled from my mouth. "I think I'm in love with you, Lucas," I confessed.

Her eyes went wide again, and I started to panic. It was too soon to tell her that, she was a commitaphobe! If she hadn't still been tied to my bed, she might've bolted, but she went slightly stiff beneath me for a second before the most radiant smile I'd ever seen broke over her lips.

"I think I'm in love with you, too, Brady," she whispered to me, leaving me in complete awe of her. This was it; this was who I was supposed to spend the rest of my life with. I swore when I got divorced that I was never going there again, with anyone, but in only two weeks, and I was ready to get down on one knee for this girl. I just had to wait until it was the right time and two weeks after dating wasn't it.

CHAPTER 21

LUCAS

I wanted to send up a thankful shout when Brady said he was falling in love with me. It had been a long time since I'd felt that way about anyone, and I was more than a little scared about what it meant for our future. I wasn't used to feeling this deeply for someone this quickly.

Hell, it took me a year to tell Preston I loved him, even though I was sure I felt it the whole time just as strongly as he did. I resisted because I was petrified. I mean, we were so young. I'm still young, too young to be thinking about forever, but every minute I spent with Brady made me want that with him. That elusive word, forever, more than I'd ever wanted anything in my entire life.

Usually, I'd run like crazy when I became conscious of the fact that I was getting into a relationship too deeply, but for some reason, the thought of running scared me more than the thought of staying and seeing what we could be.

After the words were out between us, we seemed to fall into a groove, spending every free moment we had together, including weekends. Because of the uncertainty of where we were headed, I'd held off on forging a bond with Taylor. I didn't want to be that girl who used to spend time with her if something every happened to Brady and me. That and Becca didn't seem too thrilled about the prospect of me, supposedly, replacing her in Taylor's life.

Conversely, though, Becca and Xander's relationship was starting to show cracks in the foundation. Which was why I wasn't surprised when Becca asked if we could have some one on one girl time one weekend nearly two weeks later when I was hanging out at their apartment with Taylor and Brady.

"I can tell that he really misses seeing his kids every day," Becca told me as she sat beside me on her bed after we'd finished dinner. "But every time he goes over to *her* house, I feel like he's not going to come back to me," she continued, picking at the blanket. "They weren't even married, so it couldn't have been *that* serious," she tried to justify, even though I was pretty sure the fact that Xander and his ex had three kids together meant they were serious.

"What do you expect him to do, Bec? They were together for years before all this stuff happened. Plus, the kids were used to seeing their father every day, too," I pointed out. "Should he just forget about all that?"

"Of course not, Lucy. Don't be stupid," she snapped, causing me to bristle slightly at her defensive words.

"Well, then, you've just got to find a way to get past this if you are going to be together," I leaned back against the wall and stretched my feet on the mattress.

"Easier said than done," she mumbled before we noticed Taylor standing silently in the doorway, her brown hair pulled back into a neat ponytail. "What do you need, sweetie?" Becca asked, her voice sounding sweeter than sugar.

"Lucy?" the toddler asked, looking at me with sad blue eyes, causing Becca to stiffen in repressed anger that Taylor addressed me instead of her.

"Yeah, baby girl?" I swung my legs off the bed and bent to her level as she wordlessly took my hand and pulled me behind her into the living room. Over my shoulder, I shot Becca a puzzled look and shrugged, following behind the tiny girl. A slow grin settled on my face when she led me beyond Xander to Brady and picked up his hand, too, bringing the three of us together and putting my hand in his.

198

"I was playing and I saw you aren't sitting with daddy anymore, and you should always be with my daddy," she smiled as she encouraged me to sit beside Brady on the floor and settled in on the other side of him, content to be tucked under his arm, as if we were a family.

I could feel the anger coming from Becca in waves as she watched us from behind the sectional for several long minutes, and I couldn't stop the freaked out expression that was settling over my features as the meaning of what this tiny girl had just done washed over me. If I couldn't hear it pounding in my ears, I'd wonder if my heart had just stopped beating all together. Out of the corner of my eye, I watched Becca take a deep cleansing breath before pasting a smile on her face and joining everyone in the living room after five minutes of watching the three of us sitting on the floor watching Xander playing a video game I hadn't seen before.

"What are you up to, Xander?" she ran her fingers through her boyfriend's shaved brown hair.

"Just playing this new game I picked up," he dismissed, swiping her hand away from his head. "Don't do that, it's distracting."

"I thought you were going to head over to get the kids," she prompted after another couple of minutes of silence. His rejection had to hurt, but she was trying to regroup. Her tone came out as forced nonchalance, and I could tell she was reaching her boiling point before she turned to desperation, as he seemed to be ignoring her in favor of his game.

"I was, but my ex wants to talk to me about something, so I'm meeting up with her later when she can get her sister to watch the kids," Xander shrugged his indifference in the change in plans, and Becca's face went red with anger again. It was a good thing Xander was facing the television and not her, or things would've escalated much faster.

"Oh," she choked out, curtly, when she finally got her anger under control, mostly. "I can't believe her, cheating on you and now she's got you running in circles for her," Becca rolled her eyes. Xander looked over to Brady with a look that seemed to ask if she was always this crazy; Brady simply nodded. "See Brady agrees with me, Xander," Becca droned on, taking the nod as directed at her words. "We should just go to Vegas and get married, and then she can't say anything anymore! I think she realized her mistake with Mike and now she wants you back. If we got married, then she would see that you are mine now. Not hers. We really need to send her a clear message, Xander."

My jaw dropped at her proposal. She'd only known Xander for three months, and he was just out of a long term relationship. Whether she wanted to see it or not, Xander was rebounding and only looking to get his dick wet on a regular basis, not enter into another long term commitment, not to even mention something as serious as marriage.

"Um, okay?" Xander choked out, obviously just as shocked by her words as I was. "Let's do that. That'll show her that the six years and three kids meant absolutely nothing to me," he quipped, his eyes never leaving his video game to respond or to show her that he was being entirely sarcastic.

"Really?!" Becca squealed as if he was actually agreeing to take her to Vegas and marry her. "Oh my GOD! LUCY! We have to plan!" she started to bounce from her spot on the other side of the sectional with an exuberant grin.

Brady leaned over toward me with a disbelieving look, stage whispering, "If there's a two for one special, wanna join them?" a mischievous smile on his face let me know he was playing along, probably so I wouldn't hyperventilate at his fake proposal.

"Let's do it," I laughed and stuck my tongue out at him.

"OH MY GOD! THAT'S PERFECT!" Becca was now out of her seat and grabbing my hand. "We can get married together, just like we always wanted!" she screamed, dragging me from the floor and back toward the bedroom, babbling the entire way of all of the planning that had to be done.

I shot Brady a helpless look as she yanked me behind her. I'd hoped my acceptance of Brady's fake and, frankly, unromantic proposal would've snapped her out of her reverie and recognize how fast and ridiculous this all was. However, her burning desire to be married, coupled with the desperation teeming off her to hold on to Xander, seemed to render her incapable of comprehending that this was not actually going to happen. I couldn't believe how easily she could overlook the true meaning behind his words because the false agreement had served her interests. Had this been the way she'd gotten 'engaged' all of the times before when she said she was getting married? This whole scene had been eye opening to me at how deeply Becca's delusions could go.

"Lucy?" Becca called my attention back to her as she hurled me toward her bed again. "Are you even listening?" I hadn't been because I was trying to figure out how I was going to get her to understand how stupid she was acting.

**

BRADY

Looking down at the sleeping toddler beside me, I let out an exasperated sigh. I was grateful that Becca's unbelievable power to reject reality and subsequent excitement didn't wake Taylor, especially when I, unthinkingly, proposed to Lucy. The last thing I needed was a call from Lori asking if I was really going to be running off to Vegas to marry a girl I'd only been dating a month. I was left dumbfounded by the latest development. It wasn't to say that I didn't want to get there with her, eventually, but I knew it was too soon. Surely Becca read the sarcasm in Xander's voice, right?

As if reading my mind, my friend looked over at me, scared. "Um, she knew I was joking, right?"

"I don't think so, man," I laughed, uncomfortably. "You do *not* want to play relationship chicken with Becca like that, you'll lose," I warned.

"I *just* got out of a relationship with someone I was in love with, Brady. How can she think I'm just going to get past that in like three months?" he asked, giving me a look that he can't fathom Becca's train of thought. Neither could I, but I've known her long enough to be able to predict her actions. Joking with her about marriage should never be done, because she will buy herself a ring to wear.

"I tried to advise you of her craziness in January and you didn't listen," I shrugged and pulled Taylor into my lap, resting her head against my shoulder, which caused her to snore directly into my ear. "I'm going to drop her in my bed. She's loud," I told Xander before gathering my baby into my arms.

"She snores louder than most adults!" Xander agreed. On the way, I could hear Becca's planning filter into the hall, with Lucy duplicitously trying to talk her down, while being supportive. I didn't know how she walked that fine line with Becca. It must come from being her best friend for nearly a decade, but I'd been Flynn's friend longer than that and sometimes I was at a complete loss as to how to deal with his insane mood swings. I barely settled back onto the living room floor when Xander signaled a smoke break.

"Man, I hope she doesn't think I'm actually in this for the long haul," he shook his head, after checking to make sure Becca's bedroom window was closed, as her eavesdropping knew no bounds. "I mean, the sex is good and all, but I think we've just about run our course, you know? I'm ready to find some new strange."

"Ugh," I groaned, knowing this was coming. It was exactly why I didn't want him to get involved with Becca in the first place, even though, deep down, I knew putting them on a collision course had made this unavoidable. Apparently, I'd forgotten that Becca still felt it was her roommately duty to attend to all of the guys she lived with sexually, if they were unattached. "You know if you do, you are going to make living here extremely uncomfortable for both of us, right?"

"I didn't say I was going to do it right now," he countered, leaning against the balcony railing. "I don't have any prospects right now, so I'd be stupid to cut off easy pussy without having something to take its place."

"Xander's words to live by."

"I haven't been single in years, Brady. I just think I should enjoy it while it lasts. I mean, I'm still going to be a good dad to my kids and all, and the best way I can do that is to keep girls from harboring delusions of becoming their new mommy. They have a mother, and that's not going to change."

"Are you missing her that much?" I asked.

"Didn't you miss Lori, at first?"

"Fuck no. That was over way before we split," I informed him. Flynn's words from a few weeks ago echoing in my head, was I the only guy that truly let go and moved on after a break up? "I didn't get blindsided like you did. You thought you guys were happy."

"Tell me about it," he frowned. "Mike moved out, but I can't go back there, not yet. I don't trust her right now."

"Understandable."

"I think Becca senses that you still love her. That's why she's clinging so hard. She thinks you're going to leave her for your ex," I stamped out my cigarette and threw the butt in a bag of trash sitting next to the stairwell, waiting for Xander to take it down to the dumpster. It was nice to have him as a roommate, but he was not timely in completing household chores he volunteered to do.

"But I'm not really with her. I don't call Becca my girlfriend, and I stop her if she tries to slip the 'C' word, commitment, into conversation. I've been nothing but completely honest with her," Xander leveled me with a serious look. "Aside from the *blatant* sarcasm I just displayed that seems to have been a mistake, I've never given her any hope of a future with me."

"I know that, you know that, hell, Lucy knows that, but Becca's brain is half crazy girl and half really crazy girl. She cherry picks the words she wants to listen to and how she wants the inflection to play out in her head. I don't know how she does it, but she's the Mozart of denial," I tried to explain, pretty damn proud of myself for being able to wax poetic about her insanity.

"What about what you said to Lucy? Aren't you afraid she'll do the same?"

"No, if she thought for a second that proposal might be remotely real after dating for a month, you would've seen a

204

Lucy shaped hole in our apartment door," I gestured with my words.

"I thought you guys were in love or some shit," he scoffed at me. "You think she'd just be gone?"

"You haven't known Lucy very long, but she has to be eased into this commitment stuff, very slowly. She spooks easily, like a baby squirrel or stray cat."

"Are you trying to get her to date you, or eat food from your hand?" he laughed.

"Um, maybe a little of both," I joined in on his laughter, because I was trying to cover up my own denial. I, actually, kind of wished that Lucy had taken the suggestion of Vegas seriously. It wasn't because I wanted her to run though; I wanted her to say yes to me for real. I'd contemplated what it would feel like to get down on one knee and tell Lucy about our future and ask her to be my wife since I'd first told her I was falling for her, but regardless of how clearly I could see it, the tainted images of the end of my last marriage would always come to the forefront just enough to scare me straight. I knew Lori and Lucy were nothing alike, but it was hard not to make comparisons anyway.

"You've got it bad," Xander nodded with a smirk. "It's awesome to see, though. I remember how cynical and withdrawn you became after your divorce. I'm glad you are letting in some happiness again. I mean, aside of just with your daughter. You deserve it," he finished, patting me on the back.

"Thanks man."

"I mean it. Lucy's a great girl, but she seems slightly lost in the world," he looked off in the distance toward the parking lot. "I think the two of you could be exactly what you're looking for."

I couldn't help but mull over Xander's words for the rest of the night. Were we really meant to be? I mean, we'd been friends for so long without anything happening. Up until New Years' Eve, we hadn't even had 'almost' moments. How could we have been literally under each other's noses for so long and not sense that we could be more?

CHAPTER 22

BRADY

I was too exhausted to give Lucy a proper good bye the following morning when I felt her slip out of bed to go to work.

"I'll see you later," I vaguely recalled her whispering as her lips grazed my forehead when she left. I awoke a little more than an hour later with Taylor sitting on my chest.

"Good morning, daddy! Bekfast time," she announced, her brown hair sticking out in every direction from her sleep.

"Breakfast," I agreed and shifted her to the floor so that we could set off for the kitchen together. The house seemed to be completely quiet, like Taylor and I were the only ones in the house. Thank goodness I didn't have to deal with Becca's crazy Vegas wedding talk this morning.

Glancing at the clock, I saw we only had an hour together before her mother would be there to collect her for the day. My heart sank, a little, knowing that my weekend time was going to be cut short. The apartment was always so full of life when I had Taylor, and seemed way too quiet when she was gone. "Cereal?" I asked her, shaking a box of some sugar laden crap Becca had bought the last time she went to the store.

"Cereal," Taylor nodded, her blue eyes overly bright with excitement. "And chocolate milk!"

"Okay," I smiled and set about fixing her a bowl. After breakfast came clean up and bath time, and before I knew it, Lori was knocking on my door.

"Hey," I said, ushering my ex-wife into the apartment. She and Lucy didn't have much in common when it came to their looks. Lori was short, just a few inches over five foot to Lucy's five foot seven or eight. Lori's hair was the same brown as Taylor and me, and actually Lucy's natural color, I think. I'd seen old pictures of Lucy from high school, but her hair had been blonde, red, and all the colors in between since then. I loved the black it currently was. Both women were curvy, but where Lori had more 'A', Lucy definitely had more 'T.' "I was just brushing her hair and getting her shoes on."

"Great, thanks," Lori nodded, looking awkward in the entryway to the apartment. "Can I make arrangements with you to have Taylor again for part of the weekend in a couple of weeks?"

"Sure, what's going on?"

"I'm, um, well, I'm getting remarried," she said, hesitantly, like I was going to lose my shit over her announcement. She had been with her boyfriend since a few months after we split, so this development wasn't really a surprise, though slightly unexpected that I would get only a couple weeks' worth of notice.

We hadn't been together in years, but our split had been bad. We pretty much couldn't stand to be in the same room for a while, but now? Now, I didn't feel anything for her. I wasn't in love with her, I didn't hate her anymore. Aside from the fact that she was the mother of my daughter, I felt nothing for her but indifference. But a conversation we'd had when we signed our divorce papers came filtering back through my head at her words.

"Ha!" I responded. "What happened to 'I'm never getting married again'?"

208

"I could ask you the same thing, Brady," she smiled. "I hear you and this Lucy girl are getting serious," she teased. "Taylor has been gushing about her for weeks now, and I think I need to find the time to meet her."

"That can be arranged. And yeah, yeah, yeah, we were full of shit back then, weren't we?"

"Nah, we were just young and wanted something we weren't ready for," she shrugged. "Now we are, and we've found people we are more compatible with."

"That's a good way to put it," I said, trying to get a tennis shoe on my daughter's squirming foot. "Yeah, you can have her for that, but is there a way I can pick up Taylor on Friday next weekend to make up for all this time and keep her until Monday?"

"Sure, that should even things out. Sorry I didn't give you more notice, it's kind of a last minute thing," she explained. "I'm glad you are taking such an interest in your time with Taylor again. It's good to see, Brady."

"I know, and it's cool on the notice. You know I'm pretty flexible. Is there a reason you're getting married so quick? Another baby?" I quirked an eyebrow at her. Lori had a total of five children, one from a relationship before me, our daughter, one with her boyfriend, and then her boyfriend had two kids from his previous relationship. It was a chaotic family, but I think she thrived on it. I was glad she was happy because I could've never given her that many children.

"Ha-ha," she laughed, humorlessly. "No more kids, I promise! We fixed that last year after the last one," she frowned. "It's just time, you know? It feels right and we don't want to wait."

"I get that," I said, thoughtfully, because for the first time in a very long time, I really did get it.

**

LUCAS

When I got to Brady's apartment after work the next day, all seemed to have died down on the wedding front. Becca had called me at work once to tell me all about the hotel she thought we'd all like to stay in *when* we went, but then Xander wanted to go to lunch and all was forgotten. Or at least put on the back burner now that he was giving her a little more attention. All I could say was a huge thank you to Xander for taking one for the team on that one.

"Is it safe?" I whispered when Brady answered the door for me, peeking cautiously into their living room.

"Yeah, the coast is clear, Lucy," he motioned me inside and walked back to his video game controller and, surprisingly, turned off his game. "Taylor's with her mom this afternoon because they had some birthday party to go to."

"Oh," I frowned, trying not to sound too disappointed. That little girl was amazing, and quickly starting to mean way too much to me.

"Don't worry, I negotiated a little bit of extra time next weekend so we can take her to dinner at that place you wanted to try," he told me as he sat down on the couch beside me.

"Yay! Now I'm excited," I bounced slightly at the announcement. "I really hope she likes the place, though. It's so much fun."

"I'm sure she will," he smiled at me.

210

"Has Xander brought Becca down yet?" I asked, dropping my voice down to a whisper again, even though I knew we were alone in the apartment.

"I hope so! Holy shit! She was talking about colors and dresses and going ring shopping all morning," he rolled his eyes. "You don't have those kinds of dreams right now, do you?" his voice sounded teasing, but there was an edge that made me wonder if he was actually curious.

"Um, not right now, but I do have dreams of what I'd want for my wedding," I told him. "Don't all little girls? Even the ones who have no hope that they'd ever actually *get* married know what they'd want in a perfect world."

"Is that so?" he smirked. "You don't think you'll ever get married?"

"No, I don't," I said, matter-of-fact, even though I was lying through my teeth. "What about you? Ever think you'll get married again?"

"After the divorce was final, I was adamant that I would never be in a relationship again, and I am, so I guess I'd never say never, but um, not right now," he finished, blowing out a shaky breath at his confession. There was something that rang false about his words though.

"I know what you mean," I nodded, wincing at the thought that he really might never want to get married again. "I don't see it happening tomorrow though, like not any time soon at all."

"Even though we aren't going to Vegas right now, doesn't mean that I don't want to see where we are headed, Lucas," he said, pulling my hand to twine our fingers together and looking deep into my eyes to show me he'd seen my reaction to his words. Wow, he could really see right through me.

"Well, enough of all the serious stuff!" he announced, sensing I wasn't ready to go any further with all of the wedding and commitment talk. "I've really missed you today." Brady pulled on our joined hands and yanked me into his lap in the corner of the sectional and stuck his face in my cleavage. "I've really missed these, too. You should leave them here when you are at work. The three of us could have some fun."

"Stop it!" I squealed as his tongue traced a path from the swell of my breasts over my collarbone and up to my neck, trying to squirm away from him, but he was holding me tight.

"I don't wanna," Brady nuzzled me closer and pulled me in for a deep kiss as his palms moved over my bare thighs, pulling my legs to straddle him on the couch.

"Good to see things are working out so well for the two of you," Flynn announced as he walked through the door to the apartment without knocking, causing me to jump to my feet in surprise. "This must be some sort of relationship record for you. I guess one man's trash really is another man's treasure, eh, Lucy?" he continued as he brushed past me on the way to the room he used to share with Brady.

"What the fuck is that supposed to mean, Flynn?" Brady called out behind him, sounding deceptively calm.

"I thought we already had this conversation, Brady," he answered, his back to both of us. "It just sucks that I had to lose my best friend to a whore who will never be able to stay faithful to him."

"You have no idea what you are talking about, Flynn," I said as calmly as possible. "And there is no reason you and Brady can't still be friends," I pointed out.

212

"I can't stand to be around you as much as you're here now, Lucy," he said, bluntly, finally turning towards us, his eyes blazing in barely restrained anger. "We aren't friends."

"Is it because I never fucked you, Flynn? Is that why? Because I didn't let you have a chance to work me over with your robo-cock?" I asked, folding my arms over my chest and leveling him with a challenging glare. "Could we still be friends if I'd let you into my panties just once?"

"That's not what this is about," he fired back, turning to go into the bedroom, leaving us to stare after him as he started throwing the few items he'd left when he moved out into a bag.

"Good, because I seem to remember the night you told me you wanted a chance; you fucked my old roommate and stole my last condom to do it. Not that I was going to fuck you anyway," I rolled my eyes. "It just seemed in poorer taste than anything I've ever done."

"Whatever, bitch," Flynn growled, but didn't turn around. "Look, Brady, once you get her out of your system, you know where to find me. As it is, I may need to crash here a few nights a week again cause I got a new job that's closer to here than where I've been. I'll kick in for the rent again, but my name is still on the lease, so I'm going to do it regardless. I'll let you know in advance so I don't have to run into certain people," he informed us, looking me up and down like I was carrying every disease known to man, even though I was sure his list was twice as long as mine. What a fucking hypocrite. "Just let me know when you're ready to throw out the trash and we'll make plans to go out and celebrate."

"You are being intentionally rude, Flynn. I can't stand here and let you talk about Lucas this way. She deserves better," Brady said, menacingly. I could feel him shaking

213

behind me as he stared bullets into his best friend. "She isn't going anywhere, so you need to get used to this."

"That's so bullshit, Brady. I can't believe that you've bought into this reformed slut act she has going on!" he roared with laughter. "Becca told me that the four of you are talking about taking a trip to Vegas together. Mark my words, if you marry this trollop, it'll be over before the ink dries on the marriage certificate," he prophesized before stomping back through the apartment, slamming the door behind him before we could answer his ridiculous accusations.

"And his real reason for returning to the apartment crystalizes," Brady sighed before pulling me back onto the couch.

"What is?" I asked, confused.

"Becca told him that Xander proposed. He thinks they are engaged and he wants to stop it," he explained. "I'd be angrier, if I wasn't happy to see all this Vegas bullshit come to an end."

At his words, I felt slightly wounded. I had no reason to be, and I actually should've felt relieved that he wasn't trying to get me to elope with Becca and Xander. I couldn't explain why I felt hurt that he'd basically said he didn't want to marry me, but I did. It was everything I could do to pretend I wasn't as devastated as I was, but he saw everything.

"That's not to say I don't see that sort of future for us, Lucas. Don't think that's what I'm saying," he said, desperately, turning my face to look at him, like he could sense I wasn't quite with him at that moment. "I love you, and I want to be with you. You and I definitely have a long and happy life ahead of us, it's Becca and Xander that don't. I don't want our happiness tied to her idiocy."

214

"Okay," I whispered as tears stung my eyes. I didn't know why his declaration had made me so emotional, but he'd just said the exact right thing I needed to hear in those few sentences. I knew it was my daddy issues coming through in my relationship with Brady, but I had to keep reminding myself that Brady had repeatedly chosen me and that it would be okay.

CHAPTER 23

LUCAS

After a month in honeymoon period isolation, I finally decided it was time to come up for air and resume my usual Tuesday lunch breaks with Abby. Walking into Antonio's for the first time since Brady and I started dating was weirder than I expected. Everything looked the same, Eric was behind the take out station, our usual seats were open, but everything felt different.

"Hey, Lucas!" Eric greeted me as I took the seat beside the window. "Long time, no see! How are things with the boyfriend?"

The word boyfriend from his mouth made a grin erupt on my face so big it should've been considered cheesy, but he just looked at me and laughed.

"Wow, you must have it bad, Lucas. I've never seen you smile over the use of the B word before," he laughed. "Cringed, scowled, gotten outright hostile, but never smiled."

"What can I say?" I shrugged. "I'm not myself these days."

"Wow, you've emerged from hibernation," Abby said, perching herself on the chair beside me. "How'ya been?" she asked, waggling her eyebrows in suggestion.

"I've been good," I confirmed.

"Missing our late nights yet?" Eric asked, quirking an eyebrow, causing me to look down at my hands. "I'm just kidding, Lucas, I can see from the *very* satisfied look on your face that you have been well taken care of."

"That's for sure."

"I'm glad, you deserve that," he nodded, completely serious. "It sucks that I'm missing out on some Earth-shattering sex with you, but seeing you happy makes up for it. Plus, it's not like I'm hurting for it anyway," he said, giving me a devilish grin.

"Oh, I know, you just have to pull up the next name on your contact list," I winked.

"Really?" Abby asked. "So you weren't like secretly wanting more with Lucas, Eric? You weren't trying to get her to fall in love with you?" her mouth was agape, as if she couldn't comprehend that we weren't into each other as anything more than bed buddies.

"Lucas is totally cool, and a ton of fun, but I'm not looking for that, and neither was she. Hell, you were the one that pointed out that we barely knew anything about each other," Eric explained. "It's not like that with us, never was. We were fuck buddies, nothing more."

"Those can exist without drama? I've never heard of it happening before," Abby folded her arms across her chest in contradiction to what she'd just been told.

"Not with most girls, but Lucas is special. She doesn't subscribe to the sex equals love school of thought some girls have," Eric said. "Plus, she's the best at adhering to the three W's that make for a perfect sexual partner."

"And the three W's are...?" Abby prompted.

"Wild, willing, and most importantly, wet," Eric smirked. "And by willing, I don't mean just willing in the yes means yes, no means no way. I mean, she's up for anything and doesn't expect me to stick around and cuddle."

"That's disturbing," Abby shuddered. "And so unromantic."

"It's not about romance, Abby, it's about sex," he retorted.

"It's true. Pre-Brady, I was all about getting mine and getting him out of my apartment before first light," I agreed. "There is nothing wrong with knowing what you do and don't want. Believe me, Abby."

"But you're so happy with Brady now," Abby continued, "so that shows you were, at least, thinking it might be a possibility."

"No, I'm being completely straight when I tell you Brady was 100% a fluke. Something I never saw coming," I denied. "I can't lie and tell you that I'm not happy about the development, because I am. But if you'd asked me a few months ago if this was something I wanted, I would've told you in no uncertain terms that it wasn't. Hell, you *did* ask me, and what did I say?"

"You said, '*Abby, if I ever think for a second, a relationship might be something I want, I need you to slap me across the face, hard, and knock some sense into me,*'" Abby echoed my words, with my exact inflection. "But I'm not going to do that. Seeing you happy is awesome. You seem so much less stressed."

"That's cause she's getting it nightly instead of tri-weekly," Eric chimed in.

"Alright, you guys can stop now, thanks," I mumbled, signaling to our waitress that we were finally ready to order our lunch.

"So," Abby started after we'd received our sodas, "when's the wedding?" The caviler delivery of her question had me choking on my Dr. Pepper. "You okay, Lucas? What'd I say?" she asked, pounding on my back as I struggled to get myself under control.

218

"Just all this wedding talk," I coughed out. "It's a little premature, don't you think?"

"It was a joke, Lucas, chill out," Abby chuckled.

"I know, Becca's just acting crazy again, and the M word has been broached between Brady and I, and it's way, way, way, too fucking fast. It's everything I can do not to freak out over the fact that I'm actually in a relationship, but throwing in that extra layer of commitment? Um, no thank you," I shook my head. I knew I was going to get the argument that I'm protesting too much, but I really was freaking out.

"Does he treat you well?" Eric asked, suddenly in front of us again.

"Yeah, he's great," I agreed.

"Does he care about you?" Abby asked.

"He loves me."

"It doesn't take a rocket scientist to see you feel the same, your whole face just lit up like a Christmas tree when you said that," Eric smiled. "So stop freaking out and just go with it. Follow the current, see where it takes you."

"Said the most commitment-phobic person I know," I retorted.

"Look, just because *I* don't want to be in a relationship, that doesn't mean I don't know what the fuck I'm talking about, it just means that I can't take my own amazing advice," he puffed out his chest in mock victory, before pausing slightly. "On second thought, if you freak out, you'll screw this good thing up and I'll be back in your panties within the next month, so…hmmm," he paused and stroked his designer stubble in thought, before his lips broke in a face splitting grin. "I'm just kidding, Lucas. I'm

219

glad you're doing this," he concluded, patting my arm as he walked away to answer the ringing phone.

"Eric's right, Lucas, it's great to see you so happy," Abby bounced in her seat. "So, when are we going to double date?" she asked, her face completely serious. Just as I opened my mouth to answer, our food arrived. Talk about perfect timing!

I needed to slow this whole commitment train down. I had a boyfriend, I was in love, I could see a future with him, but I really needed to take all of this one day at a time. If I didn't I was likely to shoot myself in the foot and sprint far, far away from all of the drama an engagement to Brady would bring. Between ex-wives, well, the one ex-wife, my ex-boyfriends, kids and Becca… There was a lot to consider. The only thing I was sure of was that I wanted to be with Brady.

**

BRADY

"So, I made a decision you guys," Becca announced Thursday, about ten minutes before our car pool was due to show up.

"And that would be?" Xander asked.

"Well, I'm really excited about this, so I'm hoping you guys will support me," she looked down at her hands in her lap. A small feeling of dread started to take root in my stomach at those words, and I hoped like hell Xander hadn't accidentally knocked her up. I didn't want this to become a "Papa, Don't Preach" moment for us. Did I really just make a fucking Madonna reference? What is wrong with me today? Clearing her throat, Becca brought me back

220

to the subject at hand. "I saw this ad the other day for a school to become a medical assistant, and I called."

"Okay? So you are going to go back to school in the evenings or something?" Xander tried to clarify.

"I qualified for financial aid, and the lady said if I go full time, I'll be able to graduate in six months," she smiled. "But that's going Monday through Friday from 9am to 5pm," she said, and I, instantly, knew what was coming next. "So I won't have the ability to find a full time job, and if I take a part time job, I won't have any time to spend with Xander..." she trailed off.

"Just spit it out, Becca," I growled.

"The financial aid only covers books and tuition, so I was hoping that you might be able to share my part of the rent and utilities for a while?" she asked in a small voice.

"Um," I started, slightly speechless at her audacity. "I already have a child I need to take care of Becca. I don't have the money to take care of another one."

"What does that mean?" she asked, haughtily. Did she really expect us to just be okay with this?

"It means that Brady and I need some time to discuss this, Becca," Xander said, giving me a look that didn't reflect how crazy I thought her proposal was.

"Oh," she breathed a sigh of relief. "Okay, just let me know, okay?" she nodded as a honk rang out, signaling the arrival of our carpool. "Have a good day at work," she smiled at both of us and kissed Xander good bye.

"What the fuck, man?" I asked once we were clear of the door and making our way down the stairs.

"Let me mull this over and we'll talk at break, okay?" he suggested as we climbed into the backseat of our co-worker's Jeep.

"Fine, but I meant what I said," I nodded and joined in with the conversation already going on in the vehicle, trying to forget the financial bomb Becca just dropped on me. I sent a quick text to Lucy before we walked through the gate to clock in, letting her know that I'd need to talk to Xander during my first break that night and would talk to her on my lunch break at 11pm.

By the time Xander walked up to me two hours later, cigarette in hand, I was bouncing off the walls trying to figure out what he could, possibly, be thinking. The sex couldn't be good enough to warrant this, especially when he'd said he was looking for 'new strange.'

"I know what you are going to say, Brady," Xander started, holding his hands up to stop me from talking. "And this isn't about pussy."

"Okay?" I asked, warily.

"It's about freeing myself from her, kind of," he started with a sigh.

"Explain yourself."

"First, she's going to be gone all day when we are home, and second, we are going to insist that she look for a part-time job, and that will get her out of the house on the weekend, hopefully," he rationalized. "In the meantime, she can make up for the rent we are covering for her by taking care of the household chores," he suggested. "That way we don't have to worry about grocery shopping or dishes for a while. We won't make her clean your bedroom or do our laundry or anything, just the upkeep of the common areas in the apartment."

222

"Hmmm," I contemplated. "That might actually work. And if she doesn't hold up her end of things?"

"Then she'll need to find a way to pay her part of the rent or find another place to live," he shrugged. "I'm with you; I have my own kids to pay for, too. But I think we should try this for a bit and see how it goes."

"I don't think Lucy will love it, but I'm willing to give it a try if it means we don't have to pick up after ourselves," I laughed.

"Who knows, if things keep going the way they are with you and Lucy, maybe she can move in after her lease is up?"

"Whoa, now you're slightly ahead of me," I told him. "Well, not me, Lucy. I love the idea because it would get her away from her pimp."

"*Her pimp*?!" Xander sputtered out.

"Not really *her* pimp, it's this dude that lives a couple of doors down that we are sure is a pimp," I rushed to clarify, laughing at his reaction. "I just don't trust that guy, or the dude that lives across the hall with the weird dog and penchant for never wearing anything but a threadbare brown robe and stained boxer shorts."

"Ugh," he groaned. "That does not sound like a safe place for a twenty-one year old woman to live alone with her cat. We've gotta get her out of there, even if she doesn't move in with us."

"I agree, wholeheartedly," I nodded, our new mission taking shape before our eyes.

CHAPTER 24

LUCAS

Xander and Brady were so stupid. As I listened to Becca gush her plan over the phone, I couldn't help but shake my head at how my boyfriend, who was smart, usually, and his equally intelligent friend could've been buffaloed.

"So, I'm going to look for a part time job, like eight hours a week or something, just to pay for my car, probably, but Xander likes to use my car sometimes, so maybe I can get him to pitch in for the payment on that, too," she relayed, making me sick to my stomach.

"Oh?" I asked, trying to seem engaged in what she was telling me when I was really seeing red at her presumptiveness. I wished Brady had talked to me about this before agreeing to it. It was a terrible idea. If they'd come to me, I would've been happy to relay to them the story of how Becca moved out of her parents' house with a boyfriend when she turned eighteen, without a job and begged me to deplete my savings to pay her rent when they almost got evicted. I didn't and in retaliation, she didn't talk to me for three months.

"They said I just needed to make sure I kept the apartment clean, and they'd cover me for a little bit," she continued. "But I think they'll give me a little bit of leeway, since I'm going to be in school and all, plus, Xander is pretty much in love with me. I mean, he fucking proposed! I think he'll be happy to support me while I get my education."

Fuck, I knew where this was going and I gave it…hmm? Okay, so it was almost May, so I gave it until the end over June before they decide to kick her ass out.

"You should probably make an effort, Becca. They work really hard. You know how tired they are most of the time, especially since they've been working mandatory overtime these last few weeks," I tried to tell her. "You should make sure they are coming home to what they are asking of you, at least until you find a part time job."

"Whatever, Lucy, you're such a buzz kill, can't you just be happy that I'm trying to do something with my life? I *was* going to invite you shopping with me, after all my dad sent me a grand to get school supplies," she snorted. "I'm going to go find a more *supportive* friend to go with me. Bye," she threw in before ending the call. Silently, I wondered if Becca was going to be giving Brady or Xander any of the money from her father to cover her bills, although, I already knew the answer to that question.

Rolling my eyes, I scanned my empty apartment, wishing Brady were here, but he was with his family for some kind of dinner thing. I didn't ask, because I couldn't go, even though I'd been to a few family functions with him since we started dating. I'd pulled a rare short evening shift to cover for someone and had to clock in within the next hour. With a sigh, I plopped down on my new couch and tried to enjoy the silence. It wasn't long before Shadow jumped into my lap with a short meow that said "Pet me or die, bitch." I was happy to oblige her for a few minutes before I gave in and dialed Brady's cell. I hadn't seen him since I dropped him at his apartment on Thursday and I missed him.

"Hello?" a female voice answered, already putting me on high alert.

"Hello?" I asked, a slight edge coming across.

"Lucy?" the voice laughed. "Hey, it's Siobhan!"

Breathing out a sigh of relief I didn't know I was holding in, I greeted Brady's little sister. "Hey, Shiv, how's it going?"

"Good, glad junior year is almost over though," she told me. "Brady and Parker are playing a game of chess right now. You should see them, they are super into it. It's hilarious; you want me to tell him you called?"

"Sure, but, um, actually…" I started, wondering what Brady's sister would think of me suggesting this. "I'll give you twenty dollars if you go right now and dump the board. I mean, are they almost to the end of the game?"

"It looks like it, and I think Brady's winning," Siobhan laughed before whispering my request to someone beside her, probably Celia.

"OH MY GOD, Shiv, do it! You've gotta do it!" the voice beside her said, laughing and confirming my suspicions. I was excited to hear them wanting to go along with my plan. Brady'd told me when I first started going to family functions that if his family joked around with me and gave me shit, it meant they liked me. He warned that I'd know I was in trouble if they were nice and polite to me, so I took this as a sign that they accepted me.

"I'm doing it!" Siobhan announced to me, keeping the phone with her as she seemed to walk down the hall toward her brothers' game. Suddenly, I heard a crash on the other end of the line and two male voices shouting expletives, and in the distance I could hear laughter.

"What the fuck was that, Shiv?" Brady asked, louder than before, signaling me that his phone was now in his hand instead of his sister's.

"Lucy asked me to do that," she giggled. "THANKS LUCY THAT WAS AWESOME!" she shouted, the words fading as she got further from the phone.

226

"You can't ask my sister to do things like that, baby. She loves that kind of thing," Brady said into the phone.

"I know, that's why I asked her to. That was way funnier than it was in my head," I let out a full force belly laugh at the picture that was in my head of chess pieces flying from the table.

"You're lucky we were playing with dad's plastic set and not the glass one," he admonished, but I could tell he appreciated the joke.

"You know Shiv wouldn't have done anything if you were playing with the more valuable chess set," I teased.

"Yes, I know, but you still have to pay for your transgression," he breathed into the phone. "I'll see you at your apartment after work?"

"I can't wait," I panted, already hot with the promise of whatever Brady had in mind to make me pay for ruining a game of chess he was, supposedly, about to win.

"Oh, but you will," he said, his voice sounding sinister. "Have fun at work, and try not to think of what's in store for you in a few short hours."

"Ugh," I groaned. "Why do you do that to me? Now those hours are going to feel like eternity!"

"I know," he chuckled, darkly. "I'll see you at eleven," he said, making it sound more like a threat than a promise and I pressed my thighs together at the wetness formed by his words.

"Have fun with your family," I smiled.

"I'll try," he sighed. "But I'll be thinking of all the ways I'll be having fun with you soon enough."

"You should focus on the fam, honey. I don't want you sporting wood at the dinner table," I joked.

"Ugh," he grunted. "Too late."

"On that note," I said, "I've gotta head to work now," I finished, moving to end the call.

"Okay, baby, I love you," he said, like the words were second nature, even though we'd never used them to say good bye before. Hell, we'd never used them outside the bedroom before...

"I love you, too," I said, looking down at Shadow, shell shocked, as I hit the red button to disconnect the call. What the fuck just happened?

**

BRADY

I cursed my final words to Lucy all day long. We'd been together over two months now, but I didn't know if she was ready for that kind of endearment when we said good-bye. I felt it, I knew she felt it, but I wasn't sure she was ready to hear it daily, even though I was bursting to tell her all the time. I should've known better after she'd freaked out a month ago and we lost nearly a week because I tried to rush it. What was I thinking? I was lucky she didn't call to cancel tonight. Although, with the promise I'd made, I was sure she wouldn't back out.

Using my key, I let myself into her darkened apartment. I had another hour before she was due to get off work. An angry meow at my feet startled me from my thoughts and drew my attention to the black cat trying to decide whether it was going to attack me or not.

"Hey, Shadow," I greeted. "I'm guessing you want me to feed you? Will you let me live if I open a can for you?" I asked, not expecting an answer, but the response of a sharp meow before the cat turned to walk back toward its bowl,

228

tail in the air, showed me she'd known what I'd said and agreed to let me live, this time. Just as I cracked open the can and fed Shadow, my phone started to vibrate in my pocket. Looking at the screen, I saw the number for Lucy's work. To mess with her, or not to mess with her, that is the question...

"Hey, baby," I answered.

"Hey," she said, warily, and I instantly decided to mess with her. "Have you made it to my place yet?"

"Actually, Xander asked if we could hang out tonight. It sounded serious," I told her. "Rain check?"

"Um, sure," she said, sounding disappointed by the change in plans. I tried to refrain from doing a celebratory dance in the middle of her vanity. "Tomorrow then?"

"Yeah, I'll come by for lunch after your classes, if that's okay," I soothed.

"Sounds perfect," she said, and I could hear the smile in her voice again. "Well, then, I'd better get back to work."

"Okay, call me when you get off, so I know you've made it home safe," I told her.

"Okay, I'll talk to you in like an hour then," she finished, ending the call. How could I pull a surprise together in an hour? I asked myself as I looked around her apartment.

After locating her usual package of cookie dough in the refrigerator and setting her oven to preheat, I tracked down the candles she had scattered in various rooms of the apartment. Throwing the cookie dough into the oven, I rearranged the candles to lead toward her bedroom and shut off the lights in the apartment, except the kitchen where I was working. By the time my hour was up, I'd completed

229

the caramel stuffed chocolate chip cookies, straightened up the clutter in her apartment, and cleaned up the few dishes lying in the sink.

Arranging the cooled cookie on a plate and placing it on Lucy's bed, I scurried around lighting the candle path to her bedroom and stripped down to my boxers and crawled into her bed, hoping that she'd find this romantic and not creepy. My phone rang at 11pm on the dot.

"Hey baby, I'm just headed home, how's everything going with Xander?" she asked.

"Oh, fine, he's out with Becca now," I told her.

"Oh, well, did you want me to come to you then?"

"Nah, you can just head home, we'll hang out after you get out of class tomorrow," I dismissed, hearing her truck crank in the background.

"Okay, if you're sure?" she said, sounding disappointed again.

"I'm sure. The family thing was a little heavy tonight, and I could really just use a night alone, if that's okay?" I lied.

"Sure," she agreed. "Well, then, um, I guess I'll talk to you in the morning?"

"Absolutely, baby," I said in the most placating voice I could muster, hoping it sounded slightly insincere because she'd gotten my sister to mess with me earlier, and payback was a bitch sometimes.

"Okay, then," she whispered, ending the call and making me question if I was doing the right thing, yet again. I was going to get smacked, I could feel it. I just hoped it would be worth it, to see the look on her face. A couple of minutes later, I heard her key in the lock.

"What the…?" I heard her ask into the candle-lit darkness of her apartment. "Why are all these candles lit, Shadow? And why do I smell cookies? Did you bake cookies?"

I suppressed a chuckle at the cat's answering meow. I heard the keys hit her coffee table and her purse hit the table in the dining area.

"Are you hungry, baby?" she asked the cat, but the words came out slightly muffled, even though it was closer than before. Hearing the door to her walk in creak, I knew she was right outside her bedroom door now. "No, it looks like you've already been fed," she said, and I could tell she was smiling by the obvious chipper quality to her voice. "Was that you, Brady?" she asked, finally entering the room and surprising me with the fact that she'd shed her uniform on the way to her bedroom.

"Yes, it was," I smirked. "So what would you have done if it wasn't me in here, and you're mostly naked? What if it was the guy down the hall?"

"I don't think he's going to break into my apartment, bake some cookies, light some candles and feed my cat," she laughed, reaching behind her back to unclasp her white underwire bra.

"Well, you never know."

"I decided to take my chances," she said, pulling the bra down her arms and tossing it at me, leaving her completely naked in the candle light. She'd never looked more beautiful.

"Cookies first or sex?" I asked, meaning it to be rhetorical, because there was no way she was having dessert before me.

"Did you really just ask me that? And why in the fuck are you still in your underwear? Take them off," she ordered.

"Yes, ma'am," I smiled, lifting my hips from the bed to catch up with her level of nudity.

"Perfect," she said, eying my hard on like it was her lifeline and crawling up my body from the foot of the bed. Just as her mouth was level with my dick, I yanked her up and threw her onto her back beside me.

"Me first," I growled before leaning in to devour her with my lips, leaving her panting and writhing beneath me. "Fuck, I missed you tonight," I stated. "Getting my sister to dump the chess board was so fucking hot," I started to kiss a path down her jaw to her collarbone to the tops of her breasts. "For you to be getting along with my family the way that you are…I can't even tell you how much that means to me," I finished before unleashing my tongue within her, already, drenched folds.

"I'm glad you enjoyed my little prank," she panted out before the incoherent moans started.

"Shh, baby, I'm trying to enjoy my dessert here," I scolded before going back to work between her legs.

"Sorry," she said with a low moan as I found the spot I was looking for and fucked her with my mouth and fingers until she shouted her release. I was surprised her neighbors never complained, because Lucy was loud in bed, like really loud, and usually, we were having sex well after midnight.

When the last of her orgasm was rung out of her, she grabbed a condom under from under her pillow and pushed me onto my back beside her. After rolling on the protection with her teeth, she straddled me, her breasts swinging tantalizingly in my face. "My turn," she growled as she

232

ground down on my dick with purpose. I loved making her wild for me.

CHAPTER 25

LUCAS

The far too loud tones of my cell phone woke me at some point during the night. Looking at the still dark sky beyond my vertical blinds, I cursed whoever was calling me until I saw the display on my screen.

"Hello?" I answered, groggily, with a whisper, swinging my legs out of my bed so that I didn't wake Brady. Thankfully, the phone hadn't woken him from his sex coma and as I left my bedroom, I watched him cuddle closer to his pillow and let out a contented sigh. Absently, I wished that I weren't leaving him right now to have a long overdue conversation. I was lucky I'd even heard the phone myself, considering he'd orgasmed me into a coma, too.

"Since when are you crashed out so early, Lucy?" a bright voice said from the other side of the line as I settled myself on my living room couch, soft light from the outside walkway peeking through the covered windows.

"Since I have an early class in the morning, Preston," I laughed. "What are you doing up so late? Did you take a leave day?"

"I'm on guard duty for the next hour and I was getting sleepy. I figured I'd call you and you could keep me up," he informed me.

"Isn't your Commanding Officer around there somewhere? Won't you get in trouble?"

"I would, normally, but he's talking to *his* wife right now, too," he chuckled.

"Oh, so I'm your wife now?" I joked.

"I'd like you to be," he blurted.

"What?!" I whispered, harshly, although I wasn't completely surprised.

"I talked to Parker and he said you and Brady are still together, is that true?"

"Is that why you're calling?" I asked, knowing that Preston wasn't taking the news from Parker well if he was calling me in the middle of the night. Not that the time of the call was a surprise, just the subject matter. He didn't usually want to talk about things so heavy during what we'd dubbed our twilight time.

When we lived closer together, it wasn't uncommon for Preston and I to go out to have a late night burrito or walk around the neighborhood porn shop at three in the morning. Sometimes, he would just knock on my window and slip into bed with me when he couldn't sleep. It was the time that we were just Preston and Lucy, so for him to bring up something like my relationship with Brady meant I was in for some heavy duty mind fucking.

"Is this thing with Brady serious, Lucy?" he laid out.

"Yes," I answered, quickly and honestly, knowing it was going to sting, but wanting to tell him the truth. I could hear his swift intact of air on the other end. He hadn't been expecting me to say that. It broke our protocol.

"You've never…," he stalled. "We've never admitted to something serious with someone else before… is it because I'm not there?"

"I don't know, Preston, maybe? But I'm in love with Brady, so I think it might be more than just your absence that's making this relationship serious," I disclosed.

"So even if I were there, I'd have no chance?" he sounded like he was choking on his tongue.

235

"Look," I sighed, leaning back against the arm rest and rubbing my forehead. I was fucking tired and this was not the time for this kind of conversation. "I'm not saying that, but you aren't here, so it's kind of moot at this point, isn't it?"

"So that's it? We're over?"

"We've been over for years, Preston, you and I both know that," I pointed out. "Last year was the just the tipping point on that, wouldn't you say? I'd really like for us to be friends."

"We'll always be friend, Lucy," he admonished. "If I'd known that tape was going to cost me another chance…"

"You'd what, Preston? Not make it without asking me? Not let your friends see it? You're lucky I'm still offering friendship," I rattled off, starting to get angry again. I didn't realize my voice had gotten louder until I saw Brady standing in my dining area looking tired and confused.

"All of it," Preston confessed. "I'm not going to hash it all out with you again. I'm so sorry. I was drunk and stupid."

"Yes, you were," I agreed as Brady walked over to sit on the couch with me and pulled my feet into his lap, his hands caressing my thighs. "But I'm over it as your friend, but you and I won't ever happen again, I'm sorry."

"Okay," he whispered. "I understand, but I couldn't just go down without the only fight I can wage from a thousand miles away. You know I'll always love you."

"Me, too, Preston. At the end of the day, even with everything, it's true. I'm just *in* love with Brady," I emphasized, looking at Brady when I spoke those words and I saw a flash of relief cross his features in the dark room.

236

Preston sighed, deeply, on the other end. I could tell this conversation hadn't gone the way he expected. He'd wanted me to say 'I love you, too' and 'Of course I'll marry you when you get home.' Maybe I was a bitch for saying this to him, knowing he was going overseas in a few weeks, but I couldn't give him false hope anymore. We both knew it would happen sooner or later. We'd been each other's back up for far too long and it was time to get off the carousel. I, actually, surprised myself by being the one to get off first.

"I'll write you when I get where I'm going, okay?" he said. "But guard duty is almost over, and I need to do one more parameter check."

"Okay, Preston. I'm sorry," I frowned, feeling guilt that I didn't deserve at his sunken demeanor.

"I know, me, too," he told me before ending the call.

"Does Preston make a habit of calling after two in the morning?" Brady asked when I threw my phone onto the coffee table beside me.

"Yes."

"Oh."

"It's always been our thing," I shrugged, not knowing how to explain the conversation I just had to Brady. "But I wouldn't worry about it happening again."

"Because you told him you're in love with me?" he asked, confused.

"Yes," I nodded, pulling my feet from his lap and getting up from the couch. "I'm sorry I woke you," I continued, grabbing his hand to pull him back to bed.

"It's okay," he dismissed, following me. "How can you be sure he won't call again?"

"Because I just broke the cycle," I stated, diving head first back into my bed and cuddling up to Brady.

"Okay," he said, pulling me closer as we both drifted back to sleep. I knew he'd have more questions for me when we woke up, but I wasn't sure I was ready to lay everything out for him. I was so ashamed at how I'd let my guard down with Preston all those years ago and I didn't want Brady to look at me like I really was a slut. I was still surprised that he didn't think that after knowing how many guys I'd been with.

**

BRADY

"Because I just broke the cycle," Lucy's words echoed in my head when I woke the next morning in her empty bed. Her side was long cold as her alarm clock told me I had about thirty minutes until her last class would end. Scrubbing my hands over my face and exhaling a deep sigh, I pulled myself up and put my boxers and t-shirt back on, traipsing through her apartment toward her front door to have my morning cigarette.

I wished I could get the words to fade away, but there was something about them still bugging me. If I'd woken up to her sparkling blue eyes, giving me some sort of reassurance, I'd probably be over it by now. I hadn't, though. I'd woken up alone, my last thoughts ricocheting off each other and building in my head. I couldn't believe how hard it was to talk myself down when she wasn't here.

In the distance, I heard a faint ringing when I walked back into the apartment. My cell phone.

"Hello?" I answered without checking my caller id.

"Stop freaking out," Lucy's voice came over the phone, instantly calming me. "I meant what I said last night."

Exhaling deeply, I ran a hand through my too long brown hair. "I know, but you've gotta admit, it's a lot, Lucy," I told her.

"What do you mean?" she asked, her voice sounding like she was on edge, going up a few notes.

"We'll talk about it when you get here, okay?"

"I'll be there soon, I'm just leaving campus," she sighed.

"See you soon, then," I answered, throwing myself backward on her bed, so that I was laying width-wise on the queen sized bed. I was trying not to spiral, and feel like an insecure girl about all of this, but Parker's words were now echoing along with hers. This was her cycle with Preston and she said she'd ended it, but had she really? What if he was still holding out hope that she'd only changed the game not ended it completely? What if he saw it as a challenge?

I was still cycling through all of the 'what if's' when I heard the door open fifteen minutes later.

"I stopped by Antonio's and picked us up something to eat," she called out, and I heard the sound of a bag hitting her table.

"Good," I said, moving to the dining area to join her. I wanted to pull her into my arms, but I needed to talk to her first. The look on my face must've given away my thoughts because her eyes did a slow perusal over my face, before biting her lip to suppress a frown.

"What's a lot?" she asked again, bring us back to the topic at hand.

239

"This," I answered, simply.

"Us? Preston? What?" she probed, putting an impatient hand on her hip.

"Not us, us is fine," I joked, grabbing her hand, finally pulling her into my arms. "It's them I'm worried about," I confessed.

"Them?" she asked, confusion blooming in her eyes.

"Preston, Carter, Adam, Eric, Trevor," I listed. "Need I go on?"

"No," she shook her head and rolled her eyes at me. "No need to go on, and no need to be worried either," she dismissed my confession. "If I wanted to be with them, I'd be with them. I wouldn't let us stop me," she shrugged, which was absolutely the wrong thing to say to me in that moment. I stepped away from her so fast, her mouth dropped open in shock.

"Please tell me you didn't mean that the way you just said it," I growled, stalking back and forth in her living room, trying to calm my anger. She'd basically just told me that she'd cheat on me, if she didn't care about me as much as she did. What would happen if that changed?

"I just meant that if I wanted something with them, you and I would be casual, Brady," she tried to clarify, folding her arms over her chest and popping her hip out in anger. "The fact that you have a fucking key to my apartment and I *let* you sleep next to me should be enough to know that I'm with you, and only you."

"What's that mean? I've had a key since almost day one, and I've seen a few guys sleep over," I threw back, her words not quite registering the way she was probably meaning them. I know she was trying to calm me down, but it felt like she might be digging a hole instead. Shit, this was going to be our first real fight, wasn't it?

"I asked if you could handle my past, Brady," she glowered. "I won't have it thrown back in my face," her voice was now deceptively calm.

"Look," I said, closing my eyes and throwing my head back in exasperation. "Is there any way we can have this conversation, calmly, outside so I can smoke?" I asked, knowing it was the only way I would be able to actually listen to what she was really trying to tell me.

"Sure," she clipped out, barreling to the door behind me and leaned against the railing opposite the make-shift ashtray.

"I'm sorry," I sighed after pulling in my first drag, and I was finally able to organize her words in my head and see them for what they were. Not her looking for an out or an excuse to cheat, but trying to show me how much she really was in this with me. "I didn't mean to throw your past in your face. It's just…this is hard."

"No shit," she snorted. "I know the issues with Preston are a lot to take. I get that," she said, softly. "But for a long time, I wondered if he was going to be the only happily ever after I got."

"What do you mean?" I looked at her, perplexed, wondering how she'd instantly gone from the angry, confident woman fighting with me in her dining room, to this broken girl trying to explain her fucked up relationship with her high school sweetheart to me, again.

"Well," she started, taking a deep breath. "You know I grew up without my dad around really, right?" she asked, looking up at me. After I nodded in confirmation, she continued. "Watching my mom and dad ship me back and forth for so long, I decided to give up."

241

"What does that mean?"

"It means, I stopped watching Disney movies when I was twelve, Brady. I knew no one had assigned a prince to come and rescue me. That was more than evident by the time I turned nine. So why should I keep watching something I had no hope for? How sad is that? Knowing at twelve that no one could ever really fall in love with me? That I wasn't enough for my parents to always be around, and they are supposed to always be there, you know? How could I expect someone who didn't *have* to be there to stay? I knew I wasn't destined to dance to 'Fade Into You' while some guy poured his heart out of me like in some teen romance or drama on the WB."

"That's ridiculous, Lucas. You see that now, don't you?" I asked, stubbing out my cigarette and moving to pull her back into my arms.

"I figured that Preston was going to be the closest thing I got to true love, because even though he left, he always came back, you know?" she said, resisting my embrace.

"Lucas," I called, imploring her to meet my gaze. When she did, I pulled her lips to mine and kissed her hard, spearing my tongue into her mouth and beseeching her to join in. Finally, her tongue tentatively touched mine and I almost shouted to the heavens in relief before I pulled back again. "I'm *in* love with you. I want to be with you," I told her, watching her try to mentally pull away from my words again. Desperate for her to understand me completely, I grabbed her face in my hands and forced her to look into my eyes. "When I asked you if we could get married in Vegas like Becca and Xander, I may have sounded like I was joking, but I wasn't," I leveled with her, as her mouth dropped in shock. "I'm going to marry you. I might be a

242

little frustrated with everything, but I'm in this for the long haul."

"Okay," she whispered.

"I was just making sure you were on board with the plan, too, because it seems like I'm having to battle an awful lot of exes for someone who never thought she deserved a happily ever after," I smirked.

"It's not like that with them," she tried to shake her head against my hold. "It's more about having constant access to my panties, and you are hindering that."

"You don't wear panties, Lucas," I joked, trying to keep my jealousy in check that they knew how amazing Lucy was in bed, too.

"It's a metaphor, Brady, don't be facetious," she rolled her eyes again.

"What were you talking about last night with Preston?" I asked, bravely, more of her words filtering through my head. "Something about a tape?"

"It's nothing," she dismissed, pulling her face from my hands and heading back into her apartment.

"Bullshit," I called after her, following her toward our take out.

"It is bullshit, but I don't want to talk about it right now," she admitted, pulling foil rounds from the bag and handing me my lunch. "I don't want you to hate Preston."

"It's too late for that."

"Well, I still want to be friends with him, and if I tell you…let's just say that won't happen," she said, sitting down opposite me at the card table and digging in to the Italian sub she'd got for herself.

"Hmmm, I'm thinking that's going to happen anyway, but I'll let it go," I said, conceding to her desire to stop talking about her ex. "For now, but I reserve the right to ask again in the very near future."

"Thank you," she whispered before going back to her lunch.

CHAPTER 26

BRADY

After I laid everything out for Lucy, I expected her to start spiraling, but she surprised me. She accepted my declaration in stride and we seemed to grow even closer. It seemed the knowledge that neither of us saw our relationship as a passing fancy, or whatever, settled us.

I wished all of my decisions that involved giving people a chance worked out as well as my decision to date Lucy. Unfortunately, that wasn't meant to be, because three weeks after Xander talked to me, Becca had started her program, but still hadn't located a part-time job, nor had she been keeping the house as clean as she promised it would be when she gushed her thanks at Xander and I agreeing to let her start her medical assisting program full-time.

The fact that she didn't have a job, coupled with Xander and me covering her share of the rent and utilities, should have meant that she had virtually no money to her name. However, at least once a week, she came home with her arms weighed down with bags from the mall and bookstores. She told us her father had sent her money, but insisted she spend it on herself and stuff she needed for school and not to spend it on her bills. He dubbed it 'fun money' in celebration that she'd found something she wanted to do with her life.

I felt cheated, and the only saving grace was that she *wasn't* home when Xander and I were sleeping during the day, that is when I actually spent the night in the apartment. She wasn't waiting up for us at night either, since she had to be in school early. It was nice. I was happy that she seemed to be taking the schooling seriously, which was something else I'd been worried about.

Conversely, Flynn was sleeping in my closet again (insert obvious joke here) three times a week because of his new job and because of Becca's unemployment, he'd decided to kick in more than his fair share of part-time rent. Therefore, it could be argued that we weren't feeling the pinch as much as we should have, but Becca was definitely getting into freeloading territory, since neither Becca nor Flynn contributed to the household food budget. Flynn wasn't eating at the apartment, but Becca seemed to blow through a week's worth of food in a couple of days now that she was in school. That was the worst, wanting a snack before work, and having the cupboards bare. I might as well be at Lucy's but, at least, at her house, there is always fish sticks and cookie dough.

"We've gotta talk to Becca, man," Xander groaned, flopping down on the sectional.

"I fucking told you this would happen," I rolled my eyes, leaning my head back against the top of the couch and looking at the popcorn ceiling.

"You were right. Anytime she actually does the work she promised to do, it's like she expects us to throw her a ticker tape parade or something. And even worse, she's gotten so freaking clingy now that we barely see each other," he groaned. "Good news, though, I reconnected with this chick I used to know. We've got a date on Friday," he grinned at what would probably become his "new strange" as he'd put it.

"You're killing me," I whined. "She's never here anymore, but this is going to make the times she is here unbearable, man."

"She'll be fine," he dismissed.

"No," I said, sitting up and staring him down. "She's going to spend every fucking second you aren't around drilling me for information. '*Why doesn't he love me? I thought we were going to get married! My life is over! Do you think I can get him to sleep with me again?* '" I imitated.

"She doesn't do that," he shook his head.

"No?" I laughed and pulled out my cell phone. After dialing Lucy, I put the phone on speaker.

"Hello?" Lucy answered.

"Hey baby, how's it going?" I asked, not wanting to jump right into the reason for my call and watched Xander roll his eyes and cross his ankle over the opposite knee to recline on the couch.

"Okay, you caught me headed home from school," I could hear the smile in her voice.

"Awesome, then you have time to help me out with something," I announced. "I've got you on speaker and Xander is here."

"Okay?" she said, sounding confused.

"He just told me he wants to break up—"

"It's not breaking up," Xander yelled toward the phone. "She's not my girlfriend. I'm just going to stop sleeping with her."

"Awww, man!" Lucy grumbled. "Why would you do that to me? Why? I thought we were friends!"

"Um, we are," Xander told her.

"Then suck it up, man! Take one for the team! At least until I take my last final next week," she coached.

"Is she really going to be that bad?" he asked, disbelieving.

"She's probably going to be worse," she told him. "She's still convinced you are planning to take her to Vegas," Lucy sighed.

"Thanks for your help, baby," I said. "I'll let you get back to it."

"Okay," she said, now sounding less cheerful than she had when we'd started the call. "I love you."

"I love you, too," I replied, ending the call, my eyes bugging out at Xander to portray the unmistakable message of 'I told you so.'

"Yeah, yeah, yeah, whatever," he mumbled. "But we need to sit her down this weekend and talk to her about the work she isn't doing on the house."

"I agree. I'm sick of never having food in the house right after we go shopping."

"Me too. Plus, I'm sick of all the new shit she keeps buying from the money her dad gave her, and that she still tries to get me to pay for her car payment. How about we just pick up a few things for our kids on the weekends and eat out the rest of the time?" he suggested.

"Eating out gets old, but I'd rather do that then spend $100 on groceries that I don't get to eat and have to go out anyway," I agreed, reluctantly.

"Maybe if we don't have any food in the house, it'll remind her to get a fucking job," Xander said, harshly. "Or maybe that she needs to use the money her dad keeps sending on her own food rather than bullshit cheetah print throw pillows that match nothing in the apartment."

248

"One can only hope anyway," I murmured, knowing that Becca could be completely dense at picking up social cues. Lucy said she picked them up, she usually decided to ignore them, though.

**

The starve-out took two weeks before she started to complain about a lack of food in the house while a plethora of fast food bags started to show up in the trash can. We knew she wasn't *really* starving It could also have to do with Xander finally telling her they were over and sleeping on the sectional until after Becca went to school and on weekends.

I wasn't surprised when Becca announced that Friday after she got home from school that she wanted to have a house meeting on Saturday morning before I went to pick up Taylor. Groaning inwardly, I shot a look at Xander, trying to communicate our agenda silently. She made a huge deal when the house was clean about keeping it that way, but we actually paid rent. It wasn't like we were slobs; we didn't intentionally make messes we knew we weren't going to have to clean up. We did what we'd always done; she just wasn't timely about picking up after us, so things got out of hand quickly. There were three and a half adults living in a 1000 square foot apartment, plus weekends, where we could have upwards of four kids and my girlfriend, depending on whether Xander's ex let his kids sleep over.

"Good, you guys are here," Becca breathed out a sigh and sat down on the edge of the sectional the following morning.

"Um, yeah, you called the meeting and we agreed," Xander looked at her like she was crazy.

"I just have a couple of requests," she said, softly, fidgeting with the cushion. "First, um, I'm not going to be able to clean like I have been, my coursework is so much—"

"That's not going to work, Becca," I said, cutting off her flow. "You don't clean enough now for the rent and utilities that we are covering for you."

"That's another thing I wanted to talk to you about," she heaved a deep breath. "It's just that I take the time to clean the kitchen and living room, and you guys only say 'thanks, Becca' or 'good job' to me when I ask for it. I'm kind of feel like you guys only see me as the maid."

I knew she wanted us to refute her statement, to say that we appreciated what she was doing, but her not working was costing us an additional $200 a month each, which is about what hiring a weekly cleaning lady would cost, and she wasn't even doing that much work. So I wasn't surprised when Xander and I answered her simultaneously, "You are!"

I wanted to give Xander a fist bump to celebrate the fact that we were so in sync on this issue, but now was not the time.

"But I'm going to school! You guys have to cut me some slack here!" she screeched. "Not to mention, we never have any food in the house, so Flynn has been giving me money to eat, I found out today that my car is getting repossessed because you guys told me you wouldn't help with that, and my cell phone was turned off," she listed her complaints.

"Going back to school without a job was your idea, Becca," Xander reminded her. "No one forced you to put yourself in this situation. In fact, I seem to remember there was even a part-time option for schooling, and you didn't want to take it. Besides, why haven't you been using the money your dad has been sending?"

"I have to pay my own car payment and phone bill, not to mention I have to buy food for myself and Taylor when she's here," I picked up. "I told you when you decided to do this, I already had a child, I wasn't adopting you."

"But you don't understand what it's like," she wailed. "I've got homework every night, and I'm in class all day. I don't have time to clean except for the weekends, and I want to spend what little free time I have with my friends and resting, not picking up after the two of you and your children. And you know that the money my dad sends isn't to cover my bills, it's for things I need for school."

"Hmmm, I didn't want to bring this up, Becca, but Lucas goes to school full time, works full time and still has time to keep her apartment clean. Plus, I'm not sure the purple shag rug you bought for your bedroom constitutes a 'school expense,'" I pointed out. The answering scowl on Becca's face told me she didn't appreciate being compared to Lucy.

"Besides, this was the agreement you made, Becca," Xander said, leveling her with a menacing glare. "If you can't abide by it, you need to find a new place to live."

"You can't do that! My name is on the lease," she countered, loudly, then after a beat, she sighed deeply again, this time in defeat. "Fine, you win. I'll do better, I promise."

"Okay, but this is your last chance," I said, calmly, not sure if I was buying the 180 she'd made in the span of fifteen seconds. "If things don't improve with regards to the cleaning and you don't have a weekend job to justify it, we'll give you 30 days to move out. There are ways to get you off of the lease, and I'm sure telling them you are a mooching freeloader will work."

"Too mean, Brady," Becca growled.

"You're right, but you need to be mindful of everything we've done for you these last few months. We'll buy a little bit more food than we have been if we can start to see an improvement. I promise."

"Are you picking up tricks from Lucas, Brady? This sounds like her words, and Flynn's name is still on the lease, too, so he'll fight you."

"I'll deal with Flynn if the time comes, but in the meantime, I'm only asking you to hold up your end of the agreement the three of us made last month," I reminded her and Xander nodded.

"Whatever," she mumbled before stalking back to her bedroom and slamming the door.

"Well, that went better than I expected," Xander announced and headed for the balcony, cigarette already in hand. That sounded like the best idea he'd ever had. Grabbing my own pack, I moved outside to join him. I was pretty sure that hadn't gone well at all, I just needed to wait for the other shoe to drop.

**

LUCAS

Sunday after work was my monthly date with my mom. As usually, I was excited/scared about it. I loved my mom, but she was definitely a hand full. I got my ability to speak my mind from her. Well, the lack of a socially acceptable filter part anyway. Although it annoyed me sometimes, I loved that my mom said exactly what was on her mind. You never had to guess her feelings because she'd flat out tell you.

She and my dad hadn't been together as a couple since before I was born, plus they lived in different states since I was a baby. I didn't look anything like her, well, maybe more now that my hair was black. She was shorter than me, her boobs were smaller, her eyes were green, and her skin was this nice golden color. Basically, she was my opposite, except for my hips. I definitely got her childbearing hips, which was probably the only thing I hadn't wanted.

I wasn't an only child, but I wasn't raised around my siblings much either since they lived with my dad. My mom had always been my best friend, since most times it was just the two of us. She always made it work though, and I never seemed like a burden or a mistake to her, even though my birth was the reason she had a GED instead of a diploma and had to start at the bottom where ever she worked. For the last ten years, though, she'd been working as a bank manager and was finally in a good place, financially. She was my hero.

I always felt guilty for the dread that I felt at our lunch dates, though. She sacrificed so much for me, right? The least I could do was have dinner with her when she wanted to see me, but the aforementioned bluntness always had me on edge. I never knew what she was going to bring up, so I wasn't surprised when in the middle of our orange chicken and fried rice from our favorite mall-based Chinese restaurant she said:

"Your grandma was always wrong about what it takes to keep a man happy."

"Okay?" I looked up at her, confused. She and my step-dad had been married for years, but we'd never really

253

gone 'in-depth' like this the way she liked to know every single detail about my relationships.

"I'm serious, Lucas," she said with the most severe look I'd ever seen on her face.

"I know," I nodded.

"Then don't look at me like you are waiting for the punch line," she scolded.

"I wasn't, mom. I promise. Tell me what grandma was always wrong about," I cheered, leaning forward in my plastic food court seat.

"Mom always used to say 'Miranda, the best way to snag a man and keep him, is to be a good homemaker,'" she started. "She told me if I was the best cook and could keep the house looking brand new, I'd never want for a husband. And we both know how that turned out."

"Mom—"

"What I'm trying to say is that the homemaker thing is secondary to what she didn't teach me," my mom said, a devious smile lifting the corners of her lips.

"And that would be?" I asked, already getting the hint that I probably shouldn't have encouraged this topic and I was about to be mortified.

"Blow jobs," she whispered as if it were a better kept secret than the KFC recipe. My mouth dropped open, reflexively, at her words. I was glad I wasn't taking a drink or had food in my mouth, because I was pretty sure it would've ended in a spit take. Taking in my reaction, she laughed. "I'm serious, Lucas. Cooking and cleaning are all well and good, but if you can suck a man so dry he can't walk, he will never leave you."

"I don't even want to know how you figured this out," I chuckle, uncomfortably.

"Then I won't tell you, but if you are doing what you should be doing with Brady, I should have a new son and grandbaby in no time," she nodded, sharply.

"We've been dating for just over three months, mom," I refuted. "Isn't it a little soon for that? I'm not even twenty-two yet."

"The time doesn't matter, Lucas. That boy is smitten with you and I don't want to see you muck it up with some society-based timeframe," she wagged a finger at me. "I swear, for a girl who seems to care very little about what image she projects to the world, you are completely traditional in so many other things. It must be something you get from your dad," she mumbled, going back to her lunch. After the uncomfortableness of how I could keep Brady around by giving him a good 'mouthy'- which I didn't want to tell my *mother* I was already quite skilled at- the rest of the dinner passed in relative peace, but as soon as I was safely behind the wheel of my truck, I pulled my phone out and dialed. I couldn't keep this hilarity to myself for a moment longer.

"Oh my GOD! You aren't going to believe what my mom just said at dinner," I rushed out as soon as I heard the call connect. I hadn't been able to get ahold of him all weekend, he and his mother had taken Taylor up north to visit his grandparents and cell reception there was non-existent.

"What did she just say, trader?" Becca's voice snarled through the phone.

"Why are you answering Brady's phone?" I asked, even though it wasn't entirely uncommon, seeing as they were roommates.

"Oh, we were hanging out in his room after he took Taylor home," she said, with a hint of bitchiness and blasé-ness that I hated. It was like she was in on a secret that she knew would destroy me. "He's asleep now," she sang, before holding the phone down to let me hear the snores of the person in bed with her, presumably my boyfriend. "Must've worn him out or something," she giggled. "I didn't know you guys had broken up, you should've warned me."

"We didn't," I deadpanned, trying to keep my anger in check.

"Oops!" she exclaimed before hanging up the phone. My heart dropped to my toes and shattered as I struggled to focus enough to make it back to my apartment in one piece. Was she serious? Had she slept with Brady while I was having dinner with my mother? Why had he slept with her? Had they been drinking? Did something happen this weekend? Had he found out the truth about the tape and was disgusted with me?

Or was our relationship just a ploy to get her back? He told me he loved me, that he wanted to marry me, but I'd been constantly pushed over for other girls, so it wouldn't surprise me if Brady had done the same. If that's all I was to him, why did he make me fall in love with him to? Becca was a vindictive person, so could this be a ploy to come between Brady and I?

I wanted answers, but I couldn't think straight enough to demand them now. Besides, if I called back, Becca would probably just answer again, and then I would have to cry. I didn't like crying over boys. They weren't worthy of my tears. Regardless of the intention, I needed to hear the truth from Brady, so that I could rip his balls off and move on.

CHAPTER 27

LUCAS

A few hours later, the feel of a solid body sliding in behind me brought all my senses to attention. Rolling over, cautiously, I found Brady trying to pull me closer.

"What the fuck are you doing here?" I asked, jumping out of my bed.

"Um? It's Sunday?" Brady shrugged. "I know I didn't call, but I figured our plans hadn't changed."

"How could you do that to me?" I wailed, too tired and upset to be able to speak rationally, the wounds too fresh for him to be acting like nothing happened.

"I'm sorry, I left my phone at the apartment. I knew I wasn't going to get any reception at my grandparents," he apologized.

"Likely excuse," I rolled my eyes. "You need to leave," I told him, coldly, motioning toward the door.

"What's going on?" Brady asked, finally getting out of my bed and coming over to face me. "Why are you so mad?"

"*WHY AM I SO MAD?!*" I screeched. "I called while you were napping, Brady. Becca told me what you two did. I feel so stupid," I moved away from him again, hugging myself.

"What Becca and I--? What are you talking about, Lucy?" Brady looked at me, seeming genuinely confused by my anger. Taking another step back, I decided to start at the beginning.

"Where were you tonight?" I asked.

"I had dinner at my dad's after I dropped off Taylor since I was already in the area, and then I went to my brother's to check out a new game he just picked up," he explained. "Time must've gotten away with me, because when I looked up, it was after eleven, and I didn't have my phone to call you," he continued. "After our talk with Becca yesterday, the house has been too angsty, so I decided to come straight here instead of stopping off to grab it. Obviously, that was a mistake," he finished, sitting down on my bed.

"Oh," I said, defeated, not sure what to believe, but I was leaning toward Brady because Becca had a tendency to lash out and make up stupid shit when she felt wronged. I'd forgotten that they'd planned a house meeting for Saturday morning where the boys were going to lay down the law on her lack of follow through on their agreement. "Becca said you guys hooked up," I confessed, looking down at my dingy carpeting, ashamed that I believed her when Brady busted up laughing. "It's not funny, Brady," I said with a scowl.

"Yes, it is, Lucas," he laughed. "It has to be, or I'm going to get very, very angry," he said, grabbing my phone from my nightstand and dialing.

"Lucy, I told you we were sleeping," Becca's annoyed voice answered. Brady had obviously put the call on speaker.

"Are we, Becca? Are we sleeping?" Brady asked, his voice capable of freezing over a hot tub.

"Brady," she said, her voice now full of surprise.

"What are you doing answering my phone, Becca?"

"I needed to arrange a ride to school tomorrow and Xander was out," she started. "You left your phone on the couch, so I borrowed it."

258

"That doesn't explain why you are *answering* it," he graveled out. "Why are you answering it and telling Lucas lies, Becca."

"Oh, come on, Brady," Becca dismissed. "I was joking around. I saw it was Lucy, so I answered it and messed with her. Flynn even provided the snoring for me. I mean, there is no way I thought she'd believe you'd cheated on her. We were playing around."

"Then why are you answering it right now?" The silence on the other end spoke volumes. Becca had been caught, she knew she'd been caught, now she was just forming some sort of indignant rebuttal as to why this wasn't her fault. Before she could start whining, crying or yelling, Brady continued, "You know, I don't care, just put my phone in my bedroom and leave it the fuck alone." Ending the calling, he stood from my bed and pulled his cigarettes from their place on my dresser.

"How could you believe I would do that to you, Lucas?" Brady asked when I joined him outside a few minutes later.

"I'm sorry," I apologized. "I know better than to just take what Becca says at face value, but after lunch with my mom, everything was just ugh in my head, the fact that I could hear someone in her bed, and it just hit me wrong," I tried to explain, but knew I wasn't making any sense.

"You're going to have to translate that from Lucas to English for me," Brady said, confirming he had no clue how to decipher that gibberish.

"Ugh," I groaned, leaning against the railing outside my apartment. "I had lunch with my mom and for some reason, I was feeling vulnerable when I tried to call you. Becca fed on that insecurity, with the scenario she presented. And stupid, stupid me, bought into it because it was easier than fighting her in that moment, I guess. Besides, I never feel like I'm good enough for you, so, of course, you'd leave me, too."

"What do we need to do to ensure this *misunderstanding* never happens again?" Brady asked, taking a long drag from his cigarette and giving me his most chastising look. I know he's pointing out my obvious mistake, because thinking about it then, I felt stupid.

"It won't, Brady," I waved off. "I shouldn't have let it happen this time. I know you aren't that guy."

"You are right, I'm not that guy," he confirmed, stamping out his cigarette and grabbing onto my arms to force me to look at him. "What we are building is more than she's ever had, she knows that, Lucas. She's mad at Xander and me, and this is how she knows to lash out."

"I know, believe me, I've seen Becca go to work on destroying everything someone loves just because they have something she wants," I rolled my eyes, exasperated with myself over my stupid behavior. "I am usually not this trusting when she's telling me things like this, but she did make out with a few of my exes in high school. She pursued them openly a couple of times, throwing it in my face when she finally got one of them to date her. I just...she's..." I trailed off, not knowing what to say anymore.

"Then we communicate, fight fire with knowledge and being completely open with each other, okay?" he asked, his steel blue eyes entirely focused on me.

"Okay," I agreed, looking down at my feet.

"Good, because that's the only way you and I are going to work. I've told you, I'm in this for the long haul. You need to start believing it," he smiled, grabbing my hand and pulling me toward my door again. "Now, I think you need to apologize to me, and I have just the way to do it."

"I'm sorry," I frowned. "I feel like such a dumbass, but you are right. I'm in this with you, I promise. And you know, my mom told me the best way to keep a man is to know how to give a good beej," I joked, following along behind him.

"Then you don't have to worry about me ever going anywhere," he smirked. "Now, get in your bedroom, get naked and get on your knees, wench," he said, placing a sound slap on my ass as I moved past him to do just that. "You've got some groveling to do."

"Yes, sir," I said, mockingly, as I moved to follow his instructions. I couldn't be more relieved to be wrong, even though I needed to work harder on being more trusting of the man who'd shown me nothing but absolute loyalty over the last two plus months. He deserved it and more from me.

**

BRADY

When I went back to my apartment the next day, I wanted to bring my wrath down on Becca's shoulders. I knew she wouldn't be home, and I'd have to continue to stew until Friday. Becca would try to deflect the blame to Lucy again. I knew this, she'd play it off like it was all a big joke and she hadn't tried to ruin my relationship.

"We've gotta kick her out, man!" I vented my frustrations to Xander, who was, luckily, still not back in her panties, even though her recent behavior bordered on obsessive in trying to get one of us to fuck her again. I

261

think it was more out of the desperation to not get kicked out than anything else though.

"I agree," he said, blowing out a harsh breath and running a hand through his too long brown hair. He'd recently shaved the sides, so only the top was long now. "I brought Kate over to chill yesterday and Becca threw a jealous tantrum. *Then* she "accidentally" walked out of her bedroom in her underwear, saying she didn't realize that Kate was still there, but it didn't stop her from sitting on the couch next to her and telling her about how she's been with a woman, tried to get Kate to agree to a three-way!" Xander rolled his eyes. "I'll admit, it would've been hot, if I wanted to fuck Becca again. If she weren't so fucking crazy, I think Kate would've gone for it too."

"Are we sure Becca isn't on drugs?" I asked, dubiously, completely dumbfounded to hear how busy Becca was the day before.

"I'm sure," Xander laughed, "but I am questioning whether or not she needs to be medicated, maybe in a padded room, where she spends most of her day hugging herself."

"I agree," I howled, joining in his laughter, because if I didn't, the whole thing would be just too tragic. I knew that our conversation would sound overly harsh on Becca to the outsider. I mean, both Xander and I had a relationship with her, she'd been our friend, but it only goes to show how far she'd stretched and taken advantage of our hospitality. We had to draw the line at overtly and maliciously trying to ruin our respective relationships.

"But things are okay, with Lucas?" Xander asked, his expression serious.

"Yeah, if I hadn't gone over that night, if I'd decided to go back to the apartment instead, we might be having a

262

different conversation. Something happened with Preston that broke her trust, Xander. I'm fucking sure of it, but she won't talk about it."

"Preston? You think?" he asked, scratching the back of his neck.

"I can't say for sure, but it has something to do with some video tape? I have to figure it out before he gets back though, because I want to be over it," I confessed.

"Why's that?" Xander laughed.

"Because I have a feeling she wouldn't be too happy if I kicked his ass," I frowned. "Much like I wish Becca wasn't a girl right now, so I could do the same to her."

"You sure that Lucy won't?"

"I'm sure. Lucy wants to, but she also knows it's her friend's defense mechanism and that she was lashing out for attention. Lucy says beating her ass would be a form of giving her what she wants."

"True," Xander nodded, sagely. "Bad attention is better than being ignored."

"I don't give a shit what she wants. This isn't about giving her attention, negative or otherwise. She needs to know what she did wasn't cool," I growled, shaking my head. I couldn't wait for Friday.

**

I'd fumed all week over what to say to Becca, but all my well laid plans to rage at Becca went out the window on Friday when Xander and I realized that Sunday was Mother's Day. I scowled at the thought that I'd overlooked it, because I'd been so focused on my bitch of a roommate. To top it all off, our apartment looked like shit, because she still wasn't holding up her end of the bargain. We did have a brand new set of towels and a pair of zebra print four inch heels, though, courtesy of her latest check from her father. I felt like she was thumbing her nose at our generosity because she felt slighted.

Even though we needed to talk to her again, I think we were both a little gun shy, knowing what her reaction would be and getting a better look at what kind of emotional terrorism she was capable of. So after a short morning nap, we ended up at the mall, but I still had no idea what I was going to get my mother. I was usually on top of this stuff, and it bothered me that I was letting Becca get to me like this.

After Xander found something for his ex from 'his kids', a display caught my eye and I gravitated toward it. I knew there was nothing in this store that I could get my mom, but something told me I needed to look anyway.

"Why are we going in here?" my friend asked. "I didn't think you had the kind of money for this place. I thought we were going to look for one of those dolls your mom collects."

"We are, but something keeps telling me that I need to look in here first," I said, looking over the jewels shining at me from the lighted cases.

As soon as I saw it, I knew the real reason we were in here. Sucking in a deep breath, I backed away from the most perfect ring I'd ever seen. The ring made me feel like there was only one place it belonged, and I'd never felt more like a girl than I did at that moment.

"Shit, man. I didn't know things were that serious," Xander laughed as he looked into the case I was all but running away from. Flashes of it perched on Lucy's finger raced through my head. I felt dizzy and short of breath at the sight of my future. The muted lights of the store felt hot

264

on my skin as I sucked in deep breaths. I had to get out of that fucking store.

Backing out of the store, I looked for the nearest mall exit and stalked my way to the door. After I was safely in the courtyard, I pulled a cigarette from my pack and lit it. After two or three drags, Xander finally joined me outside, but didn't say anything until I finished my cigarette. I was happy he knew I needed to get a shit load of nicotine in my body before I could process what just happened.

"That was a pretty big freak out for what looked like a normal every day ring, Brady," Xander joked. "It wasn't even a diamond."

"I know," I shook my head. "Lucy wouldn't want a diamond engagement ring. That ring would be perfect for her. She'd love it."

"Oh, well, shit!" he laughed. "I *really* didn't know things were *that* serious. I mean, I knew you loved her, and cared about her, and that eventually this might be in the future. But now?"

"I didn't know either, until fifteen minutes ago when I saw that fucking ring man," I said, pulling another cigarette from my pack. "I was on board with it being an eventuality, hell, I was on board with it being somewhat soon, like in the next couple of years, but I had no idea it was going to be a now thing."

"I thought you said it would freak her out if you went too fast?" Xander brought up, reminding me of why I needed to be extra careful with Lucy.

"I know, but after everything with Preston, I told her I was marrying her and she just said 'okay.' She didn't freak out, she didn't run, she just accepted it as the truth," I confessed, taking a deep drag and blowing it out slowly.

"Then what in the fuck are you waiting for? Let's go buy that ring!" Xander said, grabbing the butt from my hand and flinging it to the ground. With a sigh, I followed him, questioning my sanity the entire way. Was I asking for the end of my relationship? I said I was marrying her, but I don't think she was expecting the question to come now, or even soon. Was I ready for this kind of step? We'd only been together like three months, was that too soon to propose? Echoing my thoughts, Xander turned to me before we got to the store, "Look, just because you buy the ring, it doesn't mean you have to propose tomorrow. You said it's perfect for her, so don't you want to already have the perfect ring in your possession, just in case?"

Fuck, he made a really good point. Buying the ring didn't mean this was a foregone conclusion. I didn't have to ask her today or tomorrow or even next month. With that thought crystallizing in my brain, I was able to walk back into the jewelry store.

"How much for this ring?" Xander asked the woman behind the display.

"This ring is part of our Mother's day special, so it's half off today," the saleswoman explained, completely selling me on blowing my savings, down to the fact that the display ring was Lucy's size. Something I only knew because I'd helped her pick out a mother's ring for her mom's birthday last month and she told me they wore the same size. After going through all the warranty and return information, I was the owner of a beautiful ring I hoped to one day put on Lucy's finger.

Walking back into the apartment that afternoon, I went straight to our stash of vodka and poured myself a shot or five. Once my body was numb, I was finally able to process the fact that I really wanted a future with Lucy. Even though I'd been in a disaster of a marriage before, I still

266

wanted to take that risk with her. Only after coming to peace with my purchase was I able to find a great hiding spot for it in my bedroom. I couldn't chance Lucy coming across it before I was ready to ask the question.

CHAPTER 28

BRADY

In my infinite wisdom of trying to hide the ring from Lucas, I forgot about one thing… hiding it from Flynn, too. I knew I'd failed that mission when I woke up the following Saturday and he was sitting on the futon in my room that I used for Taylor's bed with the ring box on his knee. His hands were clasped on the cushions like he was stopping himself from shaking me awake.

"Hey, what are you doing?" I asked him, stretching my arms over my head.

"You guy have been together like three months and you are buying her jewelry? I know her birthday is in a couple weeks, but this is a little serious for that, don't you think?" he asked, his voice cold and emotionless. I knew he was on the brink of a blow up when he sounded that detached.

"Aren't you supposed to buy jewelry for your girlfriend?" I asked. "Especially for her birthday?" I challenged and watched a strange look come over Flynn's face before he stood from the futon, the ring box dropping to the ground at his feet.

"Holy shit, Brady, this isn't just a present, is it? It's a fucking engagement ring for that bitch!" he roared. "It all makes sense! Lucy doesn't like diamond," he pieced together.

"How do you know that?" I asked, my curiosity peaked that he would know my girlfriend's gemstone preferences.

"Don't get your panties in a wad," Flynn dismissed. "She's felt that way since high school and I have a good memory. There was something she always said," he said, looking up as if trying to remember, but it was too far from him.

"Promises made with diamonds aren't worth the shine of the stone, promises made with rubies show that you are willing to bleed to keep them," I quoted.

"You're just a game to her, a pit stop on her way back to Preston," Flynn told me. "This thing between you isn't real."

"It's more real than you could ever understand," I shook my head, grabbing the box from the floor and looking around for a new hiding place.

"I've seen her do this over and over, rope in some guy, seemingly fall in love, then when Preston's standing in front of her, begging her to come back, telling her he loves her, she just caves. She's not strong enough to not go back to him, that's why she's been single the last few years," Flynn explained, his voice still entirely too calm. I would've expected him to be in my face about this, it would've made his words easier to dismiss.

"He already tried to beg her back, she didn't go," I confessed, telling him more than I'd ever intended to share.

"He's not here; he's not looking into her eyes with that longing you can feel in their presence. It's fucking strong and it whips through the air until it fills every single corner."

"Not anymore," I said, weakly. "She loves me, and I'm not proposing tomorrow."

"I wish you could see this mistake for what it is," he sighed.

"I don't agree, Flynn," I frowned. "Now, if you'll excuse me, I have to go pick up my daughter and visit my family. I'd appreciate it if you didn't talk about what you found. I want it to be a surprise."

"Sure," he agreed, showing me that maybe my friend was in there somewhere. Somehow, though, I could see the end of our friendship coming, and I had a feeling that the Becca issues and my relationship with Lucas would be the final nail. He didn't want me to trust Lucy, but the way he protected Becca with blinders on was too much for me. Yet, there was something about what he'd just said about Lucy and Preston, something I thought I'd overcome that night he'd called her, but a nugget of insecurity took root. Would the outcome be different when he returned? *Had* it been easier to break the cycle over the phone to the point that it wasn't really over?

Doubts circled through me as I picked up my daughter and drove to my dad's house for a family barbeque. My dad had invited my mom and grandparents, so I had to try and get it together before I walked in. Taking in my mother's furrowed brows when she looked at me, I knew I hadn't been successful. One of my cousins shuffled my daughter down the hall to play and the rest of the family descended on me with questions.

"You look like you lost your best friend," Shiv said with a snort. "Although, if you did, that wouldn't be such a bad thing, Flynn isn't the best."

"What's going on, Brady? You look really deep in thought," my mom said, bringing me back from where I'd been for the last couple of hours.

"What do you think of Lucy?" I asked my mom, but everyone around us looked like they wanted to answer that question, too.

"She seems really good for you, Brady. You've been so attentive to Taylor, and I know it's because of her," my

270

mom answered. "I'd like to see the two of you get more serious."

"Me, too," my sister agreed.

"Eh," Celia said, a sour look on her face. I discounted her opinion because I knew she didn't really know Lucy, just her reputation.

"I'd hold off the seriousness until Preston gets back," my brother offered.

"Why the fuck does everyone bring up Preston?"

"Language, Brady," my mother scolded, nodding toward my grandparents.

"Sorry," I muttered before continuing. "She and I have talked about it and what they had is over," I tried to clarify.

"Yeah, sure," my brother snorted in disbelief.

"She said she can't trust him anymore, something about a video tape?" I shook my head at my brother, trying to get him to understand that I knew more about my relationship than he did.

"She knows about the video tape?" he asked, his face paling. "Well, that might change things," he nodded, his face turning from smug to thoughtful.

"*You* know about what ever this is?" I asked, dying to know what Preston had done to shatter Lucas' trust so wholly. She was a very forgiving person, but she seemed adamant that he couldn't be more than a friend because of this tape thing. In fact, it seemed like the average person might not have even offered to remain friends with him because of this incident.

"She didn't tell you?"

"No, can you? Because it seems pretty big." The family members surrounding us for this conversation seem

271

to volley their eyes back and forth at our exchange like it was a tennis match.

"If she hasn't told you, then no," he shut down. "It's not my story to tell. I'd definitely ask her though," he continued cryptically. "Make sure you get it out of her, it's important," he continued, confirming my suspicions.

"I bought her a ring, an engagement ring," I blurted out.

"Then I'd ask her about the tape sooner rather than later," Parker nodded, his mouth slightly ajar. Celia looked dumbstruck, and my mom and Shiv were trying to contain their grins at the news.

"You think it'll change my mind about wanting to marry her?" I asked, my brow furrowed that he wouldn't just tell me what this mysterious tape business was all about.

"I, honestly, don't know *how* you'll react, but knowing you, it might," he shrugged. "But you need to know for sure *before* you ask her to marry you. I can tell you that."

Scrubbing my hands over my face, I sighed, deeply and looked at my father's ceiling as my mom started to bombard me with more questions about the ring, if I was going to ask her father for permission, when I'd want to get married. It was so different from when I'd gotten married the first time when she tried to talk me out of it. Luckily, Taylor came to the rescue and distracted her enough that I could finally find some time to think.

Could Parker be right? Was there anything that Lucas could tell me about that video tape that would make me not want to be with her? That would tell me whether she was honest about stepping off the Preston carousel?

272

LUCAS

I was pleasantly surprised when Brady and Taylor showed up at my apartment that Saturday night with a box full of barbeque leftovers. I hated that my weekend work schedule kept me from being able to attend their family gatherings. Plus, with my desire to want to spend family time with Brady and Taylor, I'd even stopped hosting my parties, much to the chagrin of my regulars.

Brady's family seemed really close knit, and it was something I'd always wanted. Before Brady, I didn't mind working weekend mornings, even though I used to take one day off a month for party recovery purposes, finding someone to take over the shift was nearly impossible.

The look on Brady's face when I opened the door was pure determination, and frankly, it scared me a little bit. It reminded me of when he'd asked me about my relationship with Preston, and part of me wondered if he was finally going to bring up the one thing I'd asked him to let go of. I knew he wouldn't say anything until after we'd tucked Taylor in to bed, so I milked it for everything it was worth.

"Can't you read me one more story?" Taylor asked, after I'd finished giving her a bath and I'd read her three of the longest books we kept at my apartment.

"No, Taylor, it's bed time," Brady said, firmly, from behind me, even though I was going to cave and read a fourth.

"Okay, daddy," she said, smiling at her father sleepily as I tucked her into her bed on my couch. "Good night," she said, closing her eyes as I kissed her forehead and moved away from her so Brady could say good night.

"Night, baby," he said, kissing her cheek and ruffling her still wet hair as I turned off the living room light and headed toward my bedroom. Pulling sleep shorts and a tank top from my dresser, I started to get ready for bed as if I knew that Brady had something he needed to say. I wasn't sure if I was strong enough to tell him the whole truth, yet, but knowing that Taylor was asleep on my couch and he wouldn't want to wake her gave me the strength to be honest about the tape, if that was what he wanted to talk about.

When soft snores started to echo through the apartment, Brady finally made his way to my bedroom and stripped down to his boxers to join me in my bed.

"What's up?" I asked, looking over at him, his expression more contemplative then.

"Um, just thinking," he shook his head and settled back against his pillow. "Can I- um, can I ask you something?" he asked, looking uncomfortable.

"Of course," I encouraged, laying down beside him and turning on my side to look at him, brushing my newly re-dyed black hair from my eyes.

"Can you tell me about Preston and the tape?" he asked, confirming my suspicions. I knew he'd wanted to ask for a while.

Taking a deep breath, I went over the story in my head. I knew that he'd hate Preston after I was finished, but part of me wondered if he'd hate me, too. I'd let it happen. I hadn't paid attention to my surroundings, and, frankly, I'm not sure I'd have stopped even if I knew about the tape, because I needed the reassurance Preston had given me that night that much. I just hoped Brady would be okay with what I was about to tell him.

"Um, well," I said, clearing my throat. "Right after I turned eighteen, I was kind of dating this guy. He wasn't my boyfriend or anything, and I didn't really even like him that much, but he told me he wanted to start seeing this other girl that *wanted* to be his girlfriend. I don't know why it upset me so much, because *I* didn't want to be his girlfriend, but I'd never been dumped before. Especially in favor of another girl, and definitely not in favor of a commitment. I didn't love him or even trust him, but it hurt," I explained, hoping I didn't sound as vapid as I felt.

"Okay?" he looked over at me, confused.

"Well, Preston showed up at my work the next night and asked me if I wanted to hang out after we closed," I continued, "and he had that look in his eyes that said he was up to no good, but I ignored it. I knew that he'd help me feel better about what happened, so I went over to his house.

"When I got there, a few of his other friends were hanging out with us in his room, just surfing the internet and playing video games. I didn't think anything of it, because it was pretty standard," I shrugged.

"That's the impression I got, too, from Parker hanging out over there," he confirmed.

"Anyway, I sat next to Preston on his bed and suddenly, he was all over me. Kissing me, touching me, moving clothes aside, not caring that we weren't alone," I said, taking a deep breath. "Frankly, I didn't care either, because he always knew just what to do to make me forget anyone but him."

"So you were making out in front of people," Brady shrugged. "Still sounds like a normal hang to me."

"It was, until my shirt and bra disappeared and my hands ended up in his pants," I closed my eyes, not wanting

275

to look at him anymore. "Absently, I could still hear his friends busy doing whatever they were doing, so I thought their backs were to us. Before it went too far, the lights in his bedroom went off, and when I looked up, it was just the two of us in the room."

"So they finally got the hint to give you some privacy?" the tightness in his voice told me he wasn't as detached from this story as he wanted to be.

"Yeah, they'd already gotten a good look at their friend sucking on my tits, they had some good spank material already," I joked, flatly. "I was still a virgin at the time, and I wasn't planning to lose my virginity just because of a stupid bout of insecurity over a guy I hadn't wanted to date anyway, but that didn't stop other things from happening. Things I'd done before, but never with Preston. His fingers were places, and I ended up sucking him off. I was single, so it's not like I did anything wrong," I shrugged again, cracking open an eye to look at Brady.

"No," he said, "I'd say oral sex is a pretty normal part of the teenage experience," he agreed.

"Exactly. I got what I needed that night, so did Preston. We hooked up like that couple more times before we pushed each other away again. I ended up with my first ever hickies, and realized how freaking gross they are," I laughed.

"Yeah," he nodded, joining my soft chuckles.

"One night last year though, Preston got fucking blitzed out drunk and walked to my house," my tone changing. "He curled up next to me in bed, asked me to marry him and then proceeded to tell me that he wanted to make another tape with me, now that we'd had sex.

"When I asked him what he was talking about, he proceeded to tell me all about how his friend had recorded

276

everything that had happened that night all those years ago from start to finish. That he'd only turned out the lights and kicked out the other guys so I wouldn't stop or get suspicious," I forced the last few sentences out, because I knew that he'd wonder if their leaving the room would've effected how far I went in a room full of people. I mean, he'd seen me bare my chest at parties, give lap dances, he had to wonder if part of me wasn't exactly what my reputation implied.

"What did you do?" Brady asked, his voice sounding even tighter than before.

"He was drunk, so I ignored it and went to sleep. I thought maybe he was just rambling and was confused. The next morning, I asked him about it and he confirmed that there was a tape and that people had seen it. I kicked him out of my house, and until he left for training, I hadn't talked to him," I finished, my eyes closed again, afraid to see the disappointment in Brady's face. I wasn't surprised when he didn't say anything, just threw himself from my bed and stalked out my door for a cigarette. I willed myself to fall asleep before he came back, but I tossed and turned all night. I was crushed the next morning when I left for work and he was asleep on my couch, Taylor cuddled in his arms. He couldn't even come back to my room and tell me what he thought of me. That hurt worse than anything he could've said to me.

I came back that afternoon to an empty apartment and a letter from Brady.

Lucas,

I want you to know what you told me last night must've been hard for you. I'm so sorry that happened to you. I still love you, so don't take my disappearance as a sign of

277

anything. When I came back from my cigarette, Taylor woke up and asked me to lay with her for a few minutes. I must've fallen asleep, and I can't imagine what thoughts are going through your head right now about us.

Don't freak out, but I don't even know how to respond to what Preston and his friend did or how you ended up in that position to start with. Give me a few days to cool down and we'll talk it through.

Trust me.

I love you,

Brady

Brady's handwriting was the worst, but I could read between the lines. I knew that this was probably the beginning of the end for us. I didn't think he was disgusted by what I did, but part of me wondered that, too. The biggest obstacle was Brady not having a problem with my desire to remain friends with Preston. I knew he probably didn't understand why I allowed him back into my life.

Part of me wondered, too, but I knew that Preston was my one consistent person. Until someone else proved that to be untrue, I needed him in my life. I knew that Brady was swiftly replacing every part of my heart that had once belonged to Preston, but if he couldn't get beyond this, what kind of future could we really have?

278

CHAPTER 29

LUCAS

Things were still strained with Brady a couple weeks later. We'd talked about everything with the tape and it seemed like everything was on better ground, but I could feel him pulling back. He and I had disagreed on my role in the tape and my desire to remain friends with Preston. I thought that part of it was my fault, and he wouldn't stand for me taking any sort of responsibility.

In addition, he was being secretive and hiding his phone when he was over. I didn't know what to make of it or how to broach the subject with him until the night before my 22nd birthday. I'd asked him to stay over with me, and he'd agreed.

I was glad that he'd decided to come over, because we'd spent the last week sleeping apart and I didn't like it at all. I was trying desperately not to become clingy like Becca, calling him constantly, demanding we talk about our issues. It needed to be done, though, because I really had no clue what those issues might still be and I hated that they were keeping us apart. I'd hate to think it was still the specter of my past with Preston alive and well in the middle of our relationship.

Unfortunately, I could tell we weren't going to be in for a warm and fuzzy night when he walked into my bedroom that night, or early morning. Brady looked just plain tired, his eyes ringed with dark circles, showing he had been getting as much sleep as me. His hands were in his pockets as he made his way further into my room, not even making a move to sit next to me as he gazed at me, sadly from the foot of my bed.

"Honey," I started, moving to my knees to go to him, but he held out a hand to stop me, and I sunk back onto my bed. "You look like you haven't slept in a week."

"I could say the same about you," he smiled, weakly, his eyes moving over my own dark circles and stringy hair.

"Yeah, I haven't been sleeping well without you," I confessed, falling back against my pillow. My heart started beating faster when he didn't respond right away. Squeezing my eyes shut, I took a deep breath and waited for him to start talking. Brady was a man of few words, but I knew if I didn't say anything, he'd eventually fill the uncomfortable silence growing between us.

"Um, we need to talk," he started after another minute passed. My eyes popped open at the unbelievably obvious words he'd just spoken. Fuck yeah, we needed to talk. I pursed my lips against my desire to roll my eyes.

"Okay?" I said, sitting up from where I'd been lying. It was three in the morning, and I was usually asleep, but tonight, I could feel things were going to change. I could only hope that this was going to signal a new chapter in our story, something that would solidify our connection, but something in the way he was behaving wondered if it was the end.

"I've been thinking about a lot of things lately. I mean, we've been together, what? Not quite four months now?" he scrunched his brow in thought, looking up as if he were searching his brain.

"Yeah," I confirmed, looking toward the lighting fixture above me, dimming slightly as the air conditioner kicked on.

"I know I told you that I could see marrying you, but I don't know if that's something I ever thought I would actually want. I mean, when I got divorced, I swore I'd never be in this situation again," he babbled.

"We both know what's happening," I said, sadly. "So go ahead and get it over with."

"You promised that I could tell you if it was all getting to be too much," he started, looking down at where I was lying on my bed. "You know how much my marriage took out of me, and you knew that I wasn't sure if I could be in a serious relationship again," he sighed, scrubbing his hands over his face before pushing them through his short hair.

"I know," I nodded, feeling overcome with emotion. I loved this man in front of me more than I ever thought possible. If he was going to tell me what I thought he was about to tell me, it was going to destroy me. I couldn't look at him anymore.

"Everyone keeps saying we are moving too fast," he continued. "And I keep seeing all these signs that we should slow down or take a break."

"Oh," I managed to say, the last of my hope falling to my feet.

"I can't do this," he shook his head and stalked out of my bedroom, my jaw dropped in shock at what just happened and my eyes filled with tears. Before they could spill over the lids, I heard the first strains of 'Fade Into You' coming from the stereo in my living room and he came stomping back into my room, stopping beside my bed. A multitude of thoughts barreled through my head as I watched him stalk toward me with a renewed fervor. If the music hadn't given away his true intentions, his next actions did.

Putting a finger under my chin, he tilted my head up to look into his steel blue eyes. "I decided that they don't know anything about us," he smiled, softly, before sinking to one knee in front of me. This time, when my jaw dropped, I also gasped. "We may be moving quickly, but I can't put on the brakes. I don't want to, because I love you so much," he professed. "Lucas Spencer Dunn, will you marry me?" he asked, opening the white leather box in his hand to reveal the most beautiful ring I'd ever seen. A ruby was the center stone, instead of a diamond. It was set in white gold instead of yellow. He knew me so well.

"Yes," I whispered, the tears pouring from my eyes now from happiness instead of possible heartbreak.

"What was that?" he laughed, pulling the ring from the box.

"Yes, you asshole, I'll marry you," I joined his laughter as he slipped the ring into place.

"Thank God," he wiped imaginary sweat off his brow. "Because I don't think any other woman could've gotten through that proposal without kneeing me in the balls," he joked. "It just shows how perfect you are for me."

"Don't speak so fast, jackass," I warned. "I haven't made up my mind about that yet."

"Then let's get your naked so I can apologize to you," he smiled, pulling me off my bed and into his arms.

**

BRADY

She said YES! I'm lucky she didn't kick my ass for my brilliant proposal, but fuck it! She said fucking yes! I couldn't wait until she was my wife. I said eventually, that it didn't have to be now, but since that ring slid on her finger, I was already feeling impatient about the next step.

282

After she'd confessed what happened to ruin her trust in Preston, I knew then that nothing she could ever tell me about her past would change how I felt about her. It made me antsy to move up my proposal to as soon as possible, so I pulled back from her to make it happen. I knew she'd get suspicious and think our relationship was ending, so I played it up more than I probably should to give her a memorable proposal.

I spent a week waiting on her father to return my call so I could ask his permission. It had been hard to keep my phone next to me. Lucas wasn't nosy, but if my phone rang when I was out of the room, she always brought it to me. I could feel her getting suspicious. In the end, though, her wariness helped me truly surprise her.

"So, no more doubts?" I asked her the next morning when we sat down for a late breakfast at the Denny's across from her apartment. She had the day off to celebrate her birthday and I planned make it the best birthday she'd ever had.

"None," she smiled, looking down at her ring. "Holy shit, we're really getting married," she breathed. "Becca's going to be pissed."

"I'm not exactly worried about that right now, but I do know that I don't want to get married in Vegas," I laid out.

"Me either," she shook her head. "I know you already had a big church wedding, and we aren't exactly church goers, but I would still like a wedding," she broached. "I can see what the resort will charge or we can look for a smaller venue, but I definitely want something bigger than just our families," she confessed.

"For someone who thought they were never getting married, you sure are demanding this morning," I joked.

"That's why I want to have a wedding," she told me. "I never expected to have the frilly white dress, but holy fuck, the little girl that liked Disney Princesses when she was six really wants this."

"Okay, then, that's what we'll do," I agreed, grabbing her left hand and placing a kiss on her engagement ring. "Any thought on a date? I mean, I know I just put this ring on your finger last night, but I'm kind of antsy for the rest of it."

"Is it weird that I am too?" she whispered. "What the hell is wrong with me? When did I become the girl that not only wants to get married, but is actually engaged and setting a date? Is Hell frozen over?"

"I'm pretty sure Hell is still nice and toasty, because we are still nice and toasty here in Arizona," I pointed out.

"Yeah, that's true, um, so how about we get married on Friday the 13th?" she suggested, with a raised eyebrow. "As an in your face to superstition and bad luck? You know, since everyone is going to think we are doomed to begin with?"

"That sounds perfect," I smiled, pulling up the calendar on my phone. "The next one is in February 2004 or August 2004," I informed her, closing my phone again.

"Hmm…February might be too soon, but August is just over a year away and is totally doable," she said, looking at me with hope in her eyes.

"So, August 13th, 2004?" I confirmed.

"Let's do it," she smiled, leaning across the table to kiss me. In that moment, with her on her birthday, having a relaxing breakfast, talking about *our* wedding, everything was perfect.

"So when are you moving in?" I asked when we broke the kiss.

"When my lease is up? I can't afford to pay rent in two different apartments," she frowned.

"Xander and I are already covering the rent for Becca, Lucy, having you there wouldn't dent our pockets any further, plus, you'd actually contribute to the house food budget," I countered. "Your apartment is not where I want my fiancé to live. I'm already worried about your safety enough."

"I'll tell you what," she started. "If Becca doesn't get herself squared away and she moved out, I'd consider moving in before the end of my lease," she offered. "But I don't think I could live with Becca after what she tried to do to us."

"I accept your terms," I nodded, already formulating how I was going to make her move in with me sooner rather than later.

Leaving Denny's with her hand in mine, I still couldn't believe that in just over a year, she was going to be my wife.

BRADY

I wish that my engagement bliss would've lasted a bit longer before everything went to hell with Becca. I'd spent most of the week at Lucy's but Xander kept me up to date at work every night. We both knew something had to be done about our roommate.

Less than a week later, Xander and I had to break the news to Becca that she only had one more chance to prove she could keep living with us. We'd already talked to the management company of the complex and they said if we could find someone to take Flynn's and her spot on the lease, we'd be fine.

After the discussion about the ring, Flynn had already talked about getting his name taken from the lease, so he wasn't going to be an issue. It was Becca that would be the problem. We'd discussed giving her this last chance to prove herself so that we could gather what we needed. We had to show the history of her not contributing to the rent if she didn't leave willingly and we weren't looking forward to that.

"How'd everything go, man? Did you talk to her about moving in again?" Xander asked, meeting me at the door and signaling the need for a cigarette.

"I haven't again, because she already gave me her requirements to move in early," I told him, leaning against the balcony railing.

"Well, ask, because her," he said, nodding toward the living room, "time here is at an end," he finished resolutely.

"I knew it was getting close, but I thought we were giving her one last chance. What happened?" I asked, grumbling at the increased level of drama we'd have to deal with today.

"Aside from the fact that we live in a fucking sty right now. I mean, you and I pick up after ourselves, cause she's sure as hell not going to do it," he complained, "but she's not even picking up after *herself* anymore. I found," he stopped and looked at me with a shudder, "a half-eaten something just sitting on the fucking couch last night. It looked like throw up, and it was still there this morning, even though I went through and cleaned up my mess last night."

"I get the point, but that's not any different than before," I shook my head. "What aren't you telling me?"

"I went to take a shower this morning," he started. "I locked the door behind me and the next thing I know, she's sliding into the shower behind me, buck ass naked, grabbing at my junk!"

"Oh my God, you're kidding me right now?" I asked, hoping that this was a sick joke that she'd go this far.

"No, she kept saying that she missed me and that she wanted me. When she fell to her knees in front of me, I just left her there and walked out of the bathroom buck ass naked. I didn't even try to find my towel," he continued. "I couldn't even breathe the same air as her anymore."

"Holy shit," I said, grabbing another cigarette from my pack and lighting it.

"That's not even the half of it," he laughed, humorlessly. "She came out of the bathroom fifteen minutes later like it wasn't a big deal. When I went back into the bathroom to finish my hygiene stuff, I found her birth control pack from last month still fucking full, only one pill gone," he said. "She's been trying to get me to go bareback for the last two months, talking about how she

287

was protected, it was okay. It's a good Goddamn thing I didn't listen to her," he blew out puff of nicotine.

"Um yeah," I agreed. "Fuck!" I shouted off the balcony, knowing that Xander was right. This shit needed to stop, because she was getting way too out of control and desperate.

"Yeah," he nodded, and we finished our cigarettes in silence.

"You ready to do this then?" I asked, my eyes sliding to the door, dreading the next twenty minutes.

"Let's get it done," he said, determined, before throwing the apartment door open and stalking through. "Becca!" he called as I settled onto the sectional to wait for the fireworks to begin. I knew Lucy wanted to try to salvage her friendship with Becca so that she could be in the wedding, but part of me knew it wasn't going to happen. At the end of the day, Lucy really *was* way too forgiving.

**

LUCAS

"Congratulations on your engagement," Becca said, insincerely.

"Um, thanks?" I answered, taking a tentative step further into the living room to take a seat on the sectional.

"Did Brady ask you to move in?"

"He mentioned something about it, but my lease isn't up for another three months," I informed her. "Why?"

288

"Because Brady and Xander are kicking me out, effective next month," she growled. "They said they want you to move in because you can actually pay rent."

"Oh," my eyes widened at her words, because I knew they wanted me to move in, and I'd mentioned that I wouldn't be able to live with Becca, even though she was supposed to be my best friend. They must've used it as an excuse to do what they'd been dying to do for a couple of months now.

"You're saying you didn't know they were going to kick me out?"

"They've been talking about it for a while, but Brady didn't talk to me about the possibility of moving in until he proposed."

"You *knew* and you didn't warn me?! You are a horrible fucking friend," she roared, moving to loom over me, her finger in my face.

"I *did* warn you, Becca! Two months ago, when you decided you weren't going to try to find another job that the boys weren't happy about it," I tried to converse with her calmly, but knew this was going to escalate fast. I threw up a silent prayer that the boys would be home from the store soon.

"Yeah, but we made the agreement that I could stay rent free, as long as I cooked and kept the house clean," she folded her arms across her chest and popped out a hip in a defiant stance.

"Um, Becca, have you looked at this place?" I asked, indicating the sink full of dishes behind us, the pile of mail falling off the kitchen table, the other side of the section full of clean, but unfolded clothes and the three bags of trash visible on the balcony through the patio door.

"I'm getting to all of that today! I went back to school full time, Lucy! I don't have time to do it every fucking day. They can't expect that much from me!" she screamed.

I just shook my head and rolled my eyes at her, before leaving the couch and heading back toward Brady's room.

"What? You think you could do any better than me? You think you are so much better than everyone, Lucas, but you're not. You are going to fuck this thing with Brady up, because you can't really commit. I mean, I can't believe you think you can change and be faithful. I've known you the better part of a decade and you've always been a worthless slut."

"Wow, thanks for being my best friend, Becca. I love you, too," I said, sadly. I knew she was just lashing out, but her words stung. She wasn't the only one who thought that Brady and I wouldn't last long enough for the ink to dry on a marriage license, but I expected more support from someone who helped us get together. "I don't think I am better than you, but I do think you need to grow up and take responsibility for yourself and your choices. You chose to scream at Flynn at your work and get fired, you chose to go back to school, you chose not to pay your car payment, you chose to not find a new job, you chose to not do the work the boys asked you to do," I fired off the litany of bad decisions she'd made of the last four months. "I go to school full time, I work full time, and I take care of my own laundry and housework, too. That's not being better than anyone else, it's part of being an adult, Becca."

"Fuck you. Brynn should be here to get me by now, and she's a better friend than you've ever been," she threw over her shoulder as she grabbed her wallet and slammed the door behind her.

"Wow, how soon you forget all of the times I've rescued you from Flynn's anger and took care of you when

290

your mom forgot to pick you up after school," I said to the empty room, tears shimmering behind my eye lids. I was sitting, dejectedly, on the floor beside my fiancé's bedroom, deep in thought about how erratic Becca's behavior had become since she and Xander broke up when Brady found me sometime later.

"Hey," he called, softly, interrupting my train of thought. "You okay?"

"Becca and I got into a fight about you guys kicking her out. She railed into me pretty hard about it," I frowned.

"But it's not your fault she isn't doing her share," Brady's look mirrored my own. "Let's get out of here for a while, okay? We've got a wedding to start planning," he said, holding his hand out to help me off the floor.

"Sure," I nodded and accepted his hand, my engagement ring sparkling in the late afternoon sun shining through the patio door. Tucking me under his arm, he pulled me toward my truck. Suddenly, he stopped in his tracks with a jolt. "What?" I asked, following his eyes. My mouth dropped open as I took in the state of my vehicle. Deep gashes were present in the paint on the passenger side door, probably from a key, and my tires were slashed.

"Why didn't I notice this when I got home with Xander?" Brady asked, rhetorically.

"Wow, this is going to be fun," I muttered, sarcastically, unable to stop the tears that sprung in my eyes at the knowledge that my best friend was now placing the entire blame for the current state of her life on my shoulders. It was apparent now; that she intended to make me pay for taking what she thought was hers. Suddenly, the planning of my wedding was going to get a lot more interesting.

Acknowledgements

Thank you to my husband for being so supportive of me, always. You have been the constant rock in my life for the last decade and I can't repay you enough for the support you've given me. You know that this book is for you, and you alone.

Thank you so my awesome beta readers: Ronda, Erica, Toni, Tracy, Roseann, Samantha, Wendy and Michelle. Thank you for helping me through some ups and downs with this book, and helping me get to what was important about the story.

Thank you to authors, J.M. Stone, Brittainy Cherry and Laura Brown for being great sounding boards and giving me such incredible feedback that always makes my books so much better in the long run. I couldn't have made it this far without you guys!

Thank you to all of the blogs that have supported me in my career thus far, regardless of which of my books you've read and promoted:

Dii at Tome Tender

Chris at Chris' Book Blog Emporium

Shayna at Shayna Renee's Spicy Reads

Brinda at WiLoveBooks

Kay Dee Royal at Paranormal and Erotica Romance Musings

And Smut Book Club

And lastly, but not least (in the slightest!) THANK YOU SO MUCH to everyone who has read one of my books and has passed it along to a friend. You mean everything to me.

About the Author

Josie Leigh is an independent author who focuses on writing Romance because she loves a story with a happy ending. Writing has been an escape for her from a very young age, and she cherishes the time she gets to spend with her characters. After graduating with a Bachelor's degree in Nutrition in 2008, she pursued a challenging career in the field of nutrition insecurity and anti-hunger advocacy. She is grateful to be able to feed hungry families on a daily basis and chase her literary dreams in her off time.

Josie's second book, "The Weakness in Me," is a 2013 Amazon Breakthrough Novel Award Quarter Finalist in the Romance genre. She rereleased her first novel, "Love, but Never" in May 2013 and completed the Professor series in September 2013, her first foray into the wonderful world of Erotic romance.

Other books by Josie Leigh

<u>Never Series</u>

Love, but Never (#1)

<u>The Professor</u>

The Professor (#1)

The Student (#2)

The Widow (#3)

The Wife (#4)

<u>Drama Free</u>

Drama Free 2003 (#1)

<u>Stand-Alone</u>

The Weakness in Me

<u>Coming Soon</u>

Never Ever After (Never #2)

A Spin off of The Professor Series- Featuring Anton (currently untitled)

A Drama Free Wedding (Drama Free #2)

Made in the USA
San Bernardino, CA
06 November 2013